P9-ELR-925

Praise for the Sanctuary Island series

"*Sanctuary Island* is a novel to curl up with and enjoy by a crackling fire or on a sunny beach. It's a beautifully told story of hope and forgiveness, celebrating the healing power of love."
—Susan Wiggs, #1 *New York Times* bestselling author

"I didn't read this book, I inhaled it. An incredible story of love, forgiveness, healing, and joy."
—Debbie Macomber, #1 *New York Times* bestselling author

"A heartwarming, emotional, extremely romantic story that I couldn't read fast enough! Enjoy your trip to Sanctuary Island! I guarantee you won't want to leave."
—Bella Andre, *New York Times* bestselling author of the Sullivan series

"Well-written and emotionally satisfying. I loved it! A rare find."
—Lori Wilde, *New York Times* bestselling author

"Fall in love with Sanctuary Island. Lily Everett brings tears, laughter and a happy-ever-after smile to your face while you're experiencing her well-written, compassionate novel. I highly recommend this book, which hits home with true-to-life characters." —*Romance Junkies*

"Redemption, reconciliation, and, of course, romance—Everett's novel has it all." —*Booklist*

"Richly nuanced characters and able plotting . . . Everett's sweet contemporary debut illustrates the power of forgiveness and the strength of relationships that may falter but never fail." —*Publishers Weekly*

"Lily has a talent for metaphors that make me melt . . . and I love the way she ties the story together. I'm so looking forward to the next book in the series."
—*USA Today*'s Happily Ever After blog

"I loved learning about Sanctuary Island and I felt as if I was there seeing and feeling everything first hand. A wonderful book to get lost in for a few hours. I definitely recommend it to other readers." —*Night Owl Reviews*

"I couldn't help but fall in love with Sanctuary Island and want to move there myself. An enchanting romance that swept me away!"
—*Books N Kisses*

ALSO BY LILY EVERETT

Sanctuary Island

Shoreline Drive

Homecoming

Heartbreak Cove

Home for Christmas

Three Promises

Home at Last
(coming in March)

Close to Home

A Sanctuary Island Novel

LILY EVERETT

St. Martin's Paperbacks

ORLAND PARK PUBLIC LIBRARY

NOTE: If you purchased this book without a cover you should be aware that this book is stolen property. It was reported as "unsold and destroyed" to the publisher, and neither the author nor the publisher has received any payment for this "stripped book."

This is a work of fiction. All of the characters, organizations, and events portrayed in this novel are either products of the author's imagination or are used fictitiously.

CLOSE TO HOME

Copyright © 2017 by Lily Everett.

All rights reserved.

For information address St. Martin's Press, 175 Fifth Avenue, New York, NY 10010.

ISBN: 978-1-250-07405-8

Our books may be purchased in bulk for promotional, educational, or business use. Please contact your local bookseller or the Macmillan Corporate and Premium Sales Department at 1-800-221-7945, ext. 5442, or by e-mail at MacmillanSpecialMarkets@macmillan.com.

Printed in the United States of America

St. Martin's Paperbacks edition / February 2017

St. Martin's Paperbacks are published by St. Martin's Press, 175 Fifth Avenue, New York, NY 10010.

10 9 8 7 6 5 4 3 2 1

For my father,
who knows how hard it is to start over.

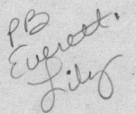

Acknowledgments

I've had this story, or parts of it, in my head for a long time. Some of my favorite romances are the ones that acknowledge that not every story ends at the wedding vows—sometimes, that's just the beginning! Big thanks to my editor, Rose Hilliard, for helping me get this story out of my head and onto the page while keeping it passionate and fun and exciting, and special credit to Elsie Lyons for the lovely cover art.

Major thanks to Sarah MacLean, who gave me the key that unlocked Johnny's heart. This would be a very different book without her!

Thank you to my sister, Georgia Edwards, for stepping up and being an incredible source of emotional support when I needed it most.

And, as always, my biggest thanks go to my husband, Nick, along with my whole heart. I might be able to do all of this on my own . . . but I wouldn't want to.

Chapter 1

"Here he is, the man of the hour. Johnny Alexander, everyone!"

He blinked, thrown for a bizarre, stomach-tightening instant by the sound of his real name, as all around him the agents and support staff of the Washington Bureau ATF office stood up from their desks and clapped.

Alex—no, damn it, Johnny—consciously relaxed his sore shoulders and forced his mouth into the easy smile that had gotten him out of uglier situations than this. A tense shootout followed by an all-night debriefing was nothing compared to living for eighteen endless months as someone else, surrounded at all times by violent criminals who would cheerfully slit his throat if they knew he was a special agent with the Bureau of Alcohol, Tobacco, and Firearms.

Today was supposed to be his victory lap, for God's sake. Not a test of endurance already strained to the breaking point by a year and a half of deep undercover work.

But as he moved through the smiling throng of co-workers he barely recognized, shaking hands and accepting slaps on the back, Johnny wished he could be someplace else.

With every beat of his heart, every breath of his body, he wanted to be walking into the tidy little town house he shared with Terri.

The thought of his wife's shy half smile and downcast eyes warmed something deep in Johnny's chest—a place that had been frozen solid for months. Months he'd survived by locking away the memory of Terri's long, light brown braid curving over her shoulder, or the shine of tears in her green eyes when she'd seen him off on this assignment to stop a ring of gun runners.

Maybe most people wouldn't understand the Alexanders' marriage. It hadn't started as the love match of the century—in fact, you could argue it wasn't a marriage at all, more of a marriage in name only. But it was everything to Johnny.

For eight long years, since the night he found a terrified seventeen-year-old girl sobbing and shivering in his family's barn, Johnny had wanted nothing more than to protect Terri. From her parents, from the harsh, cold world—from himself.

Terri was sweet. Clean. Pure. Everything Johnny wasn't, after six years of heavy deployment with the army and two years in the ATF.

He needed that now more than ever. When he'd been posing as Alex Santiago, he'd kept his memories of Terri on total lockdown along with his worries about her safety. It was the only way to fully immerse himself in the role. Any slipup could've meant his life—and would've blown an op that was years in the making and responsible for the ATF's best hope of getting a huge number of illegal guns off the streets.

"Johnny!" A tall man with a receding hairline and eyes that crinkled at the corners came forward, hand outstretched, and Johnny felt his smile turn real for the first time in a long time.

"Brad. How are you, man?"

They exchanged a brief, back-thumping hug before Brad pulled back with a grin. "Not as good as you, Mr. Hero. It's great to see you in person. And all in one piece."

"More or less." Johnny shrugged, exhaustion weighing him down as if his bones were made of lead. At the same time, though, he felt twitchy, like he was about to jump out of his skin. Johnny scraped a palm over the short bristles of beard he'd grown to rough up Alex Santiago's look. He couldn't wait to take a hot shower and shave it all off. Now that the danger was past, his skin itched with the need to shed every bit of Alex Santiago he could.

Of course, Alex's memories wouldn't be as easy to wash away.

Ignoring the sharp scrutiny Brad swept over him, Johnny rolled his neck and gave him a grin. If there was one thing Johnny was sure of, it was his ability to deflect suspicion. "I'm glad there's at least one guy from the old days still kicking around this office. It's been less than two years, but I swear to God, I don't recognize anybody else. And when did the ATF start hiring high school kids?"

"I know, they're infants." Brad slung an arm around his neck and started leading him toward the glassed-in office at the rear of the floor. When they got close enough to make out the name on the placard beside the door, Johnny turned to his handler with genuine happiness.

"Bradley Garner. ASAC. What the hell, man? Why didn't you ever say anything?"

Brad shrugged modestly, but there was a well-deserved light of pride in his eyes. "Oh, sure. I guess I should have mentioned my promotion to assistant special agent in charge during one of your calls, in between making sure your cover wasn't blown and you weren't about to get shipped home in a body bag."

"There wasn't a lot of time for small talk," Johnny agreed. "I didn't get much news from home."

The deeper Alex Santiago had gotten embedded into the gang, the harder and more perilous it had been for Johnny Alexander to get word out about their activities. Phone calls on burner phones and coded e-mails sent from library computers—and getting any info back from the home office had been even harder. Johnny could count the messages he'd received from Brad on his fingers, and most of those had come during the final days of breakneck preparation for the big takedown.

"Listen, you know I haven't been home yet. How's Terri doing?" Johnny paused, a nameless emotion gripping his insides. He'd had even fewer messages from home, and not a single one in the past year, but he knew Brad would've been looking out for Terri.

"She's fine." Brad's smile was wide and easy, but tight at the corners. "Hey, come check out my new digs. Swanky, right?"

Johnny glanced around the cramped office of the new special agent in charge, taking in the immaculate desk and the old-fashioned file cabinets while trying to tell himself he was reading too much into the way Brad held his gaze with the steadiness of a man who knew how to lie and make it convincing.

"Nice. How many nights a week do you spend on that couch, and how bad does Donna make you pay for it each time?" Johnny smirked at his old friend to hide how closely he was studying Brad's expression. "Wives. Gotta keep 'em happy."

There it was again, the slight tightening at the corners of Brad's eyes, a tiny twitch of muscle at the back of his jaw.

Johnny's guts clenched. He dropped the grin. "Tell me."

Wincing at the flat command, Brad sighed and flipped the venetian blinds over the glass walls closed. He rounded his desk to pull something out of the top drawer. "This is for you. It'll explain everything."

Johnny watched his hand take the thin white envelope with a strange, detached feeling.

"For what it's worth," Brad was saying as Johnny opened the envelope and pulled out a sheaf of papers, "I told her she was making a huge mistake."

Every ache and pain faded under the cold rush of

numbness that crashed through Johnny like an avalanche.

Dear Johnny, he read. *I want to start by thanking you for everything. You've been my savior and my guardian angel since I was almost eighteen. But I'm not a teenager anymore, even though I know part of you still sees me that way. I've come to realize that you always will. To you, I'll always be that helpless young girl you rescued. I get it, and I get why you'll never see me as someone you could want to be with for real. I don't blame you—it's just how things are between us. But I want more. I deserve more.*

Whew. Even writing that down was hard for me. I'm still working on believing it. But I know for sure that the first step for me is to release both of us from this marriage.

I'm sorry for putting this in a letter, but I don't want you to feel like you have to argue with me about it or make promises you can't keep. I want a new life, a life I can be proud of, on my own terms and without relying on anyone else to save me. I hope you can understand that.

I'll always be grateful that I met you when I did. I don't regret the years we spent together, and I hope you don't, either. I know you'll finish this mission and come home safely, because you're the strongest, smartest, best man I've ever known. I won't ever forget you, and I sincerely hope you find someone who makes you happy the way I never could.

With all my heart,
Theresa

The sound of paper tearing startled Johnny out of

the cold, gray fog the letter created. He looked down at the rip in the paper where his clenched fist had crumpled it. Behind the top page, behind the letter, was a stack of official-looking documents. He didn't need to read through them to know they were divorce papers.

"When," he growled, clamping down on the urge to rip the pages to shreds.

"She left the package with me almost a year ago." Brad's reply was prompt but his tone was cautious, as if he were aware how close Johnny was to melting down. "I wanted to call you, but it was right after Valdez put you on his personal security detail, and I couldn't have you distracted. Plus . . ."

Brad grimaced and broke off, but Johnny had to know. "Plus what?"

"She begged me not to tell you. I think she was worried you'd endanger yourself rushing home to talk her out of it."

Anger flashed red-hot through Johnny's chest, burning away the numb ache. "Maybe I would have. Damn it, Brad."

"That would have been a bad call," his handler said firmly.

Johnny slammed his hands down on Brad's fancy new desk, everything inside him burning for Terri, desperate to get to her. "It should've been my bad call to make."

Brad's eyes flicked to the door of his office, and Johnny realized how loud his voice had gotten. Breathing hard around the constriction in his chest, he stood upright and backed off a step or two. He needed information. As much as part of him wanted to beat it out of Brad, the rest of Johnny knew he'd get further by controlling himself and the situation.

"Listen, I know you're pissed," Brad said quickly, holding up his hands in surrender. "I get why. If I came home and found Donna had up and moved out, left town—"

"She moved away?" Johnny's head spun. He couldn't imagine the quiet woman he'd left behind having the guts to pack up and start a new life, the way she'd written in the letter. Not that Terri was weak, exactly. She'd lived through hell as a kid, and Johnny was of the opinion that surviving her childhood meant Terri was stronger than she even knew. But the fact remained that when he was home on leave, he'd have to coax her into going out to dinner. And when he was gone, he knew she barely went farther than the grocery store or library.

Brad was nodding, a complex expression darkening his friendly eyes. "A new start, she said. For both of you."

Feeling trapped, Johnny prowled the perimeter of the office. "A new start. Was she really that unhappy? I mean, I know I was gone for a long time, but after the navy, that was nothing new. We've spent most of our marriage apart, but I thought we were solid. That we understood each other."

Except they hadn't, obviously. Johnny hadn't understood anything.

Unless it was the opposite . . . that Terri understood more than he knew. His blood went icy cold. Oh, God. Had she figured out his secret? Was that why she left?

"This is a shock." Brad was all sympathy and gentleness. Johnny wanted to punch him in the mouth to get him to stop sounding like the shrink they wanted to make him talk to about the aftermath of the undercover assignment.

"She thinks I don't want to be with her." For some reason, the words grated at Johnny's throat on the way out. "That's what she said, in the letter. How messed up is that? Why would I have stayed married to her if I didn't want to be with her?"

The problem had nothing to do with whether Johnny wanted Terri. He'd never wanted anything in his life more than he wanted his wife. The problem was that he couldn't let himself take advantage of her. He couldn't touch her. No matter how much he lay awake at night, his palms aching to trace the lines of her slim body.

"I can't speak to why you married Terri," Brad said, clearly choosing his words carefully. "People get married for all kinds of reasons. Sometimes it's about companionship. Security."

"So I married her to keep her safe. To take care of her. Is that so awful?"

"It's not awful." Brad paused. "But it's not exactly true love, either."

Johnny cursed, low and filthy, and dragged his hands over his face. "True love. Please. Love is for puppies and kids' movies. You sound like that moron shrink."

"Dr. Reeves isn't a moron. She's a valued member of the department and she's here to help you transition back to your real life."

"You have to say crap like that now that you're ASAC."

Brad shrugged. "Doesn't mean it's not true. Deep-cover missions tend to scramble people's brains. Whatever we have to do to unscramble you, we want to do it."

"My brain is fine. It's my life that's a mess." Johnny leaned over the desk, spearing his handler with a glare. "And you're going to help me clean it up."

"Maybe you should sit with this for a few days, try to process. Take some time off, do your mandatory talk therapy with Dr. Reeves . . ."

The rage that had propelled Alex Santiago through countless challenges of his loyalty to the gang filled Johnny's gut and tightened his hands into fists. "I'm not talking to a damn shrink. I'm going after Terri and I'm going to get my wife back."

Alarm widened Brad's eyes and he shifted in his seat. The hot, furious part of Johnny took a grim satisfaction in the knowledge that he was making his friend nervous. To Brad's credit, though, his voice stayed steady and low, like he was talking a jumper off a ledge.

"Johnny. Think about what you're saying. Terri left you. She doesn't need you to take care of her anymore—maybe you should think about taking care of yourself right now, instead."

"Where is she? I know you kept tabs on her, Brad. Tell me where she is."

"You're not even listening to me. Johnny, man, you've got to calm down."

Johnny slammed his hands down on the desk, the

sound like a gunshot impacting muscle. His brain flashed white-hot, his focus narrowing to the man in front of him—the information Johnny needed. Before he knew what he was doing, he'd shoved the desk aside to wrap his hand around the man's throat.

"Tell me where my wife is," Johnny snarled. "Right now."

He didn't even recognize his own voice, guttural and wrecked, and the shock of that was enough to loosen his grip. Brad never flinched and never broke his gaze. All he said was, "You need to let me help you, Johnny."

Johnny froze, heart pounding. What the hell was he doing? He backed up a step, raising his shaking hands to show he wasn't a threat. His vision was swimming, the back of his throat coated with the peculiar metallic tang of adrenaline, and he wasn't so sure he *wasn't* a threat. But Brad didn't call in security, or one of his baby agents out there in the bull-pen. Instead, Brad regarded him with eyes that saw and understood way too much.

"Okay. Maybe I do need some help," Johnny admitted, reluctance drying his mouth out. "But I need this more. Please, Brad."

His handler—the man who had been a reassuring voice in Johnny's ear for the past eighteen months—studied him for a long moment while Johnny tried not to look like a basket case. He didn't even know why he was pushing this so hard. It was Terri's choice to leave, and maybe it was time to stop torturing himself with wanting what he couldn't let himself have.

But first, Johnny had to see her for himself. To

know for sure that she was okay. And if she wasn't, he'd convince her to come home where he could keep her safe and close.

Close enough to touch. Not that he ever would.

With a sigh that seemed to come from the soles of his feet, Brad reached into his desk drawer and withdrew a file folder. Setting it on his desk, he tapped his blunt fingers on it and regarded Johnny thoughtfully.

"I had a feeling you were going to want to follow your wife, so I put together this file. It contains Terri's new address and some intel about her new life."

Johnny reached for it immediately. He had to suppress a growl when Brad flattened his palm and anchored the file to the desk. Forcing himself to stand down, Johnny crossed his arms over his chest in resignation. He knew the score. You can't get something for nothing.

"What do I have to do to get that file?"

"Make me a promise." Brad eyed him like an appraiser pricing out a shipment of semiautomatics. "Go to Terri. Talk to her, set your mind at ease, work out your marriage or don't, but I'm putting you on administrative leave. And you're going to complete the program I'm assigning you—ah, ah, just wait. You can do both things simultaneously because the program is based on Sanctuary Island."

Everything inside Johnny went still, as if a bell had been rung in the silence of his mind. "Sanctuary Island?"

Nodding slowly, Brad slid the folder across the desk. "That's where your wife is."

Johnny looked up, determination quickening every

muscle like a predator sensing prey nearby. "Then that's where I'm going."

Sanctuary Island was going to be the place where Johnny found out what the rest of his life would look like. Whether he'd spend it alone or with the woman he'd married. The woman who made his blood pound with forbidden lust, at the same time as she soothed his soul with her quiet presence.

The woman he'd sworn he'd never touch.

Chapter 2

Sanctuary Island turned out to be tiny . . . and chilly.

Johnny was glad for his leather jacket, even though the walk from the ferry landing to the address he'd memorized from the file took less than five minutes. It was five minutes of walking along a winding, hard-packed dirt road with the cold wind off the water scouring his cheeks with salt. Five minutes added to the hours of nonstop travel since he'd let himself into the empty, echoing town house he'd shared with Terri, to shower and pack before heading right back out the door.

He'd been glad to leave. The dust and silence of their home haunted him. He'd gotten through five deployments and nearly two years undercover by picturing Terri going about her life, safe and warm and *there*.

Without Terri, the house meant nothing. It wasn't the home he'd longed for.

And now here he was, not so many miles from their tidy little place in northern Virginia . . . but Sanctuary Island felt like another world.

The air smelled like saltwater and sunshine, threaded through with the scent of the budding rose garden he'd passed as he strode down Main Street toward the center of town. He passed a florist, a library, and a family-owned hardware store with two grizzled old men playing a lazy game of checkers out front. The old guys clocked Johnny's movements with interest, clearly gathering intel to grease the town's gossip wheels.

Johnny paused, unwilling to pass up the chance to gather a little intel of his own.

"Afternoon, gentlemen," he said, giving them his best, nonthreatening smile.

Judging from the wary glance they exchanged, Johnny could stand to work on his nonthreatening smile.

"Hello, there," the younger of the two old men said. He was wearing a plaid flannel shirt under his overalls, and Johnny was startled to notice a battered, dull gold crown glinting from the gray curls wreathing the man's head. "What brings you to our fair island?"

Johnny hitched his backpack a little higher on his shoulder. "I'm looking for someone. Do either of you gentlemen know a Terri Alexander?"

The older man scratched at his grizzled beard and squinted across the street and the quiet town square. "Can't say I do. And I know near about everybody in town, I woulda thought. King, what do you say?"

The man called King was, unsurprisingly, the one

with the crown. Sure. He frowned, more in confusion than anything else, Johnny thought. "I don't know any Terri. Pete? Is there a stranger?"

Sanctuary Island really was tiny if two old guys could be so sure of knowing absolutely every single person on it. Johnny had a fleeting thought about how freaking impossible it would be to go undercover in a place like this, where everyone knew everyone else and everyone else's family—and everyone else's business—probably for generations back.

"I think she's working at a bakery," Johnny offered offhandedly, from the file he'd memorized on the ferry over to the island. "Patty's Cakes?"

King's troubled expression cleared. "Patty Cakes," he corrected, sounding relieved. "Great sticky buns. You must be talking about Tessa. Right? Moved here a year ago to help Patty retire?"

Tessa. Not Terri. But Tessa was another nickname for Theresa, his wife's full name. It could be her.

Johnny didn't betray the sudden jump of his pulse by so much as the flicker of an eyebrow. "Mind pointing me in the direction of this Patty Cakes?"

To his surprise, King frowned again. And the other man stood up from his rocking chair, bones creaking and popping, to lean against the porch railing and stare down at him forbiddingly. "You're not here to make trouble for our Tessa, are you?"

The depth of his own reaction to the casual possessive stilled Johnny. Instead of growling that she wasn't their Tessa, she was Johnny's, he managed to pull together a semblance of a reassuring smile. "No trouble, sir. I'm just here to catch up, see how she's doing."

"Don't worry, Pete," King said in a loud undertone. "If he's a bad guy, Miss Patty will take care of him."

Johnny was starting to get the idea that there was something a little off about King. First that weird fake crown, now this conviction that a retirement-aged old lady was some kind of match for anyone who might want to harm Terri? It was a damn good thing Johnny was the only one who'd showed up looking for his wife, if that was her only protection on this podunk island.

To his surprise, though, Pete didn't laugh. Instead, he gave Johnny an appraising glance and nodded once in agreement. "True enough. Keep heading down Main Street, mister. You'll find the bakery on the corner, just past Hackley's Hardware."

"Try the apple fritters," King added, smiling and carefree once more as he sat and returned his attention to the checker game on the table. "They'll change your life, guaranteed."

Johnny nodded his thanks and started down the sidewalk, his mind swimming with new information. He was still in mission mode, making connections and coming up with and discarding potential courses of action as he walked, feverish and strung tighter than a guitar string.

It was a problem, the fact that he hadn't come down from mission mode yet. He knew it, Brad knew it, Dr. Reeves—the department shrink—had definitely known it. But Johnny couldn't help it.

Until he saw Terri with his own eyes, alive and safe and smiling that tiny half smile that barely lifted the corner of her generous mouth, part of Johnny was still tangled in the nest of vipers he'd lived in for the last two years. He couldn't get free until he knew she was all right.

But when he walked past the hardware store and found himself nose to glass with a wide display window showcasing cake stands topped with towering white coconut layer cakes and vibrant yellow buttercreamed confections, the tension inside him coiled even tighter.

The woman behind the counter inside was achingly familiar—but a stranger, at the same time.

Instead of his wife's long, brown hair, this woman's hair was short. Wisps and feathers of bright blond framed the delicately angled face Johnny had dreamed of over and over. But instead of the almost-smile he used to work so hard to coax from her, this woman's pink-glossed mouth opened on a laugh so big and happy it made her throw her head back.

It was Terri. Intellectually, Johnny knew it was her. But she was laughing in a way he'd never seen her laugh. And even when the laugh faded, the smile that was left behind pierced to the center of Johnny's chest. He'd never seen that particular smile before, either.

That smile turned her into someone new. Someone beautiful and vibrant and full of life. Someone Johnny could hardly believe was the shy, timid girl he'd found hiding in the barn behind his parents' Maryland farm eight years ago.

To his dismay, his body responded to her even more fiercely and undeniably than it usually did. Desire flared, bone deep and aching with frustration. Blood racing and heart pounding as if he'd taken a shot of adrenaline, Johnny stared at Terri.

He'd assumed he'd find her alone, miserable, in need of help—the way she'd been when he first met her. He never pictured her like this. She seemed . . . happy. And she definitely wasn't a kid anymore.

Terri bumped hips with the woman working beside her at the counter and sashayed into the back as the customer she'd been helping pocketed his change and scooped a brown paper bag off the counter. Johnny stepped aside to let the man exit the shop on a waft of warm, cinnamon-scented air.

Johnny caught the edge of the door with his hand and stood for a moment, breathing in while glancing around the interior of the bakery. It was second nature by this time to catalogue potential threats and size up the situation without letting on. The steel-gray-haired woman behind the counter returned his easy smile with a curious glint in her friendly gaze.

"Welcome to my store. I'm Patty Cuthbert. Don't believe I've seen you in here before. Are you in town visiting family or friends?"

Johnny kept his smile firmly in place, biting down on the desire to say he was here to collect his runaway wife. "How do you know I'm not a tourist?"

The woman's eyes narrowed, deepening the crow's feet fanning out to her temples. Patty was in her seventies, Johnny guessed from the crepelike quality of her tanned skin and the lines of a life well lived scoring grooves in her handsome face. Her dark gray hair was threaded with strands of white, silver, and black, pulled back from her face and knotted into a complicated, soft-looking bun at the back of her neck. Despite the flour-streaked red apron covering her yellow polka-dotted shirt and what looked like a pair of denim overalls, there was an aura of regal dignity about the bakery owner that made Johnny classify Patty as . . . not a threat, exactly.

But not someone to be trifled with, either.

"We don't get a lot of tourists on Sanctuary Island," Patty said slowly, leaning both elbows on her glass countertop and studying him with frank interest. "Considering we have no hotel and only one single restaurant."

"You have a world-class bakery, though," Johnny pointed out with his most disarming grin. Instinct had him working to charm Patty and get her on his side before Terri came back out. "Or so I've heard."

Flattery was always a good tactic. Patty visibly preened. "Oh? What have you heard?"

"I'm told your buns are the best in the world." Johnny wasn't above pressing his advantage by strolling over and leaning casually over the counter, close enough to shoot Patty a wink.

The older woman went faintly pink with pleasure. "Oh, go on with you. I'm old enough to be your grandmother! Our sticky buns are good, though. We already sold out the first batch, but a new tray should be coming out in a second. Not that I believe for a minute that a man like you eats sticky buns for lunch."

Patty's appreciative gaze swept down his body, making Johnny grin. "Hey," he said, throwing his arms out and pretending to be hurt. "I like sweet things as much as the next guy."

"I'll just bet you do." Patty fluttered her lashes, good humor quirking her mouth.

"Miss Patty, are you flirting with the customers again?"

Everything inside Johnny went still and alert at the laughing voice calling from the back of the shop. He couldn't stop it or hide it, even as he registered the sharpening of Patty's glance—his head came up and he was staring hard at the doorway Terri had disappeared behind.

The instant she stepped around the corner holding a huge rimmed baking sheet laden with butter-soaked rolls topped with brown sugar, Johnny felt his heart give a hard kick against his ribs.

It was her. His wife. Almost close enough to touch for the first time in a year and a half.

He wanted to vault over the counter separating them and seize her in his arms, feel her warm, beating heart and living body against his. He wanted . . . all the things he'd never allowed himself to want from Terri, who was vulnerable and soft and so in need of protection.

She looked up and met his eyes, and everything Johnny thought he knew about his life and his marriage went up in flames.

Shock rounded her lips into a gasp and drained her face of all color until she was as pale as the flour dusted over her apron. The tray dropped to the floor with an almighty crash, splattering syrup and making Patty cry out in alarm.

Johnny barely registered the older woman hurrying to grab the tray from the floor and investigate whether any of the sticky buns could be saved. He had no attention to spare for anything or anyone except his wife.

His wife. Who was staring at him in tense silence. The trembling hand she brought up to cover her mouth was sun-kissed. A shiny scar crossed the back of her knuckles above the old, faded scar on the side of her wrist.

New burn scar, Johnny's brain reflexively spat out. She works in a bakery.

It made logical sense. But all Johnny could think was that it was yet another way he didn't recognize the girl he'd married in the woman standing before him.

For instance, he was used to Terri being glad to see him. In her quiet, reserved way, sure—but he knew he hadn't imagined the fact that her wary, wounded eyes would light up when he walked through their front door.

He'd held on to that memory through nearly two years of living life as someone else, desperately clinging to his sense of self with everything he had. Somewhere along the way he'd convinced himself that if he saw that look in Terri's eyes once he got through to the other side of the assignment, he'd know for sure he'd come through it in one piece.

He'd been counting on it, all the way back to their house, and then all the way to Sanctuary Island and this moment, right here.

Johnny stared into his wife's eyes, and all he saw was dismay.

Please, Terri, he begged silently. *Please be glad to see me.*

She dropped her hand and ran the tip of her tongue over her bottom lip in a sharply familiar way. But then she shook her head, the soft tufts of her short, high-lighted hair glinting gold in the warm bakery lights, and a wave of vertigo swamped him.

"Johnny," she said. Her voice was the same, throaty and soft, but the tone . . . He put out a hand to steady himself against the countertop. She sounded strong. Sure of herself, in a way he'd never heard her before. Above all, she didn't sound happy to see him. She sounded . . . almost as if she were afraid of him.

Johnny, who'd spent the last two years convincing himself he wasn't the violent, dangerous man he was pretending to be, suddenly discovered the limits of his endurance. He'd held on for Terri, for the look of welcome in her green eyes.

He couldn't take her fear.

Without a single word, Johnny turned and walked out of the bakery.

Chapter 3

"Who was that man?" Patty demanded breathlessly, appearing in front of Tessa's dazed face with a mop and bucket.

How to answer that? The man who saved me from poverty and illness? The man I've loved for nearly a decade? The man who married me but never did more than kiss me on the forehead?

She swallowed and went for the basic truth. "That was my husband."

"Your husband!" Patty exclaimed, eyes wide and cheeks flushed a hectic, excited pink. "I thought you told me you were divorced."

Tessa eyed her boss and friend with wary concern. At her last checkup, Patty's doctor had warned her against too much excitement. She'd been slowing down for a while—hence the ad for bakery help that had brought Tessa to Sanctuary Island—but recently, Patty seemed to get out of breath more quickly.

Reaching to take the mop out of Patty's hands, Tessa explained, "Technically, we're not quite divorced yet. But we will be, very soon. I'm sure that's why he's here, to get things all settled. Maybe he wanted to hand me the signed divorce papers in person."

Patty's gaze sharpened under her arched brows. She clutched the mop to her chest and lifted her chin in defiance. "Oh, sure. I suppose that's why he came in here, stared at you like he'd never seen a woman before, and then scrammed without saying another word?"

"I don't know why he did that," Tessa admitted, making another grab for the mop. "But I'm going to find out . . . just as soon as I clean up this mess. I'm so sorry, Patty, can we salvage anything from this batch?"

Stubbornly independent as always, Patty waved her away. "Nah, don't worry about it. You should go after him now. He looked shook up, maybe you can get some more alimony out of him. Unless . . . are you sure you want to divorce that man? I wouldn't kick shoulders like that out of my bed for taking up both pillows, if you get what I'm saying."

Despite the maelstrom of emotion churning in Tessa's stomach, she had to laugh. "I get what you're saying, but I'm not asking for any alimony—Johnny's already done more than enough for me."

He'd certainly never done anything to get himself kicked out of her bed. He'd never even gotten near her bed. Which was half the problem.

"So he's a good guy, then." Patty looked satisfied. "I thought so. I can usually pick 'em."

"He *is* a good guy. One of the best." Tessa untied her apron with fingers that wanted to tremble.

In fact, Johnny Alexander was the kind of guy who married a girl he barely knew, just to get her out of trouble. He was one in a million.

And Tessa had loved him from the first moment she set eyes on him. So what was she doing asking him for a divorce?

The old fears and doubts nipped at her heels, trying to trip her up, but Tessa shook them off. She couldn't just sit back and wait for Johnny to figure things out and let her know how it was going to be. Her new life was at stake here, and she couldn't let herself back-slide now.

She wasn't asking for this divorce. She was giving it to Johnny as a gift, the way he'd given her the security and stability to grow into the kind of woman she'd always wanted to be.

"Go on then!" Patty flapped her apron at Tessa in a shooing motion. "Go get your man."

"He's not mine," Tessa called over her shoulder as she hurried for the door. "At least, not for much longer."

And if the thought stung, well, that was just too darn bad. Tessa reminded herself that Johnny had never really been hers to begin with. Not in any of the ways that mattered.

She rushed out of the bakery and swiveled her head, taking in both sides of the quiet Main Street of downtown Sanctuary. There was Mrs. Ellery, trailing scarves and wafting the scent of patchouli as she walked her golden retriever; down on the corner by the bank, Anne Marie Harvey stepped out into the street with her nose stuck in a book and nearly got herself run down by a pickup truck on her way home from her teller job.

Normal, everyday Sanctuary Island stuff was all Tessa saw. Nowhere did she see the lean, muscled form of her soon-to-be ex-husband.

Tessa had learned a few things in the year since she moved to Sanctuary Island, however. Just like the locals, she knew exactly where to go for the latest in current events—and it wasn't the *Sanctuary Island Gazette*.

Turning toward Hackley's Hardware, Tessa didn't need to do more than glance up at the two grizzled old men at their never-ending checker game before King Sanderson nodded vigorously in the direction of the town square.

She waved her thanks and darted across the street, heart pounding double time with her steps. The oncoming summer trailed warm fingertips down the back of her neck, making her skin prickle with heat. It was a relief to reach the shade of the big, old maple trees that dotted the grass of the town square. Without the bright sun glaring down, she could see better, too. Tessa shaded her eyes and tried to calm her breathing as she searched the small park.

There. A darker shadow inside the white gazebo. And when the shadow moved to lean one broad shoulder against the entrance, Tessa recognized the lethal grace, the predatory smoothness of the movement.

Against her will, a searing thread of long-denied desire coiled around her body and squeezed. Alone in her separate bedroom, Tessa had dreamed of Johnny knocking on her door, bearing her down to the mattress and claiming her in every way a man could claim a woman.

But no one could live on dreams forever. Eventually, you had to get up and live your life.

The reminder that she actually had a life to live now got Tessa's feet moving across the late-spring grass. He saw her coming, she knew. Those dark eyes of his never missed a thing. He didn't straighten from his casual slouch against the gazebo stair railing, but when she got closer, she could see he was tracking her every step with an intense hooded gaze.

Fighting down a shiver of pure feminine awareness, Tessa lifted her chin and gave him a determined smile. "Let's try that again. Johnny, I'm glad to see you."

The corner of his mouth tightened. Could've been the start of a smile or a scowl. "Are you."

It wasn't a question, and Tessa had to work not to stiffen up at the desert-dry flatness of his tone. "I am, as a matter of fact. I got a few updates on how you were doing from Brad, but it was never enough to keep me from worrying about you."

Eighteen months of the kind of worry that could suck a person down into a vortex of panic, if she let it. But Tessa had lived enough of her life in fear. To survive, she'd had to believe that Johnny would be okay.

Something shifted in the darkness of his heavy-lidded stare. "If you were that concerned, you could have stuck around long enough to see me safely home instead of letting me walk into an empty house."

Tessa flinched a little. "Johnny—"

"You wrote me a Dear John letter," he interrupted harshly, raking a hand through the dark brown waves of hair falling over his glowering brow.

"Your name is John," Tessa pointed out, trying to lighten the mood.

But Johnny wasn't about to see the humor in the situation, apparently. "That's not the point. And you know it. I guess it was too much to expect you to have the guts to deliver the news to my face."

Tessa took it on the chin, knowing she had that one coming, even though the contemptuous curl of his lip made her want to crumble in a heap at his feet. "You're right. I took the coward's way out, and I'm sorry about that. I've been a coward all my life and I'm used to running away. It's hard to break a habit that saved your life when you were a kid."

For the first time, the granite line of Johnny's jaw softened. "Damn it. I didn't mean . . . I'm sorry, Terri."

She held up a hand. "I'm not trying to guilt you with my past, Johnny. And I'm not trying to make excuses, here, but honestly I'm kind of thrown."

Johnny sighed and dropped down to sit on the top step leading up to the gazebo, his mile-long denim-clad legs stretched out in front of him. "Did you seriously think I'd open that letter, shrug, and move on with my life?"

"Yes." Tessa spread her hands helplessly, truly bewildered. "Absolutely. I thought if anything, you'd be grateful."

He turned to stone right in front of her. "Maybe I don't cast aside eight years of marriage as easily as you do."

"For nearly two of those years, we didn't see or speak to each other! And for the first six years . . ." Tessa paused, overcome by a sudden, vivid memory of the way she'd felt on her wedding day when they signed the papers at the courthouse. Like a death row prisoner granted a reprieve.

But she hadn't taken her pardon and gone out into the wide world. She'd hidden in Johnny's house while Johnny went off to war, and she'd turned her marriage into a different kind of prison.

She'd lived for his brief visits between deployments, always hoping something would have changed or that he'd realize she was growing into a woman who could be a true partner to him. But with every soft good-night kiss pressed to her forehead, Tessa realized she wasn't any kind of partner to Johnny. She was more like a little sister. Or a helpless, adopted puppy.

"I know how loyal you are, Johnny. No one knows it better." Tessa smiled up at him and had to hope it was more sweet than bitter. "But one good deed shouldn't be repaid with a lifetime shackled to a woman you don't love. It's high time I freed us both."

"Come on, Terri—"

"That's not my name anymore," she said firmly. "I always hated the nickname Terri. I go by Tessa now."

Johnny stared down at the familiar stranger who was his wife. She believed every word she was saying. Truth echoed through every sentence and shone in her clear, hazel eyes.

This wasn't just some self-sacrificing stunt she was

pulling. Terri—Tessa—actually wanted a divorce. For his sake, which was nuts, but for her sake, too.

That required some more thought, because Johnny was ready to refute whatever she had to say about how much he deserved to find a woman he loved—who the hell needed love? They cared about each other. That was real. To expect more than that was to buy into the fake crap Hollywood packaged and sold as happiness.

But he couldn't look at the woman standing at the foot of the gazebo steps and deny that a year and a half on her own had been good for her.

Hell, until thirty seconds ago, he hadn't even known what name she preferred to be called—because she'd never said a word about it throughout their entire marriage.

Drawing his boots up to rest on the step below his seat, Johnny propped his elbows on his knees and felt a wave of exhaustion sweep over him. He realized he'd been awake and running on adrenaline fumes for about fifty hours straight. Well, for months actually, if he was honest with himself.

Terri—Tessa, damn it—sighed and mounted the steps to perch next to him. He didn't look at her, but the soft weight of her seared into his side.

"Are you okay?" she asked quietly.

Johnny rolled his shoulders. "Nothing a good night's sleep—or ten—won't cure."

"Is that what Dr. Reeves would say?"

Johnny could feel his wife's skeptical look. He should never have complained to her about the departmental shrink. "I don't give a damn what Reeves thinks."

The hint of growl in his voice would have been enough to make Terri duck her head and back down easily. Tessa, on the other hand, gave him a hard stare and said, "Don't be an idiot. You've been through something intense. It's okay to accept a little help in dealing with it."

I'd accept help from you.

He didn't say it. It wouldn't be fair to put that on her. Johnny knew exactly how to use emotional manipulation to subtly steer other people in the direction he wanted them to go; it was a mainstay of any undercover operation. But he'd slit his own throat before he used tactics like that on his wife.

Instead, he told her the truth. "I'm going to have help, whether I like it or not. Brad sent me down here to some program he's all worked up over. Something to do with horses, maybe? That sounds weird. Can't be right."

But Tessa brightened. "The Windy Corner Therapeutic Riding Center! I volunteer there on weekends. It's a wonderful placc, they do great work with all kinds of people and problems, everything from physical rehab to couples therapy. I can't believe you agreed to it."

"It was the best way to get extended paid leave." And it would give Johnny time to assess the situation with Tessa, to make sure she was okay and figure out if he needed to step in and help—or if she'd be better off without him.

"So . . . you're going to be sticking around then."

Tessa's tone was carefully neutral, but Johnny didn't delude himself. His wife wasn't ready to welcome him into her new life with open arms. But he'd made vows to her, and Johnny Alexander kept his promises.

He'd never be like his father, a man who ran out on his family and left them to get by on their own.

"For how long?" Tessa asked into the taut silence. She cleared her throat. "I mean, how long do you think you'll be staying on Sanctuary Island?"

Johnny gave a grim smile. "As long as it takes."

"And . . . where are you staying?"

Another small hope flickered and guttered out. "I was hoping I might be able to stay with my wife," he said slowly. "But I take it that's out."

"I can't ask you to stay with me, there's no room. I mean, I only have the one room—I'm renting from Patty, staying in her house while I save up for a place of my own. Sorry."

She didn't sound sorry, she sounded relieved. A muscle clenched behind his jaw. "Don't worry about it. I'll figure something out."

"Okay," Tessa said doubtfully. "There's no inn or B and B here, but there are a couple of summer-houses that might be available for rent. Although with summer around the corner, they might all be booked already. Whatever is available should be listed in the weekly newspaper; I'll see if Patty has her copy."

Johnny nodded his thanks, weary and heartsore at the stiff, formal way they were talking to each other. They'd never been a chatty couple; Terri had been quiet, reserved, and Johnny wasn't exactly a guy who relished long conversations about his feelings or whatever, but there used to be an ease between them. Casual familiarity, a shared understanding.

Now there was only distance and awkwardness.

She was sitting right beside him, close enough to touch, and she'd never felt farther away. He had to find a way to bridge this gap.

Or he was going to lose his wife without ever really knowing her.

"Why are you here?" Tessa asked suddenly.

Johnny blinked. "For the bureau's mandated therapy, like I said."

"You could have gone to a million programs, a million other places." She huffed, wrapping her arms around her raised knees. "I'm trying to do the right thing and let you out of an obligation you never should've had to shoulder. Why are you fighting me on this?"

"I don't want an out." Johnny turned to her without thinking, grabbing her shoulders and savoring the way her soft lips parted in surprise. "I want my wife back."

There it was. Cards on the table. Johnny stared down into her startled face, searching for the light of dawning comprehension. But instead, she shook her head, clearly still confused. It took everything he had not to shake some sense into her.

I can't be the guy who abandons his wife and his responsibilities. Please don't make me be that guy.

"We're married," he ground out, feeling desperation burn a hole in his gut. "I want it to stay that way. Nothing has to change."

"Things have already changed," she cried, wrenching away from his touch and standing up. "I've changed."

Clenching his fists against the chill emptiness, Johnny got to his feet and stepped down a few stairs to put him eye to eye with Tessa. "That's not what I mean. I can see you're different, believe me."

Unable to resist, he reached out to brush his fingers through the short, feathered locks of bright blond hair framing her face. "I like it."

He heard her breath catch as he traced the sensitive rim of her ear, exposed by the new haircut. Satisfaction ripped through him, dark and rich as chocolate. She could say whatever she wanted about ending the marriage, but Johnny could make her want it. He could make her want him.

Now, there was an idea. He'd held himself back from taking advantage of Terri's vulnerability and innocence for years. Maybe it was time he took her at her word and started treating her like a woman with the right to make up her own mind.

Just so long as she knew everything she'd be giving up if she went ahead with this divorce.

"There's more to the new me than some highlights and a trim," Tessa said, her voice gone throaty. "I'm not the meek, mousy weakling you married."

Frowning, Johnny slid his hand down to cup her tense jaw. "I never thought of you that way."

Her eyes darkened. She turned her head away from his hand. "You would never have said that, because you're too kind. But I'm not an idiot, Johnny. You've always seen me as a child."

"I see the woman you are now," he rasped, already

missing the silken texture of her skin under his fingertips. "And I like what I see."

She swallowed audibly, her brow crinkling in confusion. "I don't understand why you're talking like this. Why are you making this so difficult? It wasn't even a real marriage."

The words were a body blow, knocking the wind out of Johnny. But he'd never been good at going down easy. "It was real to me."

"I swear, Johnny, you should have just adopted me and made yourself my guardian officially. That would have been more accurate than calling yourself my husband."

Registering the disgruntled shake of Tessa's head, Johnny realized he'd been worrying for nothing. Tessa didn't know. She had no idea how much he'd ached to touch her, since the moment three years into their marriage when he came home from Afghanistan on leave and saw a woman smiling back at him instead of the young girl he'd left behind.

"I know I'm no one's idea of a fantasy woman," Tessa continued, mouth turned down. "But that doesn't mean I want to spend the rest of my life with a man who doesn't want me."

Oh, he'd covered his desires well. Too well.

"Believe me, sweetheart." Johnny took her hand and lifted it to his mouth, brushing a kiss over her knuckles. "You're every fantasy I've had for years. Give me a chance to prove what kind of husband I can be."

Tessa's head came up, her eyes searching his face. "What? What do you mean?"

She was right to sound wary. Johnny had gotten his second, or maybe third, wind. And with it, an idea.

"Give us a month," he said impulsively, guided by the same gut instinct that had kept him from blowing his cover. "We spend four weeks together, and I'll court you, the way I would have done if we'd met some other way."

He could see the rapid flutter of the pulse in the base of her slim throat. "Johnny, this is crazy. I don't understand at all. And four weeks . . . why four weeks?"

"Well, that's how long I have to be here anyway," Johnny pointed out. "For the stupid horse therapy thing Brad is making me do."

Tessa stared up at the sky, blinking furiously as she thought it over. Johnny held his breath for her response, but when it came, it was nothing he could have predicted.

"Okay, Johnny. You're on. Four weeks. But instead of dating like we're not married, we use the time to face reality. We are married. So let's turn your therapy sessions into couples counseling."

Hell, no, was Johnny's knee-jerk response, but when he saw the clear challenge in the tilt of her dark brows, he swallowed it down.

Tessa expected him to bail. She expected to scare him off with this, but Johnny had dealt with worse things than a stupid shrink. He could handle it.

"You're on," he told her. The shock on her face made up for the way his stomach sank at the prospect of committing himself to deal with a therapist.

"You understand that's going to mean talking.

Openly." Tessa raised her brows significantly. "About our feelings."

More sure than ever that he was on the right track, Johnny crossed his arms over his chest. "I've faced down a warehouse full of illegally armed gunrunners. You're not going to scare me off with feelings."

Tessa blew out a breath. "Fine. Then I guess we have a deal. Four weeks. I owe you that much, at least."

She thought she owed him. The idea settled uneasily in Johnny's stomach, but he refused to argue the point since it was getting her to agree.

Save it for our first session, he told himself ironically, allowing a feeling of optimism to creep in.

"Four weeks of couples counseling," he said. "And at the end of it, if you still want out . . . I'll sign the papers. But I'm telling you right now. Terri, Tessa, no matter what you call yourself or who you become. I'm not letting you go without a fight. I want our marriage to work. And this time, I'm not talking about a marriage in name only."

Chapter 4

Tessa felt the hinge of her jaw go loose with shock. Snapping her mouth closed, she retreated into the shadow of the gazebo's roof. But Johnny's penetrating stare followed her, hot and intent.

He didn't want her. No man, not even Johnny, could live as man and wife with a woman for eight years without giving her more than a peck on the cheek—not if he actually wanted her.

This was something else, it had to be. She'd been so sure he would be glad to be free of her. Not that he ever would have abandoned their vows on his own—Tessa knew him, and his uncompromising sense of honor, too well for that. But honor only went so far. Surely now that she was making it clear that a new start was what she wanted, Johnny could allow himself the same freedom.

"What happened to you out there?" she asked, the words spilling out in a rush of bewilderment as she wrapped her arms around herself and tried to make sense of the situation.

He stiffened minutely, his warm, brown eyes clouding over like the sky before a storm. "What do you mean?"

Tessa knew that tone. It meant "Danger ahead, back off," and two years ago, that's exactly what she would have done. The urge to avoid conflict was still there, but Tessa was in control of it these days. She could make her own choices, based on more than fear.

"Something has obviously changed," she insisted, forcing her voice level and calm. "Do you even remember how things were between us before you took that assignment?"

Quiet. Distant. Two people living in the same house, but miles apart in all the ways that mattered.

That's what Tessa remembered. That was what she couldn't bear to go back to.

But Johnny was smiling, a slow, knee-weakening curve of those lips that had tasted every inch of Tessa's body.

Her heart jumped up into her throat, cutting off her breath and making her light-headed. That was the only reason she had for standing stock-still, like a deer in the headlights, as Johnny prowled up the steps and stalked ever closer.

"I remember everything," he said, his low, gravel-and-honey voice licking over her nerves. "I remember wondering if a touch, right here, would make you sigh."

Reaching out, he cupped her elbow in his palm and

brushed his thumb across the thin, tender skin inside the bend. Tessa felt her breath catch.

Fierce satisfaction lit Johnny's eyes for an instant before he bent his head to nuzzle at Tessa's temple.

"And if a kiss like this," he murmured against her skin, "would make you shiver."

Warm prickles raced down Tessa's spine, raising the hair on her arms and sending a fine tremor through her mesmerized body. Johnny gave a pleased, wordless hum, which caused another shiver and a spread of heat sharp enough to bring a flush to Tessa's cheeks.

Their chaste embraces and frustratingly passionless good-night kisses had never felt like this. Tessa was caught up, ensnared by years of unrequited longing for the kind of desire she never thought she'd see in her husband's handsome face.

"I should have done this every day," Johnny whispered, dragging his mouth along the curve of her jaw and up to her trembling lips. "I should have kissed you and held you and showed you exactly how gorgeous you are to me, sweetheart. Every day. Every night. Let me make up for it now."

The fading light slanted into the gazebo, golden and enveloping. Tessa heard the birdcalls and the rustle of leaves overhead, the far-off rush of the waves against the sand, like the background to a particularly nice dream. And right here, in her arms, was the best fantasy she'd ever had, come to life.

Johnny was here. And he wanted her. As the hunger and longing she'd buried came surging up to propel her into their first kiss, nothing else mattered.

And for the first time since Johnny Alexander hauled scared, meek Theresa Mulligan out of a bad situation and into his life, Tessa had the courage to go for what she wanted.

Spearing her hands into his thick, dark hair, Tessa boldly tilted her head and deepened the kiss. Their bodies crashed together like ocean waves, primal and elemental, surging on the tide of passion rolling through them both. With an incoherent groan, Johnny's grip on her hips tightened, hauling her closer until her legs spread and clenched around his muscular thigh. Hunger tugged into a hard knot at Tessa's core, pulled tighter and tighter with every stroke of Johnny's wicked tongue, every rub of his hard, male body against her melting softness.

Blood thundered in Tessa's ears. The sound of her heartbeat nearly drowned out Johnny's voice as he framed her face in his palms and groaned, "God, Terri."

The sound of the hated nickname severed the taut coil of desire, releasing Tessa from her mindless greed for more of Johnny's touch, his kiss, his body. She jerked back, shoving at his shoulders hard enough to make his eyes go wide with surprise.

"It's Tessa," she panted, her voice harsh with lingering passion and the need to make him understand. "You came here looking for Terri, but she's gone. And she's never coming back. Not if I can help it. If you can't accept that, you might as well sign those papers right now and head back to D.C."

Johnny bit back a curse. Of all the boneheaded mistakes to make. It was nothing but a slip of the tongue, he wanted to argue, but if he said the word "tongue" out loud to his wife right that minute, he might not be able to stop himself from reaching for her and getting another hit off her addictive lips.

How had he never kissed her before? The heady taste of her lingered on his palate, stoking the fire raging in his blood. When did the girl he'd do anything to protect turn into a woman he'd do anything to have?

He stared at Tessa's stiff, closed body language. Her arms were crossed over her chest, her chin tilted up, and her brows drawn down. She was in no mood for more kissing right now.

Johnny licked his lower lip where it was tender and sensitive from the force of Tessa's response to him, and allowed himself a moment of hope. There was something between them, something that demanded to be explored and savored. Tessa wouldn't be able to deny it forever, and he had time to make her see the light.

Four weeks, to be exact.

Four weeks to remind his wife that eight years of marriage couldn't—shouldn't—be so easy to erase. But if he was going to do this, he had to get smart. Strategic. Like infiltrating a motorcycle gang or working his way up the ranks of gunrunners to get the dirt on them—he hadn't just waltzed in on day one and demanded that the boss intro him to his South American contacts.

No, he had to lay low. Bide his time. Maneuver himself into position . . .

"Understood," Johnny said now, showing her an easy smile. "Tessa, not Terri. I like it. I like the new name, the new hair—everything."

She pinked up, but her chin lifted determinedly. "Okay, then. Good. Because I like the new me, too." Tessa's pink tongue came out to flick over her bottom lip, and Johnny had to concentrate extra hard on his strategy for a second.

"I want to get to know you all over again," Johnny told her. "But in the meantime, I'd better go find someplace to stay. Since I'm going to be sticking around for the next month or so."

"Sorry I can't offer you my couch." Tessa did look sorry, or at least conflicted about it, which Johnny found heartening. "But I wouldn't feel comfortable. Patty has been so good to me, taking me in and teaching me about running a business. I can't repay her with an uninvited, long-term houseguest."

Part of Johnny, the impatient part, would have loved to argue and push and point out that he wouldn't be in Patty's way if he were sharing his wife's bed. But it was too soon for that, and he knew it. "No worries. I'll find a copy of that newspaper you mentioned and look up a few possibilities. There's bound to be something that'll be better than where I spent the last year and a half."

A vision of the residence motel where "Alex Santiago" had bunked rose up in Johnny's mind's eye. Convenient to the docks and with enough foot traffic to camouflage the comings and goings of both his shady targets and his agency contacts, the Palmetto Inn had served its purpose as a home base for Johnny's undercover alias. But it hadn't come close to being a home.

He blinked the memory away and refocused on

Tessa. She opened her mouth as if she wanted to ask more about that, but instead she shook her head a bit and said, "Come on. Walk me to the bakery and I'll ask Patty for her copy of the *Gazette,* then I've got to get back to work."

"Maybe we could go the long way around the square," Johnny suggested, offering Tessa his arm. "I'd love to see a little more of this cute town you've discovered."

She gave him a suspicious look as she placed a cautious hand in the bend of his elbow, but Johnny blinked innocently and waited. He was counting on Tessa's pride in her new home to help him extend his time with her by a few minutes, and he wasn't disappointed.

"Well. I guess that would be all right." She laughed suddenly, fond and warm, and the sound made Johnny's heart swell. "It's not like even a comprehensive tour of the entire island would take longer than a couple of hours. A walk around the town square, which is our version of downtown, will hardly make a difference to Patty. Come on, then. I'll show you around."

Johnny took a firm grip on himself and prepared to be delighted by every kitschy, cutesy detail she pointed out, but to his surprise, Sanctuary was an undeniably beautiful place. From the stately old Victorian mansions lining Island Road along one side of the village green to the courthouse and the white-brick bank at the head of the park, Sanctuary looked like something out of a picture book from fifty years ago.

"And over here on this side is the main drag,

helpfully called Main Street," Tessa said, towing him around the corner and waving at the line of small shops and businesses that contained the bakery where he'd found her.

"I know, it's not exactly Tysons Corner," she went on, naming one of the largest shopping centers in the D.C. area. "But it's everything we need. In fact, that's the motto of the hardware store down the street from Patty's—if Hackley's doesn't have it, you don't need it!"

Johnny grinned, the smile coming easier and feeling more sincere than he could remember in a while. "I like it. Sometimes having a lot of options and choices is more paralyzing than helpful."

"I'm glad you feel that way, because you're not likely to have a ton of options when it comes to places to stay. There are very few apartments available for rent, and people are just starting to get their summer cottages fixed up for the season. You really might have a hard time finding anything."

"Why isn't there a hotel on the island? I would think they'd want to bring in tourists, and tourist dollars."

Tessa shrugged as they strolled past the tiny stone castle of a public library on the corner. "I don't know. Patty says there's never been a hotel here, and there never will be one."

As Johnny glanced down a side street, a man on a ladder caught his eye. Something about the guy pinged at the back of Johnny's brain, something that made him seem out of place or . . .

Johnny frowned, watching the guy tip way over to

hang a sign above a door into a building behind the bookstore. The man hung suspended in midair, back torqued and shoulders straining, but the heavy-looking sign never wobbled. Neither did his denim-clad legs, braced against the sides of the ladder.

The man hung the sign and swung down from the ladder, landing like a big cat, silent and graceful.

The hairs on Johnny's arms lifted as he clocked what bugged him about the scene. The way that guy moved—the looseness of his shoulders combined with his ramrod-straight posture. No wasted motion. From the set of his head, Johnny could tell the guy knew exactly how many people were standing at the entrance to the alley behind him, and how far away they were.

He acted like a man with a lot of advanced training, probably ex-military. Johnny ought to know—he was one, himself.

Johnny knew what he himself was doing on sleepy Sanctuary Island—what was this guy's angle?

Johnny paused in his tracks, startling Tessa into stopping, too. She cast him a questioning glance, forcing him to come up with a good reason for his sudden halt.

"Huh," he improvised, jerking his chin toward the narrow side street. "Then what's the Buttercup Inn? Sounds like a hotel to me."

"No way!" Tessa peered down the street—more of an alley, really. "Patty said there was a scheme afoot to bring in a hotel a few years ago, but the whole town basically revolted against the idea. I can't believe the council would allow it. We should check it out."

The ferocious need to protect her rose up Johnny's spine, stiffening it. Tessa didn't need to go anywhere near that ex-military guy until Johnny knew more about him.

He schooled his expression to calm, instinctively aware that this new version of his wife would react badly to being hustled out of harm's way. Not that he could be sure there was anything to protect her from, he reminded himself.

But for the last eighteen months, Johnny's life had literally depended on his ability to size up potential threats and pick out the most dangerous guy in a room, at a single glance. His gut hadn't failed him yet, and right now, his gut was telling him that the man in the alley was someone to steer clear of.

So Johnny cocked his head at Tessa and said, "I thought you needed to get back to work."

Curiosity warred with the obligation she obviously felt toward her employer. "Wellll, that's true. But you know, Patty is on the town council. I bet she would want to know what the deal is with this inn. Maybe I should go with you, just to see what it's all about."

"Or maybe you should head back to the bakery." Johnny curled an arm around her shoulders and used the leverage to turn her steps away from the alley and back down Main Street. She fit under his arm perfectly, her lithe body snugged against his as if she were the missing piece of him. Johnny shook his head, forcing himself to concentrate.

"Wait, Johnny," she protested, craning her head to look behind them. "Stop it, would you? I said stop!"

Startled by the impatient but firm command in her

tone, Johnny slowed and stared down at her. Flags of color darkened the skin over her cheekbones and her eyes sparked with some inner flame he couldn't remember seeing before.

"What's wrong?" he asked.

"This!" She pulled away, gesturing jerkily at the empty air between them. "You can't come down here after all this time apart, and start making demands and trying to run my life. Because for the first time ever, this *is* my life, and I'm not going to give that up!"

"I'm not asking you to." Johnny ran a hand through his hair, frustration burning in his gut like a bullet hole. "I just don't want you talking to that guy. There's something off about him."

Her brows drew together. "Can you hear yourself? You haven't even spoken to the man. You sound like a paranoid crazy person!"

Johnny clenched his jaw, fighting not to react. Tessa wasn't saying anything he hadn't said to himself, especially in the last few weeks of the undercover op when lines blurred and tensions soared and it became ever more crucial to be able to tell friend from foe. Maybe he was being paranoid. Probably, in fact.

But a healthy dose of paranoia was all that had kept him alive. He saw no reason to give up on it now.

"Stop trying to roll me in bubble wrap! I'm not made of glass," she snapped.

"Come on, Terri," he started, then broke off, rubbing his forehead. "Tessa, damn it, I mean Tessa."

But her face had gone cold and still. "There's no point to this if all you see when you look at me is *her*.

I'm not Terri anymore, and I never will be again. I'd rather be dead."

Before Johnny could ask what the hell was so wrong with Terri, the woman he'd married, Tessa turned on her heel and marched off down the street. He watched her go with a familiar feeling of bafflement.

Women. Before, he never knew what was up with his wife because she was so quiet and reserved. He'd ask how her day was and get one-word answers. Now she had plenty to say, but none of it made a lick of sense to Johnny.

At least he'd diverted her attention from the Buttercup Inn.

Yeah, great strategy there, Johnny mused with a grimace. *Get her to drop the idea of investigating the new guy in town by making her furious with you. You have four weeks to fix this. After that . . .*

He paused, catching a glimpse of himself in the front window of the bookstore. Johnny stared into his own hollow eyes, dark and empty in the reflection. As dark and empty as his life would be, if he couldn't convince his wife that they belonged together.

7046241

Chapter 5

Marcus Beckett closed the ladder with a clank. He leaned it against the crumbly brick wall and stared up at his handiwork with satisfaction. Sweat trickled between his shoulder blades and his upper back ached from all the heavy lifting, but both those sensations were satisfying in their own way.

When was the last time he worked with his hands to do more than fieldstrip a weapon while blindfolded, or used his body for more than standing around and looking imposing?

Grim memories bubbled up, threatening the numb detachment Marcus had worked so hard for. He pushed them down and scowled at his new sign.

"The Buttercup Inn," said a male voice behind him.

Marcus went tense all over, one hand twitching with the automatic need to lift to his ear and find out why his piece wasn't working: How had someone got the drop on him, where was his spotter—

ORLAND PARK PUBLIC LIBRARY

That life is over, he told himself harshly, swallowing the bitter, metallic tang of adrenaline on the back of his tongue. He turned, casual and nonthreatening, to see a tall, scruffy guy with a duffel over one shoulder and an easy grin. There was something about his eyes, though, something watchful and wary that prompted an equal wariness in Marcus.

Not that he had to show it. He was home now. Nobody on this island had it in for him.

"We're not quite ready to open our doors yet, but we're getting there," Marcus said gruffly, wiping his hands on the rag hanging out of his back pocket.

He offered his right hand to the guy, and got a firm handshake and a wide smile that seemed at odds with the stranger's sharp gaze. "So you're opening a hotel?"

Marcus raised his brows. "Nah, it's a bar. Or it's going to be, if I can ever get finished with the reno."

"I get it. Like a pub. Sort of old-fashioned."

The guy's frown lifted a bit, although he was still watching Marcus's every move like Marcus was a rattlesnake he'd stumbled over. Marcus was used to scaring people, but this guy didn't look scared, exactly. And he was supposed to be working on being less intimidating, he reminded himself.

"Sure." Marcus wasn't about to discuss the origin of his bar's name with a stranger. "Listen, I'd better get back to work. Feel free to stop by in a week or two, hopefully we'll be open by then. Or, I guess I should say *I'll* be open then. Since I haven't managed to hire any help yet."

"You're doing all this work on your own? Sounds

like a big job. I'm Johnny Alexander, by the way. In town visiting . . . family."

"Marcus Beckett." Marc lifted a brow. "And if your family is anything like mine, the opening of a bar that serves hard liquor on this island is relevant to your interests."

Instead of laughing or agreeing, Johnny cocked his head to one side. "Have we met before? You seem kind of familiar."

Marcus didn't tense up, but he had to exert a real effort about it. He knew his face had been caught on camera a couple of times, after it all went down, and the damn news channels repeated the same footage over and over, ad nauseum. "Nah, don't think so. If you went to Sanctuary High, you must have graduated a few years after me."

The younger man shrugged, appearing to shrug off his questions and concerns at the same time. "I didn't grow up here. The person I'm visiting is a recent transplant."

"Huh. I thought I was the only one." Marcus was making a conscious effort to get himself back in the swing of small-town life. People talked to each other. It had never been his favorite part of living here, but he'd promised to try and let people in more. He was grimly determined to keep that deathbed promise. "I missed this place while I was gone. From what I can tell, it hasn't changed much in the years since I left."

That subtle tension returned to Johnny's posture, although his expression never changed from polite interest. "Yeah? It's my first time visiting, but I'll be here about a month. Hey, you wouldn't happen to have a line on a place I could stay, do you?"

Marcus frowned. "You're not staying with your family?"

"No room." Johnny shrugged the shoulder carrying the backpack. His eyes traveled up to the bank of second-floor windows above the sign with a speculative gleam. "This place is pretty big. Where did you get the money to buy the building, if you don't mind me asking."

Marcus did mind, as a matter of fact. "None of your damned business."

"You know," Johnny said, not seeming the slightest bit intimidated, "I'm pretty handy with a hammer. If you wanted some help with the renovation, I'd be glad to pitch in. In return for a place to stay."

Stiffening, Marcus bit back the automatic refusal that sprang to his lips. He didn't want a stranger in his space, hanging around and wanting to talk to him . . . but he did need help with the bar. "If I wanted help, I'd hire some," he retorted. "Professionals with construction experience."

"Sure. But you haven't yet." Johnny tilted his head, narrowing those brown eyes that seemed to see more than Marcus would like.

"It's the interviews." Marcus grimaced. "Finding the right person to hire, talking to a bunch of people who want the work bad enough to maybe lie about themselves. It sucks."

Johnny smiled sunnily. "And here I am, willing to work for room and board and give you the chance to avoid that whole boring process."

It wasn't the boredom that bothered Marcus. It was having to deal with people. Easier to do it all on his own . . . except there *were* a few projects he'd been putting off because they required more than one pair of hands.

As if sensing his waffling, Johnny smiled confidently. "I promise not to get in your way. Come on, man. I've been on my feet for what feels like a week, and if I don't crash soon, it's not going to be pretty."

Not my problem. Marcus actually opened his mouth to say it. But a gust of wind blew around the corner from the direction of the ocean, salty sweet and fresh. The breeze caught the newly hung sign, swinging it on its cast-iron hooks, and Marcus shut his mouth with a snap.

Reluctantly meeting Johnny's imploring stare, Marcus grunted, "Fine. There's a studio apartment next door to mine, upstairs from the bar. It's small, only one room, but it's got its own kitchenette and bathroom. You're liable to get woken up by hammering every so often—I get up early, and the walls are paper thin. But it's yours if you want it."

Lips quirking as if he were repressing a smile, Johnny gave him a serious nod. "Thanks. Sounds cozy."

Marcus hefted the ladder over his shoulder and turned to head back inside. When he turned his head, Johnny was on his heels, clearly not one to wait for an engraved invitation.

"Stairs are that way." He hooked a thumb left, continuing past the staircase to stash the ladder in the crawlspace under the stairs. "Your room is the one on the right. Head on up and look around, if you want. It's open. Keys should be on the counter."

A hand on his shoulder stopped Marcus in his tracks. It took everything he had to control his hard-wired reaction, but Johnny seemed like a nice guy. He didn't deserve to get thrown over Marcus's shoulder and body-slammed to the ground.

"Seriously, man, thank you," Johnny was saying, oblivious to his near brush with major bodily harm. "I could come back down after I drop off my bag, help out for a few hours."

Marcus gave him a look. "You said you needed to crash. So go crash. You're no good to me sleep-stupid and slow. You'll only make dumb mistakes I'll have to fix later."

Mouth doing that weird twitch again, Johnny only nodded and turned to head upstairs. "Thanks again. You won't regret it."

That remained to be seen. Marcus shut the door on the closet under the stairs with a little more force than necessary. He wasn't going to tiptoe around, just because his new tenant might be sleeping. He had too much crap to do.

Grabbing up his electric drill, Marcus stalked back out front to the controlled chaos of the bar itself. The antique zinc bar shone dully under a layer of construction dust, the fading light of the spring day glinting off the mirrors he'd installed behind the liquor shelves that morning. On his way to snag the box of hooks he planned to screw underneath the bar for la-dies to hang their purses and whatnot, his work boot knocked into a stack of papers and sent them cascading over the floor.

Cursing, Marcus squatted to gather them back up. First draft proofs of the beer list. His eye caught on the name of the bar scrolled across the top with a stylized flower in the corner.

Grief and guilt caught him like a kick to the balls, sudden and sickeningly sharp. *I'm doing my best, Buttercup,* he said silently, ignoring the way the paper fluttered in his shaking hand.

I'm going to make you proud. If it's the last thing I do with my worthless life.

Tessa half expected Johnny to be waiting for her outside the bakery when she finally got done prepping for tomorrow's morning shift and closed up. But he wasn't.

Telling herself she wasn't disappointed, she shrugged into her denim jacket and wound her light scarf around her neck. She loved her new short hair, but after years with much longer hair, she shivered at every breeze on the back of her neck as she walked the four blocks home from Patty Cakes.

She ought to be glad to have the time to think through what it meant that Johnny had followed her to Sanctuary Island. When Johnny was actually around, sucking all the air out of the world and lighting her nerves on fire, Tessa wasn't usually thinking very rationally.

Heat prickled across her cheeks as she remembered that incredible, spine-tingling, toe-curling kiss. Maybe she didn't need the scarf, after all, she mused as she climbed the front porch steps of Patty's two-story brick house. With memories like that to keep her warm, she couldn't imagine ever being cold again.

"Is that you, Tessa girl?" Patty called from the kitchen at the back of the house.

Tessa savored the feelings of warmth and welcome that bloomed in her heart every time she stepped into Patty's home. "Yes, ma'am! And you better not be back there working. The doctor said you're supposed to take it easy."

The silence from the kitchen didn't bode well. Tessa hurried through, hanging up her coat and scarf, and hustled down the hall on feet that ached from standing all day, measuring out batter and testing cakes' doneness and scrubbing down the giant industrial mixer. And if she was this exhausted after a full day of work at the bakery, how tired must Patty be after doing it on her own, all day, every day, for the last fifty years?

Not too tired to fix dinner, apparently. Tessa paused in the kitchen doorway and watched Patty chop bell peppers with the same precise, efficient motions she used when she rolled out one of her famous all-butter pie crusts.

"No lectures." Patty slanted her a stern glance, her hands never faltering in their work. "I feel good today, plenty of energy, and you've had a rough time of it. Let me take care of you, for a change."

"You've done nothing but take care of me since you met me," Tessa protested, taking a reluctant seat at one of the pair of bar stools pulled up to the butcher block in the middle of the spacious kitchen.

Patty scooped up the chopped vegetables with a quick swipe of the flat of her blade and waved away Tessa's words. "Let's call it even then. We can take turns. Tonight is my turn, so have the glass of wine I wish I could drink and tell me what happened with that handsome husband of yours."

They'd been slammed when Tessa finally got back to the bakery to relieve Patty; the evening rush of after-work foot traffic and customers looking to take home a treat for dessert, or one of their savory quiches or a loaf of bread to go with dinner. There hadn't been time to do more than shoo Patty out the door to go home and rest.

Tessa wasn't a big drinker, but she dutifully picked up the bottle of Patty's beloved chardonnay and poured a healthy glug into the single, waiting glass. "Why don't you switch to red? I bet you could convince Dr. Hathaway that one glass of red wine a night would be good for your heart. Aren't there studies?"

"Red wine might be good for the heart, but it's hell on my head. Bourbon is better." Patty peeled the translucent skin off an onion with a practiced flick of her knife and started dicing it. "Now quit stalling and spill. I'm pretty sure gossip is good for the heart."

Grinning through the sharp pinch of concern over Patty's casual attitude toward her own health, Tessa propped her elbows on the butcher block and took a sip of wine. "I don't know where to start."

"Start with why I didn't know you were still married!"

Tessa squirmed uncomfortably. "I should have told you the whole truth, Patty. I'm sorry. In my own defense, I was certain it was only a matter of time until I was divorced."

"You *were* certain." Patty pounced on the past tense. "But now?"

"Now . . ." Tessa blew out a breath that ruffled the fall of bangs over her forehead. "Now I guess I'm not certain of anything. I just never imagined Johnny would come here, looking for me."

Patty whirled, pointing the tip of her chopping knife at Tessa with a narrow glare. "Why on earth wouldn't he? You're his wife! And you're absolutely adorable. Of course he wants you back."

"I wasn't his wife. Not in the ways that counted." Tessa pressed her lips together against the bitter outburst, but it was too late.

Cocking her head inquisitively, Patty set down the knife and wiped her hands clean on her checkered apron before coming over to perch on the other bar stool. "Sugar. What does that mean?"

Tessa struggled to find the words. She'd never meant to lie to Patty or any of her new Sanctuary Island friends and neighbors. But she had desperately wanted a clean break from the life she'd left behind in northern Virginia. So she'd cut her hair and bought new clothes and showed up to answer Patty's "Help Wanted" ad with a new name to match her new self.

No one on Sanctuary Island had ever met Terri, and Tessa wanted to keep it that way. But if Johnny planned to stick around for a whole month, the situation was obviously going to require some explanation.

Patty reached out and laid her strong, big-knuckled hand over Tessa's. "Oh, sugar. You don't have to tell me anything you don't want to. But I hope you know that there's nothing you could say that would shock me, or make me think less of you. I know you."

Tears rose up to clog Tessa's throat. "That's just it," she choked out. "There's so much you don't know about me. So much I should have told you already . . ."

"I know everything I need to know." Patty squeezed her hand for emphasis. "For a year now, I've watched you take to island life like a sunflower stretching up toward the sun. I've seen how eager you are to learn about running a bakery, how hard you work, how much you care. I've taken you into my home and never had a single moment of feeling anything other than grateful for the day you appeared in my life. I may not know everything about your past, but I know you, sugar pop. Never doubt it."

Tessa blinked. Her cheeks were wet with tears, but they also hurt from smiling too widely. "I can't get over how lucky I am. At the hardest moments in my life, the exact perfect person comes along to lift me out of it. This time it was you, and I couldn't be more grateful and glad."

Clearing her throat, Patty blinked too, and her voice was a little thick when she said, "Oh, stop it. Come here and give me a hug."

The feeling of Patty's thin arms closing around her melted a part of Tessa's heart that had been frozen since childhood. She dropped her head to Patty's frail shoulder and sniffled, breathing in the scent of vanilla mixed with the sharpness of chopped vegetables, and the clean linen of Patty's blouse. Maybe this was what home smelled like.

"So this time it was me who helped you—although I still think we could quibble about who's helping who here. Regardless, who was it last time?"

Trust Patty to cut straight through the bull and pinpoint the exact heart of the issue. Tessa sat up and scrubbed at her cheeks before taking a big gulp of wine. "Last time, it was Johnny."

Patty registered a complete lack of surprise. "And how old were you?"

This was the part where it got weird. "I was almost eighteen."

The beginnings of a concerned frown puckered Patty's steel-gray brows. "And how old was he?"

Cringing a bit, Tessa said, "Twenty-two. I know! It sounds bad, but it's really only a four-year age difference. That's nothing."

"It's nothing now, when you're twenty-six and he's thirty," Patty said sharply, outrage bristling all over her like a cat with its hackles up. "But you were a baby when you met him. He took advantage of you."

"No, he absolutely did not." Tessa was glad she could look Patty in the eye and be completely firm about this point. "Johnny saved me. He didn't do anything wrong. None of this is his fault."

Patty shook her head slowly. "Sugar, I hope you know you sound like every battered woman or abused wife in the world."

"Maybe so, but that's not how it was between Johnny and me." Tessa ran an agitated hand through her short hair, rumpling it up. "I can't let you think that, even for a second. Patty, my life before I met Johnny was . . . well, it wasn't easy. My family lived on a commune in rural Maryland. I was home-schooled, never left the community. It was all I knew for the first sixteen years of my life. I was mostly happy there, but looking back, it was a strange upbringing, very isolated and closed off from the world. Johnny was one of the first people I ever met who wasn't from the community."

Tessa snuck a glance at Patty, but instead of the pity she'd feared seeing, Patty looked thoughtful. "Go on," she said.

Encouraged, Tessa took another sip of wine and tried not to get sucked into the memories. "It was a nice place, truly. I don't want you to think it was some weird cult, or something. A lot of the community was just about living close to the land and sharing resources. My parents, though . . . they'd been brought up in the community. My mother's parents were pretty easygoing—they even let her learn to drive—but my father is descended from the founders, and he was pretty hard-core."

Patty's brow furrowed again. "What does that mean?"

"A few of the other families shared a pickup truck to go the twenty miles into town, but my parents thought that was extravagant. We walked or bicycled, in all weather. They didn't believe in the trappings of modern life. We didn't have electricity or running water. In the winter, our heat came from a woodstove. In the summer, we had to jump in the creek to get cool. But I didn't mind any of that, really."

"So what changed?"

Remembered fear clutched at Tessa's stomach. She

swallowed, the sour aftertaste of the wine coating the back of her tongue. "When I was sixteen, I started having these episodes. Every day, usually just as I woke up, there would be thirty seconds or a minute where I didn't know what I was doing or saying. I looked like I was awake, eyes open, sometimes I'd get up and move around, but I was just . . . absent."

"That sounds terrifying." Patty reached out and clasped Tessa's hand again, and Tessa squeezed her fingers gratefully.

"It really was. I'd blink and suddenly I'd be on the other side of the room, or my mother would be asking me what was happening and I couldn't answer her. I thought I was going crazy, or maybe I was possessed. I had no idea, but I wanted to go to a doctor to get checked out."

In the pause that followed while Tessa tried to figure out how to say it, Patty's frown steadily blackened. "Let me guess. One of the trappings your parents didn't believe in was modern medicine."

Tessa nodded jerkily. "I was only sixteen. I couldn't go by myself—I'd never been anywhere by myself! So it just went on, for almost two years. Until one day I blinked and when I came back to myself, I was standing next to the woodstove and it felt like my hand was on fire."

Chapter 6

She turned her hand in Patty's loose grasp until the side of her wrist was facing upward, exposing the curved silver scar in the shape of the new moon.

"That scared my mother," Tessa remembered, thinking of the lines bracketing her mother's thin, hard mouth. "She waited until my father went out to the fields and then she borrowed the keys to the neighbors' truck and drove us into town. I was light-headed with the pain, which ebbed and flowed but never got any better even though we kept stopping to pack it with fresh snow from the side of the road."

"Merciful heavens," Patty murmured. "But at least your mother finally took you to get treatment."

Tessa sighed. "Well. For the burn, yes. But when the doctor asked how it happened and I started explaining about my episodes, he got very serious and wanted to run a whole bunch of tests. My mother refused. I don't know, maybe she was worried about paying for it. We didn't have health insurance. Or maybe she just didn't want to know what was wrong with me—sometimes she acted like if we ignored the rest of the world and the things we didn't like about it, it would all go away. But as we were leaving, the doctor pulled me aside and told me my episodes were called seizures, and that they could be very serious—but they could likely also be treated."

Without a word, Patty slid off the bar stool and went to get another wineglass. She poured herself a half portion, her lowered eyebrows daring Tessa to comment. Tessa kept her mouth shut and Patty sat back down. Taking a ladylike sip, she said, "Okay. Go ahead. Tell me your parents refused to get you treatment."

It was even worse than that. Tessa bit her lip. "I hate the way this all makes my parents sound—they aren't bad people. They hold their beliefs very close to their hearts, and they endure a lot of hardship to adhere to those beliefs. My mother, especially. It must have been a huge blow to have a child who needed more than she could give, more than she believed any person should need."

Patty set her wineglass down with such force, it was a wonder she didn't snap the stem. "You are a sweet girl and I love your forgiving heart. But I swear by the Almighty, sugar, if you make any more excuses for those people—"

"I'm not making excuses," Tessa protested, even as Patty's fierce protectiveness warmed her heart. "My father was a hard man, and the amount of control he wanted over our household—I know now that there are other ways to live, and I can't imagine going back to that oppressive, domineering . . . But you know, I've spent a lot of time trying to understand their reasoning, to see the situation from their perspective, to understand what it was that forced them to react the way they did."

To understand how they could be willing to see their only daughter die rather than submit her to the care of medical science.

Frustration flattened Patty's mouth into a grim line. "Finish the story. I won't interrupt again."

Blowing out a breath, Tessa bolstered her courage with another sip of wine. "The whole ride home, I argued to be allowed to take the tests. I was really afraid—I don't know how to explain how terrifying it was to feel so out of control of my body. I hated those seizures, and the idea that I could find out more about what was going on and maybe even get treatment . . . But Mother gripped the wheel and stared straight ahead. She wouldn't even look at me. When we got back to the commune, it was late and my father was waiting for us. He took one look at the bandage on my wrist and sent me straight to bed, but I could hear him yelling at Mother about betraying their way of life, giving in to temptation and fear, stuff like that. But instead of agreeing with him, for the first time ever, I heard her talk back."

The moment was emblazoned on Tessa's memory. She'd crawled out of her bed and inched over to the edge of the loft, where she could peer down into the cabin's main room. Her mother had been down on her knees, hair straggling around her shoulders and a look of raw misery on her lined face. "She told him what the doctor said about the seizures and she . . . she pleaded with him. On her knees, she begged. The look he gave her, I'll never forget. Contemptuous, disgusted. He sneered at her that she wasn't the helpmeet he thought he'd married, if her principles and morals could be shaken so easily. He grabbed her by the arm and yanked her up to her feet and I remember being sure he was about to hit her, but he didn't. He shoved her toward their bedroom and slammed the door behind them, and I knew . . . I had to leave. My parents never fought. Ever. They were united about everything, except this. I was the thing tearing my family to pieces, and I couldn't bear it."

Tessa peeked at Patty, who appeared to be holding her breath. "It's okay," Tessa said, attempting a smile. "It was a long time ago, and not to ruin the ending but obviously, I did get away."

"You ran away," Patty corrected. "At what, seventeen years old, with no money and no resources and no experience of the world outside your community."

"It could have gone so badly." Tessa shivered. "When I think about it now, the kinds of people I could have met up with, the kinds of things I could have fallen into—I really am the luckiest woman alive. Because the person I met was Johnny."

"Now we're getting down to it." Patty settled in, eyes bright and interested.

Tessa nodded. "I waited a couple of hours until I

was sure my parents were asleep. Then I got up and dressed in my warmest clothes. I went down the loft ladder as quietly as I could and let myself out of the cabin. It was so dark, but when the clouds shifted, the moon and starlight reflected off the snow, and I could see my way forward a little bit. I didn't have a plan, exactly, except to get back to town and be at the doctor's office the next morning to have those tests. I was putting one foot in front of the other, not looking any farther ahead than that—and I hadn't reckoned on how cold it was. I'd only gotten a few miles when I started stumbling and falling down because my feet were numb inside my boots. I realized I was slowing down, and I'd lost my way in the snow. Part of me wanted to just lie down in a snowbank and go to sleep, but I knew if I did that, I'd never wake up again. So I kept putting one foot in front of the other until, finally, I saw a light in the distance."

She paused, caught in the memory of that shambling, painful half run toward the tiny light that represented hope to a girl with none. The welcome sight of that red-sided barn whose safety lights had been her beacon. The shock of sudden warmth and the exhaustion that overtook her when she finally allowed herself to stop running.

"It was a barn on the edge of a neighboring farm," she told Patty. "Johnny's family's farm, as it happens. And when he came out to milk the cows the next morning, he found me huddled in the hay, in the middle of one of my fits. I came to in the arms of the handsomest young man I'd ever seen, being carried to his truck and bundled into the passenger seat. I told him I was better, that I was sorry for trespassing, but he waved it all away and took me straight to the hospital. I had my tests, and when I came back out . . . Johnny was still there, waiting for me."

Tessa closed her eyes, reliving her complicated joy at the sight of a familiar face when everything in her life was in such turmoil. "The whole story came tumbling out of me, right there in the emergency room reception area, and Johnny never hesitated. He was amazing. He had a solution for every problem—I had juvenile absence epilepsy, I needed treatment. My parents wouldn't pay for the medicine, Johnny would. He didn't have the money . . . but he'd joined the army upon graduating from college, and if we got married before he shipped off to basic training, I'd share in his health benefits. I wasn't quite eighteen? Well, the age of consent in Maryland was sixteen. Johnny took my hand, and swore to me that all he wanted was to help me."

Patty made a noise in the back of her throat. "Oh, sugar."

"I know. I was inexperienced, but I wasn't an idiot. Of course I was scared, but what could I do? What were my options? The doctor was very clear with me about what I needed to do to control the seizures, and what the consequences would be of letting them go unchecked. I couldn't stand the thought of going back to the commune, and I knew my father would never relent about the medications anyway—and here was this boy, enough older than me to seem like he knew everything and had all the answers. And he was so handsome, so kind. I took a chance. A crazy chance."

"You were only a baby," Patty said gruffly. "When I think what could have happened, I could strangle those parents of yours."

"But nothing terrible did happen," Tessa pointed out. "I got married, to a good man who wasn't lying when he said all he wanted was to help me. I got the treatment I needed, and when I was nineteen, the seizures stopped all by themselves—but by that time, I was taking my GED and keeping the house for when Johnny came home on leave, and I just . . . stayed married to him."

Patty's mouth worked for a moment, silently, before she finally managed to say, "Sugar. When you say all Johnny wanted was to help you . . ."

Tessa could feel the sting of bitterness in the corners of her smile. "I mean, that's all he ever wanted. He never touched me. At first I was relieved, but oh, Patty, as the years went by . . . He was gone so much of the time when he was in the army, but when he was home, it got harder and harder for me to pretend I didn't want more. We weren't husband and wife, we were roommates. I'm not proud of how long it took me to leave, but I was sure I was doing the right thing . . ."

She paused, uncertainty welling up in her belly and mixing unpleasantly with the chardonnay. Patty's gaze sharpened. "And now you're not so sure. Because he came for you."

"I don't understand how he could want to stay married to me! I'm nobody to him, just some waif he rescued almost a decade ago. It's long past time I let him out of this deal, so he can find someone he can have a real relationship with. And so I can find a man who actually wants to be with me!"

Taking a last, savoring swallow of wine, Patty leaned her elbow on the butcher block and regarded Tessa consideringly. "Are you certain Johnny doesn't want you? I would think his actions in pursuing you to Sanctuary Island indicate otherwise."

Tessa's mind flashed back to the way he'd kissed her in the park that afternoon, tender and fierce . . . and hungry. Was it possible Johnny could actually want her? It was hard to believe, after years of being looked through as if she were invisible. Tessa wasn't sure she was brave enough to let herself believe Johnny's desire was sincere.

"Johnny's always had a thing about loyalty," she explained dully. "He would never leave me, even if he wanted to. I had to be the one to do it. So I did it."

Even though it had felt as if she were tearing out her own beating heart and leaving it behind. But that was a pain she was sure she could overcome, given enough time—unlike the insidious, soul-killing pain of living every day knowing that she was desperately in love with a man who could never see her as anything other than a vulnerable child to be protected.

That kiss wasn't real, Tessa decided as she accepted Patty's fierce hug. That kiss just couldn't have been real. What Tessa had to remember was how it felt when Johnny kissed her forehead and sent her off to her lonely bed, night after night. She refused to go back to that. She wanted more out of life. She deserved it. And goodness knew, so did he.

But as Patty went back to cooking dinner, finally allowing Tessa to help chop and stir, it was the kiss in the gazebo that kept replaying in Tessa's head.

Johnny paced the deserted beach, sand crunching under his leather boots and the rush of waves almost drowning out the thunderous silence on the other end of his phone call.

Losing patience, Johnny said, "Brad. Are you still there?"

A sigh. "I'm here, Johnny. But I was kind of hoping you were kidding."

The back of Johnny's neck felt hot. "I know how it sounds, but there's something going on with this bartender, Brad. I've got a gut feeling."

"Much as I respect your gut . . ." Brad paused again, seeming to choose his words carefully. "I have to wonder if this is hypervigilance left over from spending the last eighteen months in an incredibly stressful, high-pressure situation where your life was literally in danger every second."

"Not everything in my life is a reaction to the past eighteen months," Johnny growled, staring out over the ocean.

"I sent you to Sanctuary Island to get some rest and reconnect with your wife, not to get embroiled in another investigation."

"I slept fourteen hours straight last night," Johnny countered. It was the truth. Waking up had been like coming to after a coma. He still felt groggy, although the sea breeze was helping to clear away the mental cobwebs.

"That's good. And what about your wife? How's it going with Terri?"

This time Johnny was the one who paused, replaying the memory of that spectacular kiss. After years of dreaming about the softness of her lips, years of imagining the surprised sound she'd make in the back of her throat and the way she'd wrap her arms around his neck and kiss him back, Johnny's dreams had come true. And the reality had been even more devastating than anything he could have dreamed up.

Maybe he'd been wrong to keep their relationship chaste for so long. But after the way they met, how young she'd been, he would have felt like he was taking advantage of her. The idea of pressuring her into something she didn't want was the surest way Johnny knew to kill his own desire.

But now that he knew Tessa left because she thought he didn't want her, all bets were off. Maybe that kiss was fighting dirty, but Johnny was fighting to save his marriage. He'd use every weapon at his disposal.

"She goes by Tessa now," was all he told Brad. "And she's my number one priority here. I'm not going to let anything get in the way of that, not even looking into Marcus Beckett. But I'm not going to ignore my gut and pretend the guy doesn't ping every one of my internal alarms. He lives on the same tiny island where my wife lives, Brad. I need to know who Marcus Beckett is and what he's doing here."

Brad finally snapped. "Let it go, for the love of—Johnny, come on. This is textbook paranoia, man. Dr. Reeves talked about this. It's one of the most common reactions when someone is trying to reintegrate from undercover work back into civilian life."

"It's not paranoia if Marcus Beckett is actually a danger to the people in this town!" Johnny stopped, breathing hard into the phone and wishing he couldn't hear the way he sounded like a raving lunatic just then.

Brad, because he was a stand-up kind of guy, didn't bother to point it out. All he did was say, very gently and with no trace of judgment, "Your first session with the therapeutic riding center is this afternoon at one. Let me know how it goes."

As if Brad didn't have a line on that information already, Johnny mused resentfully. He probably had Johnny's new therapist on speed dial.

Reminding himself that was fair, since the ATF was footing the bill for Johnny's therapy and Brad was his boss and had to account for that money in his budget, Johnny forced a calm tone. "I'll be there. Don't worry about me."

"It's my job to worry about you."

The fond exasperation in Brad's tone pulled a reluctant smile out of Johnny. "Oh, in that case, I'm happy to keep you busy. I'd hate for you to get bored at work."

"You don't need to dream up new reasons for me to worry! I've got plenty already!"

That pulled a reluctant smile from Johnny as he

ended the call. The smile faded quickly, though, when he went back to brooding about his new landlord.

So Brad refused to help out and run a background check on the mysterious, surly Marcus Beckett. Well, special agents with the ATF were broadly empowered to investigate criminal activities on their own, and Johnny had every intention of doing just that. He'd already embedded himself in Beckett's home base. He'd figure out what the man was up to, soon enough.

Johnny turned to trudge back up the beach toward the town square. He'd slipped out of the Buttercup Inn while Beckett was drilling something in the back, and headed out looking for a place where he could be sure of making a private phone call.

Johnny knew better than to ever say anything confidential in a closet or a locked, so-called private office. He'd taken advantage of enough hiding places in his day, and he'd overheard plenty that he wasn't supposed to.

No, if you want to have a completely private conversation, look for an open field or a stretch of empty sand where you'll see an eavesdropper coming for miles before they're close enough to hear anything.

Luckily for him, Sanctuary Island was a sleepy sort of place, not exactly bustling with activity on this spring morning. Other than a dark-haired woman watching her little boy on the jungle gym and an elderly man walking a bulldog around the rose garden, Johnny hadn't passed anyone.

On his way back up to the town square, things were a little busier—more cars, more pedestrians, a couple of people on bikes. The lunchtime rush, maybe.

The thought of lunch got Johnny's feet moving faster. He hadn't eaten anything in what felt like years, and those cinnamon rolls he'd smelled at Patty Cakes the day before were calling his name.

Chapter 7

The instant Johnny hit Main Street, he caught the scent.

Melted butter and caramelized sugar, the warm spice of cinnamon . . . Johnny licked his lips and jogged the last block to the bakery.

Patty was behind the counter again, but she was busy with another customer when Johnny entered. A young woman with strawberry-blond hair and freckles stared down at the glass display case like her choice of pastry was the key to world peace.

She looked to be around Tessa's age, but something about the way she tapped the dimple in her chin as she pored over the sweet treats made her seem younger than twenty-six.

"I don't know what he'd like," she was fretting. "Everyone likes the sticky buns. But what if he's the one-in-a-million person who somehow doesn't like them? Some people have no sweet tooth at all.

Maybe a loaf of bread is a safer choice. Do you still have the jalapeño cheddar?"

Patty met Johnny's gaze over the girl's head and closed one eye in a slow wink. "We sure do, honey. Is that what you want?"

"I'm not sure," the girl moaned, clasping her fingers on top of her head. "Welcome Neighbor presents are the hardest! How do you know what he'll like when you haven't seen him since you were ten years— Oh, hello!"

The girl had turned far enough to nearly take out Johnny's eye with a gesticulating hand, and now she flushed bright enough to make all her freckles disappear.

"I'm so sorry! I didn't hear the door. You should go ahead of me, I need to think about this some more."

"That's all right," Johnny said, amused. "Take all the time you need. I'm in no rush."

He'd rather wait for Tessa to come out, anyway.

As if she'd heard his thought, Patty said, "I sent Tessa home early today. She worked a double yesterday and opened for me this morning, so I decided she needed the break."

. . . *After the day she had yesterday,* Patty didn't add, but Johnny understood her tone loud and clear. "I appreciate that, Miss Patty. I'm glad to know that Tessa's had someone like you looking out for her."

It was true, too. As much as Johnny might wish he could have been the one looking out for his wife, he'd made the choice to leave her to take that undercover assignment. He had to own that, and he couldn't regret it because it had been necessary. The world was a safer place with those guns off the streets.

And, of course, at the time it had seemed like the only way to resist his need for his wife was to take any mission that would get him out of the house and away from temptation.

Patty gave him a nod and went back to helping the indecisive girl, who was wringing her hands and peering woefully between the sugar-crusted gingersnaps and the marbled cream cheese brownies.

"Everything in that case is delicious," Patty declared. "You can't go wrong, sweetie."

"Oh, I know! I love everything you and Tessa bake." The girl glanced up with an earnest smile. "Those salted caramel shortbread bars, oh, my gosh! But what I don't know is what Marcus Beckett will love."

Johnny's ears perked up, but he didn't show his immediate surge of interest. But how the hell did a sweet, innocent girl like this have anything to do with a gruff, possibly dangerous bartender?

"That's right, I heard he was back in town," Patty said, darting a glance at Johnny. "I haven't seen him since his mother's funeral, right after his college graduation."

"I don't think he's been home since, and that was fifteen years ago. I was only a kid, and I remember worrying that cancer was contagious and my mom might catch it since we lived right next door."

Early death of a parent, Johnny noted, trying not to let the pang of sympathy interfere with inferring what that might have done to a young man at a formative time in his life. Most criminals, in Johnny's experience, boasted some traumatic childhood or adolescent event that "pushed" them into a life of crime.

Johnny's own catastrophic childhood tragedy had shoved him in the other direction, straight into law enforcement.

"Such a sad thing, what happened to that family." Patty sighed. "What a bright future Marcus had ahead of him, and then . . . Didn't he go into the army?"

Johnny felt an internal rush of satisfaction. He hadn't lost his ability to spot military training. Now, the only question remained—was Beckett a veteran who should be honored for his service to his nation? Or had he turned the training Uncle Sam gave him into something shady as hell?

"Yes, and that was the last anyone heard from him. I'm sure he turned out wonderfully!" The girl bit her lip. "Except for the part about how he hasn't visited his poor father in years and years. But maybe Marcus was busy. With work, or something."

Yeah, or something, Johnny thought grimly. *Something illegal, maybe.* The way Beckett had warned him off the subject of where he'd gotten the money he seemed to be spending like water . . . There was a secret there. Johnny was sure of it.

And where there were secrets about money, there was usually criminal activity.

In fact, maybe it was time to warn this sweet young thing off her mission of welcoming Marcus Beckett home. Johnny put on his most charming, trustworthy smile.

"You know, I couldn't help but overhear you talking

about Marcus Beckett—and as it happens, I'm staying in the apartment next to his, above the bar he's opening."

Quinn turned to him with a dazzling smile at the coincidence. "Oh! Do you know if he likes cream cheese brownies?"

"Um, I don't. Sorry. But I'd be happy to bring him whatever you pick out. Save you a trip."

Her face fell. Johnny hoped to God she never tried to play poker for money.

"Gosh," Quinn said. "That's really nice of you. But I couldn't impose . . . Oh, and I have to go see him anyway, because I'm going to ask him for a job! So I might as well deliver the cupcakes myself. Yeah, cupcakes, I think. The yellow cake ones with chocolate buttercream."

The relief in her happy smile was equaled only by the alarm Johnny felt at this turn of events. "You want to work for Beckett?"

For some reason, that made her blush again. "Well, I bartended in college, and I'm kind of between jobs right now, so I was sort of thinking it might be a good fit. Why, does he already have a bartender?"

She looked so anxious at the thought. Johnny hated to crush her dreams, but he hated the idea of this nice girl getting mixed up with Beckett even more. "He's probably a good week away from opening up, but I'm pretty sure he plans to tend the bar himself."

Her brow cleared. "Oh, that's all right, then. No one wants to work seven days a week, and I'm good with part-time. It's sort of my thing."

"Here are your cupcakes, sweetie." Patty handed a

plain brown box tied with red ribbon across the counter. "Tell your parents I said hi, the next time you talk to them."

"I will!" Quinn bounced on the soles of her sneakers as she counted out change. "They're loving the vagabond life. I haven't heard from them since they hit Yellowstone, but I think they're getting to the lodge in the next day or so, and they should have better reception then. I'll give them your love. Thanks, Miss Patty!"

With that, she wafted out of the bakery on a cloud of shiny optimism bright enough to make Johnny's head hurt. Part of him wanted to run after Quinn and keep her from going to talk to Marcus Beckett, but Johnny consoled himself with the realistic understanding that there was almost no way Beckett would be interested in hiring Little Miss Sunshine to work in his bar.

Again showing an uncanny, discomforting ability to read his mind, Patty shrugged. "No use trying to talk that girl out of anything. For such a flibbertigibbet, she's got an obstinate streak a mile wide."

Flibbertigibbet? Who said that?

"She seemed very sweet," Johnny said after a short hesitation.

"Oh, very. Always has been. But she's twenty-five years old and she's never had a real job. No idea what she wants to do with her life, no direction, nothing permanent. Even her living situation—she's house-sitting for her parents while they take an extended RV trip out West." Patty shook her salt-and-pepper curls. "In my day, most girls were married by her age.

And if you weren't married, you'd better have a good backup plan like my bakery here. Not that I'm saying women today ought to get married young. That's usually not a good idea these days."

Johnny stared at her. "I guess I don't need to ask where you stand on the subject of Tessa and me."

"Don't be too sure."

What was it about older women? How did they perfect that mysterious, cryptic, all-knowing attitude? Johnny was pretty darn sure his instincts had been correct about this one. Patty could either be a valuable ally . . . or an adversary Johnny didn't need.

When he was pretending to be Alex Santiago, he'd gotten in good with the second in command of the gang. Sometimes it was more fruitful to go around the top guy and get to the right-hand man, to convert the person who had influence with the top decision maker.

It felt weird to apply the lessons he'd learned undercover to the problem of seducing his own wife, but Johnny was prepared to be ruthless.

To that end, he dredged up a grin and a twinkle for Patty. "That's good to hear. I can use all the help I can get convincing Tessa to give me another chance after the way I left her."

A strange look came over the older woman's handsome, laugh-lined face. "You know she's not angry with you. Don't you? She didn't leave to get back at you."

That brought Johnny up short. On some unspoken level, that was exactly what he'd thought. He felt his lips twist ruefully. "She seemed plenty mad when she stomped off yesterday, after I slipped and called her Terri. I didn't mean to, but it's automatic. She's been Terri to me for a long time."

"It's not about the name." Patty folded her lips together and shook her head, as if she'd said too much. "Look, John. I'm not here to be your go-between. I'm here for Tessa. End of story. If you're what's going to make her happy, then I'll be cheering you on all the way. But if you can't get your act together and figure that out, well, I'll be the one who keys your car and leaves that bag of flaming dog poop on your front porch. You hear?"

From the pugnacious tilt of her chin and the snap of defiant pride in her deep brown eyes, Johnny thought Patty expected him to get pissed off. Instead, all he felt was gratitude.

"I hear you. And I'm glad she has you. Tessa's gone a long time with no one but me in her corner. The people who should have put her first, before everything else in their lives . . . well, they weren't nearly as strong as you. I'd include myself in that group." The admission hurt, the words sticking in his throat like he'd swallowed a bone. "But I'm here now. And I'm trying. In fact, we've got our first couples-therapy appointment this afternoon at the Windy Corner Therapeutic Riding Center. That's what I came to tell her."

For the first time since he met Tessa's new boss, Johnny saw Patty's sharp gaze soften a bit. She harrumphed and hit a button on the cash register to pop the drawer out. With a great whack, she broke open a roll of nickels and dumped it into the drawer. "Well.

Good. That's something, at least. Here, have a cheddar pecan scone. You need to keep your strength up."

Johnny took the crumbly wedge gratefully. It was still warm from the oven, and the first bite shocked him with a burst of savory flavor he hadn't been expecting. Not that he was some expert on scones, teatime not being a big hobby at the ATF, but he'd had the impression that they were a dry, sort of tastelessly sweet type of biscuit.

This scone was sharp with cheddar and rich with the buttery taste of toasted pecans, with a fiery kick of cayenne at the back of his tongue. Johnny basically inhaled the thing without even pausing to say thank you.

When it was gone and he was seriously considering licking the crumbs from his palm, he blinked his eyes open to see Patty watching him with a proud gleam in her eyes.

"That was amazing," Johnny said honestly, brushing his palm on his jeans. "I see why this bakery is such an island institution. You're a great baker."

"Oh, I didn't bake those. Your wife did. In fact, those scones are her original recipe. She won a prize for them at the county fair, had her picture in the papers and everything. I guess you didn't see it."

Johnny blinked. Tessa had cooked for them most nights, and he'd certainly never had any complaints about the simple, nutritious meals she'd provided. But she'd never produced anything as knock-your-socks-off delicious and unexpected as that cheddar pecan scone.

"I had no idea she could cook like this," he said blankly.

"When she first came here, she couldn't." Patty went about straightening her display case, filling in holes in the trays of muffins and rolls from the tall, wheeled racks behind her. "At first, all she'd do was follow my recipes. But after a few months, I started noticing that those old pastries that I've been making forever . . . they came out a little differently when Tessa was the one doing the baking. I watched her one morning, and I saw that without even seeming aware of it, she was tweaking the recipes as she went along, adding a pinch of this and a dash of that, and every single time it was an improvement. Well, I won't fib, at first I was a little put out. I mean, those recipes are tried and true! I've been making my cinnamon-streusel muffins the same way for twenty-five years! But when Tessa started folding a little dab of sweetened cream cheese into the cinnamon-brown-sugar filling—boy, I tell you what. I saw the light in a quick hurry! She's got a real knack for this work, and a real passion for it, too."

Johnny stared down at what looked like little round knots of sweet, white dough, baked to golden brown and scattered with crunchy sugar and cinnamon-laced crumbs. "There's cream cheese inside there?"

In answer, Patty pulled out one of the rolls and broke it open, releasing a warm, spicy scent. White cream oozed in the center of the roll, ribbons of dark cinnamon sugar running through it, and Johnny's mouth watered.

Taking pity on him, Patty handed him half the roll

and took a big bite out of the other half. Johnny had to hold back an obscene groan at the decadent richness of the yeasty, light pastry wrapped around warm, tangy-sweet cream cheese. They finished their treat in the silence that accompanies food so delicious that the eaters want nothing to distract them from their enjoyment.

"Incredible." Johnny gave in to temptation and licked his fingers clean. "I never knew . . . and she must love it. No one could create something this delicious without enjoying the process."

Patty's smile widened. "There may be hope for you yet, boy. Yes, she does love it. And the bakery customers love her. She's been happy here, John."

He wanted to argue, to deny it. He'd been miserable every day they'd been apart. How could Tessa have been happy? But he'd seen it for himself. The way this island had set her smile free and unlocked her laugh. The way she'd grown into herself once she was out of the shadow of their unusual marriage.

"She has a life here," Patty continued, gentle but implacable. "One she can be proud of. And I won't lie, I have my own reasons for wanting her to stay—but if you convince her to leave Sanctuary Island with you, you'll be denying her the chance to live the life she built with her own hands and talent and heart. I'm asking you. Please don't take her away, John."

There it was. The answer he thought he'd come here to find . . . and now that he knew that Tessa was fine without him, that she was happy, what was he supposed to do next?

"I want what's best for her." The words scraped

painfully on their way out of his constricted throat. "That's all I've ever wanted, since the moment I met her."

Patty's answering gaze was full of solemn sympathy. "What a coincidence. That's what I want, too."

Behind Patty, a muffled thump sounded from the other side of the door to the kitchen.

With a sense of inevitability, Johnny watched as Patty glanced over her shoulder to see Tessa standing in the doorway, fingers cramped white-knuckled around the shoulder strap of her purse.

Eyes flashing and lips pale, Tessa lifted her chin and said, "Maybe one or both of you should take a minute to ask me what *I* want."

Chapter 8

Tessa couldn't catch her breath. All the progress she'd made toward independence, being her own woman, and here were the two people who mattered most to her in the world, standing around deciding her future without any input from Tessa herself.

It was maddening and humiliating, at least partly because Tessa didn't actually know what she wanted her future to look like.

"Oh, sugar!" Patty looked startled, one thin hand fluttering up toward her chest as if her heart were thumping erratically. "You startled me. What are you doing back here?"

"I came to check on the focaccia dough," Tessa answered mechanically. "It's almost done with its first rise and I didn't want you to be the one who had to pound it down. And that's not the point! You two. What are you doing, talking about me like I'm a child who can't make decisions for myself?"

Patty flinched and Johnny held up his hands as if Tessa had turned a gun on him.

"It's not like that, sugar—"

"Come on, honey, I didn't mean it like that—"

They were both so apologetic, turning pleading eyes on her and raising "who me?" brows in her direction. Instantly flushed with guilt, Tessa struggled to stick to her point. "I know neither of you meant to run me down or make me sound like an incompetent infant—and I know I've needed you both to take care of me in the past. I'm not denying that. But I thought I'd made it clear how important it is to me to start making my own way in the world. Johnny, this is a huge part of why I left, and Patty, I didn't settle here so I could trade one guardian angel for another. Thank you, both, for everything you've done for me and the many opportunities you've given me, but please, just . . . stop."

Patty and Johnny exchanged pained glances, and Patty shooed him forward with a flip of her blue-veined hand.

"I get it, sweetheart." Tessa had never heard that tone from Johnny before, rough and graveled, but careful. "At least, I'm trying to."

Tessa couldn't help it. She melted like a lemon glaze over a hot buttermilk pound cake. "Well, I realize this is a big shift that I kind of threw at you all of a sudden. It's understandable that it would take some time to get used to the new me."

"I promise, I'm working on it."

Tessa's heart felt tender inside her chest, like a bruise. "I know you are. And I promise you I'll try, too, with the couples counseling. I mean it. So let's just see where this goes, okay?"

The slight smile Johnny gave her didn't seem to reach his beautiful dark eyes, but before Tessa could do more than frown in concern, Patty cleared her throat.

Tessa looked over at her new friend and mentor, and felt the tips of her fingers go cold and numb at the sight of the usually vibrant, vivacious woman hunched against the counter. Most times, Patty seemed more like a force of nature than an older lady whose doctors were worried about her health. But every now and then, Tessa caught a glimpse that reminded her that Patty was doing the work of a woman half her age, and it was wearing on her frail body.

"Why don't you close up early today, Patty?" Tessa urged, stepping up to the counter to wrap a tentative arm around the older woman's shoulders. Patty's bones felt frighteningly prominent under the bulky weave of her oatmeal-colored linen sweater, and Tessa held her gently. "Or I could clock back in and take the afternoon shift. Give you a rest."

Out of the corner of her eye, Tessa saw Johnny shift his weight. He bit down on whatever he was about to say, though, locking eyes with Patty. Who sighed wearily under Tessa's arm and said, "That's sweet of you, sugar, but you've already got an appointment this afternoon. To talk about your marriage while learning how to braid a horse's mane, or some such."

The spark of gratitude in Johnny's gaze made Tessa bite back a sigh. He and Patty were still conspiring to

run her life, in some way Tessa couldn't quite understand. Well, it was something to bring up in their therapy session, maybe.

"Before we head out," Johnny said, "I think Patty's
got something to say to you."

"What's up, Patty?"

Tessa frowned when Patty hesitated. It wasn't
like her forthright boss to hold back on saying her
piece. She glanced at Johnny, who seemed to know
something about it, but he merely shook his head
slightly and pulled out his wallet.

"I'll wait outside. What do I owe you for the scone,
Miss Patty?"

"You already paid," Patty argued. "Straight talk
and a new understanding. I'd say that more than com-
pensates me for a scone and half a cinnamon muffin."

They regarded each other for a quiet heartbeat, and
Tessa had the strange feeling that they knew each
other better than should be possible after meeting only
the night before.

Finally, Johnny nodded and stuck his hands in his
jacket pockets before heading for the door. He stepped
out, turning his face up to the sunshine, and Tessa
dragged her gaze back to Patty.

"Okay. Tell me what's going on with you."

"I wasn't planning to say anything just yet." Patty
fiddled with an empty coin wrapper, her knobby-
knuckled fingers uncharacteristically nervous. "I know
you're not really in a position to do anything about it
right now, and I keep hoping maybe I'll get all the way
back on my feet."

A chill of dread skittered down Tessa's spine. "Tell me."

Patty waved away her concern the way she always did. "Nothing new, just the same old, same old from Doc Hathaway. Shouldn't stress, shouldn't work too hard, shouldn't be on my feet all day." She snorted. "Man's clearly never run his own business. Or baked a loaf of bread."

"That's what I'm here for, though. To take some of that burden off your shoulders." *And off your poor, tired heart,* Tessa finished silently.

Patty reached out and clasped Tessa's hand. "And you do it beautifully. When I set that ad for help a year ago, I didn't really expect to find someone. I had no hope that I'd be able to find anybody who I could stand to work beside every day, to train up and share my precious recipes with—but then there you were. And you were perfect."

Tears burned at the backs of Tessa's eyes, but it was the fear clutching at Tessa's throat that choked off her voice.

It sounded an awful lot like Patty was saying goodbye.

"Goodness, don't look like that!" Patty's other hand came up to join their clasped hands so she could tug Tessa toward the stool behind the counter and press her to sit down. "I'm not dying or anything. Well, I suppose I will eventually, but in the meantime I intend to live a good, happy life with as much health as I can cobble together. Which is where you come in."

"Anything," Tessa said desperately, squeezing

Patty's fingers tight. "Whatever I can do to help you, I'll do it."

Patty laughed a little, but her thin lips were turned down at the corners. "Not so fast, sugar. What I'm asking isn't a small thing, and you might not be ready. But your man is right—I need to talk to you about it now so you have all the information you need to make a real decision about your future. Keeping it from you wouldn't be doing you any favors. And you were right, it wouldn't be respecting you as the woman you've worked so hard to become."

"Thanks, Patty. That means more to me than you can possibly know."

Patty leaned in for a short, strong hug, dropping her grip on Tessa's hand to clasp her shoulders and look her straight in the eye. "Okay, here goes. On my doctor's advice and after taking stock of these old bones of mine, I've decided I'd like to retire."

The bombshell rocked the foundation of Tessa's new world. "But . . . Patty Cakes can't exist without Patty!"

A wry look came into Patty's shrewd eyes. "Oh, sugar. Patty Cakes has been more yours than mine for at least half a year. You already do most of the baking, all the heavy lifting, and the books. All I do anymore is help customers, and some days, to be honest, even that feels like too much for me."

Remorse mixed with worry to form a toxic cocktail in the pit of Tessa's stomach. "I'm so sorry, Patty. I can take on more front counter work!"

"With what time? You're already here from dawn

till dusk, most days." Patty shook her head. "That's no kind of life for a young woman. It doesn't make sense to ask any employee, no matter how devoted, to work like that. You'd burn out inside of a year."

"So we hire more help! Or we reduce our open hours—except we can't afford to do that, can we."

It wasn't a question. Tessa had been taking care of the bakery's finances, with Patty's help, for three months. She knew as well as anyone the delicate balance of work hours and sales needed for a small business like Patty Cakes to turn a sustainable profit.

"I have another solution," Patty said slowly. "Something I've been thinking about for a long time now, and I want you to consider it carefully. It might not be what you want—but you've more than earned the chance to make up your own mind about it."

Hope shafted through Tessa's chest like a ray of sunlight. "Patty, come on. The suspense is killing me, here! What's this big solution?"

Patty's dark eyes were bright with the moisture of unshed tears, but the tremulous smile on her lips was genuine.

Then she opened her mouth and changed Tessa's life.

Marcus held his breath and flicked the main breaker.

Nothing happened.

Cursing on a long sigh, he let his head drop against the metal box holding the breaker switches. God only knew what he'd tripped this time. He was starting to think there were mice in the walls, snacking on different wires all day long.

"Careful you don't get sweat on those switches," an unfamiliar female voice sang out from behind him. "You could get electrocuted and thrown halfway across the room! And then I'd have to do CPR, which I don't really know how to do, although I don't see how it could be that hard and I watch TV so obviously I know the basics. But . . ."

Marcus straightened and rounded on the intruder. Second time in as many days that someone showed up here unannounced, getting the drop on him. Unacceptable.

He had no idea what his face was doing, but whatever the girl saw there cut off her babble like she was connected to the switch he'd just flipped.

"We're not open," he said, eyeing her. With her fresh-faced, freckled complexion and her red hair pulled up in a simple ponytail, she looked like she was barely old enough to be standing in a bar at all.

"Oh, I know." The quick, wide smile lit up the room. Marcus refused to be charmed. "I'm here to welcome you to the neighborhood! I mean, to welcome you *back* to the neighborhood. Welcome home, Marcus."

Every muscle went taut, adrenaline flooding him with no outlet. He had no idea who this girl was. How did she know his name?

Her blinding smile faded into a rueful wince. "You don't remember me. I mean, why would you? My name's Quinn, not that you called me that. Not that you called me much of anything! "

The slightly nervous babble of her voice faded in Marcus's ears as she held out a hopeful hand with something dangling from it. In the darkness, it was just a solid shape at the bottom of his field of vision and his body reacted without conscious thought.

Marcus stepped smoothly forward, directly into the girl's personal space, close enough to foul her aim and make their two bodies into a single target. She gasped as he simultaneously snagged the package from her loosened fingers, registering only that it was light and the contents shifted inside with the movement.

He blinked and realized he had his other hand curved around the base of the girl's slender, white throat. His thumb rested against her fluttering pulse, tracking the hummingbird-fast beat of her heart. He felt it when she swallowed, first in his palm and then, a moment later, in his groin.

What the hell?

This close, he could make out the red-gold gleam of her hair and the darker sweep of her eyelashes framing wide, indigo-blue eyes. Her lips parted and he caught the flicker of her pink tongue, wetting her bottom lip. If he tightened his hand, he could crush her windpipe— but she didn't struggle or pull away. She only watched him with that fathomless stare, as if . . . God.

As if she trusted him not to hurt her.

Which he wouldn't, because his rational mind categorized her as Not a Threat in the next instant. An instant or so too late to keep from looking like an antisocial monster, unfortunately.

Marcus stepped back abruptly, dropping his hand and releasing her. He should apologize. He wasn't an idiot. He knew it was weird, at best, to react like that to someone bringing—what was in the box? Crap, it was from the bakery.

"They're cupcakes," she offered, her bright voice a little thready and faint now.

Of course they were cupcakes. Marcus pressed his eyes closed for a brief moment. "Thanks . . ."

"Quinn," she prompted, that smile peeking out again. Was she crazy? Or was she just trying not to rile up the nutjob by mentioning the way he'd come within a hairsbreadth of taking her down like an armed assailant?

"I don't eat cupcakes," he said bluntly, thrusting the package back toward her. He wasn't embarrassed. He just didn't have time to fool around with whatever this visit was.

"Oh." Face downcast, Quinn took the box back. "I knew I should have gone with the cream cheese brownies."

Unwilling amusement caught at Marcus's breath, but he didn't let it show. "I don't eat brownies, either. You take the cupcakes home. Enjoy. I appreciate the thought."

Her nose wrinkled in a way Marcus did not find adorable at all. "I never liked that phrase, about it being the thought that counts. I mean, thoughts are nice, but not as nice as chocolate! At least, if you like chocolate, which I guess you don't. You're probably one of those people who always orders the lemon dessert at a restaurant. Oh! Miss Patty has lemon bars, sometimes!"

Something like desperation was simmering under Marcus's skin. He needed to get rid of this girl before she did something awful. Like making him smile. "I don't have much of a sweet tooth. And I've got a lot of work to do here, so . . ."

"Sure, of course." The sunny smile didn't seem to have been dimmed by Marcus's bad attitude. "Actually, that's what I'm here about. Work."

He frowned. "I don't need any help."

Especially not from a slim wisp of a redheaded girl. Although his keen observational skills informed by his up-close glimpse of her had showed her to be older than he'd thought at first. Not a girl, but a young woman, emphasis on the *young*. Mid-twenties, he'd estimate.

She would've only been, what, ten years old when he left home that last time? The thought teased at his memory. A little girl, red braids tied with pink ribbons to match the bright pink of the bicycle that was always lying on its side in the front yard of the house next door . . .

"Harper," Marcus rasped, putting it together. "Quinn Harper. I remember you. You've changed."

Pleased, Quinn clutched the box of cupcakes to her chest. Marcus's eyes dropped to it automatically, then lingered for an uncomfortably warm second. That *definitely* had changed.

"I grew up," she said cheerfully. "Well, sort of. Depends who you talk to."

He was willing to bet it did. There was something almost unbearably young about Quinn. Not a sense of immaturity, exactly, although he'd bet good money that she was pretty inexperienced when it came to some of the harsher realities of life.

"Oops," she was saying, rolling her eyes good-naturedly. "Probably not the smartest thing to say to a prospective employer, huh? But it's not like it's a secret and you'd be bound to find out eventually."

Wait. Prospective employer. What? Marcus shook his head, feeling like he'd gone a few too many rounds in the sparring ring. "Find out what?"

"Let's just say my work history is a little . . . eclectic," Quinn said, as if she were confiding in him. "Like, we're talking patchwork quilt, not solid down comforter. Personally, I think it's a strength. I know a little about a lot of subjects, and I'm a quick learner! Plus, this time I have actual experience. I went to college—to be honest, a lot of college, because it took me a while to settle on a major— and I paid my own way after the first four years."

Marcus was starting to feel as if he'd been asleep through the first half of this conversation. He'd obviously missed some key information. "Look, I've got things covered here. So why don't you run along home to your mommy and daddy like a good girl."

"I don't live with my parents!" Quinn propped her hands on her hips, indignant. "Well. Okay, technically that's because they're out of town or I guess I would be living with them since I'm living in their house, but I'm hoping to be able to afford a place of my own by the time they come home! Which is where you come in."

She was relentless. "I'm not hiring you. Get out."

"How do you know you don't want to hire me unless you give me a tryout?"

Marcus blinked, blinded by her smile and the cheery pragmatism in her expectant gaze. "What are you planning to do for a tryout? Rewire my lighting?"

Actually, if she could do that, he might have to reconsider. But no, she was shaking her head and laughing, a gurgling hoot of a laugh that should have been irritating. It *was* irritating. Marcus was nothing but irritated, damn it.

"No! Although I know how to stretch a canvas over an easel, identify poisonous mushrooms, and count to a thousand in French if any of that's relevant. But for my tryout for the bartending gig, I thought I'd, you know, mix you a cocktail."

"It ain't that kind of bar, little girl."

"I know how to pull a Guinness, too," she wheedled. "And I pour a perfect ounce-and-a-half shot without looking, every time."

Against his will, Marcus felt his interest piqued. "Bull. Prove it."

He knew it was a tactical blunder the instant Quinn's face lit up. "I will! And if I can do it, you'll hire me?"

Marcus snorted. "If you can do it ten times in a row, without looking, I'll think about hiring you. On a probationary basis."

Without waiting for further invitation, Quinn ducked around behind the bar and grabbed a bottle of Jack.

Five minutes later, she leaned her elbows on the polished zinc bar and waggled the bottle sympathetically. "That makes fifteen. I can keep going if you want, but we're going to need a new bottle."

Marcus stared down at the fifteen glasses of bourbon. Some were shot glasses, some were tall, slim double shots. There was bourbon—a perfect ounce and a half, to be exact—in wineglasses and beer steins, pilsner glasses and highballs. He shook his head, still having a hard time believing it, even though he'd measured each pour himself.

He might be a monster, he might be terse, bad tempered, and antisocial, with a past so ugly even he didn't like looking at it . . . but he was a man of his word.

Putting out his hand with a sense of impending doom, he looked Quinn straight in the eye. "I guess this means you're hired."

Chapter 9

"I've never been out here before. Funny how you can live on an island so small, and still find new things to discover."

Johnny put the rental car in park and undid his seat belt. *Play it cool,* he told himself.

It was tough, though, because those were the first words Tessa had spoken since she wandered out of Patty Cakes with a dazed look on her face.

"I can see why you love this island," Johnny said, studying her face as she got out of the car. "It's beautiful."

She laughed softly, tipping her head back and wrapping her arms around her torso. "It's like a miracle. People think small towns are boring, but honestly, I never know what to expect from day to day."

"I would have thought, after the way you grew up, you'd hate small towns."

Johnny spoke without thinking, caught up in the

sudden realization that he was going to have to contend with how much Tessa liked Sanctuary Island while he tried to get her to come home to D.C. But the minute he mentioned her childhood, he froze. It was something they never discussed, and only partly because Johnny didn't want to remind Tessa of the hell she'd gone through.

"I'm sorry," he said immediately. "Ignore me, I'm still not caught up on my sleep."

But to his surprise, instead of tearing up or ducking her head in remembered fear, Tessa reached for his hand. Her eyes were clear and direct, her voice gentle, as she said, "No, I won't ignore you. That would be a terrible beginning to our couples therapy!"

A keen sense of admiration pierced Johnny's chest. She had truly grown into an amazing woman, this girl he married so long ago. "I know I've never been a big fan of the idea of therapy, but I want you know I plan to take this seriously. I could hardly do less, when this is practically the first thing you've ever asked of me, since the day we got married."

"How could I ask for more than you were already providing? A home, a life, a future—my health! I owed you everything. I'll never stop being grateful for what you gave me."

This gratitude, again. He hated that she felt like she owed him anything. "Don't make me out to be some kind of hero," he snapped.

Tessa's brows arched in surprise. "But you've always been my hero," she offered tentatively.

"Trust me, honey, I'm no hero." Johnny pulled away from her to lock the car and pocket the keys, taking advantage of the distraction to get his expression under control. "We're going to be late."

"Johnny, wait—"

But he strode off toward the big wooden barn, grimly determined to get this over with. A hand-lettered sign out front proclaimed the place to be the WINDY CORNER THERAPEUTIC RIDING CENTER, so at least they were in the right place.

The right place for Johnny to make a last-ditch effort to save a marriage based on mutual affection, respect . . . and gratitude. He didn't know why the thought soured his stomach, but it did.

A tall, angular woman in jeans and a dark green flannel shirt greeted him at the open bay doors leading into the barn, just as Tessa caught up to him.

"Hi! Y'all must be the Alexanders. I'm Dr. Adrienne Voss. Very pleased to meet you."

Johnny shook hands with the psychologist who'd be telling them all about how their marriage sucked. She was younger than he'd expected, but there was a serenity about her that made her seem older than her years. She wasn't beautiful, exactly, with her scrubbed-clean face, plain brown hair, and wide-set eyes . . . but when she smiled gently at Tessa, Johnny felt a part of himself relax into acceptance.

"It's nice to meet you," Tessa was saying, a little nervously now that they were actually face-to-face with the doc. She'd never been big on doctors, Johnny remembered now. Probably because she associated them with the terrifying seizures from her teenage years, and the break with her parents.

He'd wrapped a protective arm around her shoulders before he knew he meant to do it, and to his relief, Tessa leaned into him instead of retreating. It felt good, safe and familiar, to have her there tucked against his side.

"We appreciate you being willing to change the focus of the therapy I'd signed up for," Johnny told the doc. "I know it's not what the bureau originally contacted you about, but—"

"No worries at all. Adaptability is one of the strengths of equine-assisted therapy." Dr. Voss tucked her clipboard under one arm and lifted her chin amiably toward the interior of the barn. "Come on, we've got a lot to do and only an hour carved out today. We'll start with the two-penny tour, but I'm going to want to get into our first exercise before y'all leave today."

"What sorts of exercises will we be doing?" Tessa asked, nerves fraying her voice a little.

"For today, we'll really just be getting to know the horses and each other." Dr. Voss led them into the warm barn, their footsteps muffled by sawdust strewn across the floor. A wide corridor flanked by stalls on both sides opened out to a view of the pine copse behind the barn, and a sloping green hill down to another structure in the distance. Sunlight streamed in the open doors, catching on dancing dust motes and making the hay bristling from the feed troughs glow.

The smell of the barn, sweet bran mash and horse, dug memories out of Johnny's brain and threw him back to the past. He inhaled deeply, feeling the muscles of his shoulders unbunch. "I haven't smelled that since my mom sold the farm," he murmured, gazing into one of the stalls.

A gray-dappled white horse poked his head out over the low half-door to eye him with the curious optimism of an animal that gets a lot of treats from strangers.

"This is Clover," Dr. Voss said, pausing to hook an affectionate arm over the horse's neck. "He's one of our best therapy horses."

Clover tossed his head as if he were nodding along, and beside him, Tessa laughed. Johnny wished he'd thought to bring an apple with him. "Sorry, fella, I've got nothing for you."

"Um, I brought something," Tessa said shyly. "I know horses like sugar cubes, so I thought maybe this would work. It's okay if not, though . . ."

She dipped into the pocket of her denim jacket and pulled out a plastic baggie full of little brown candies. They were irregularly shaped, as if they'd been pressed into ovals by human fingers.

"Did you make those?" Johnny demanded, delighted.

Tessa flushed. "They're just maple sugar candies. Easy as pie. Well, easier than pie, actually. All you need is maple sugar and a candy thermometer. So if the horses can't eat them, it's totally okay!"

"Maple sugar is fine," Dr. Voss assured her. "Clover will love it, he's got a real sweet tooth. Just give him one, though, or he'll get addicted! He's already likely to follow you around like a duckling, begging for more. You're shameless, aren't you, Clover? Here, hold your hand flat with the treat on your palm. Don't curl your thumb up! He's liable to think it's another treat and chomp down on it! That's perfect. You're a natural."

Tessa glowed a bit under the praise, or maybe it was the satisfaction of watching the eager way the horse lapped up the candy she offered and then snuffled across her palm, hoping for seconds. "That tickles!"

"There's nothing quite like a horse's nose," Johnny agreed, stepping forward to rub his hand down the long, silken-furred face. Clover nudged him hard enough to knock him back a pace, his breath whuffling loudly as he searched Johnny's torso for pockets that might hold more treats.

Laughing, Dr. Voss said, "I think you two are going to be very popular around here. Come on, I'll introduce you to the rest of the crew, but I think we'll work with Clover later. You made a good connection with him."

Johnny was careful not to lift a skeptical eyebrow. Growing up on a farm, he'd learned early on not to take a romantic view of the livestock. The horses at his parents' farm had been older, ornery, and not terribly interested in a kid who wanted to ride like John Wayne and Clint Eastwood, and Johnny had grown out of the cowboy phase pretty young. Angie was the horse-crazy one . . .

Cutting that thought off at the root before it could dig in and reach down to places he didn't want to go, Johnny tuned back in to Dr. Voss's explanations about the way the therapy center worked.

"They brought me in about six months ago when

they started getting requests for more types of therapy than physical therapy. The Hero Project helped to underwrite the cost of expanding the center's mission."

At Tessa's questioning glance, Johnny filled in. "The Hero Project is what brought us here, too. They're partnered with the ATF, among lots of other organizations, to get help for people who need it."

"For heroes," Dr. Voss said, as if she sensed Johnny's discomfort with that word. "Our heroes of all shapes, sizes, backgrounds, and experiences. The Hero Project has sent me firefighters, cops, army veterans, FBI agents—you name it, we've dealt with it."

Tessa's eyes were bright. "What an awesome initiative. I've thought a lot about how to help the people who dedicate their lives to serving others, often at great personal cost. I'm so glad to know the Hero Project exists, and proud to be part of it, even in a small way."

"That's exactly how I feel, too. So when Ella Wilkes offered me the job here, how could I refuse?"

"Ella, that's Jo Ellen's daughter, right? So you know the owners of the barn." Tessa nodded as if that made sense. "But still, to leave your practice in New York and come all the way to Sanctuary Island—it must have been a big adjustment."

Dr. Voss shrugged one shoulder. "It could have been, I suppose. But Ella is one of my dearest friends, so I already had the start of a wonderful support network here. She needed me. And the work is very worth doing. Equine-assisted therapy is a thriving, growing field with a lot to learn. The bonds between people and horses are ancient and undeniable. For centuries, we needed each other to survive. Even now, here on Sanctuary Island, the wild horses depend on the laws we pass to protect their habitat and to keep them safe. And we, for our part, turn to them for help with all sorts of troubles."

She paused beside a stall holding a small chestnut mare. "I don't mean to go on and on, but it occurs to me that the circumstances that brought you to us are somewhat unusual. Most clients I work with have chosen us, out of a range of similar options—or they live on the island and are fully aware of what we're doing here, and why. You two are different. John, your boss mandated this work, as I understand it. And Theresa, you're living on the island currently?"

"I am," she said, lifting her chin slightly. "And call me Tessa, please."

"And I'm Johnny," he added. He gave the doc a high-beam smile. She'd reminded him that he wouldn't be heading back to his job without getting a green light from her, and he had no intention of being assigned extra talk therapy with the departmental shrink. "We're not living together at the moment, but I'm hoping to change that."

"Oh?" Tessa crossed her arms, drumming her fingertips anxiously. "You're thinking about relocating to Sanctuary Island, are you?"

"I wish I could, but I can't. You know I can't. My job—"

"You're not the only one with a job, Johnny. I mean, I know it's not as important as your job, but it's important to me."

"Tessa. Have I said once that your job matters less than mine?"

Deflating like a pricked balloon, Tessa sighed. "No. You haven't. And I realize how much your job matters, to you and to the world. It's literally life and death, keeping illegal guns off the streets and out of the hands of criminals. Not quite the same as putting cinnamon buns in the hands of eight-year-olds."

There was no way to argue with that, and Johnny didn't exactly want to argue it—but he hated to see the defeated hunch of Tessa's shoulders. All the spit and vinegar and fire and life he'd seen in her through the bakery window had drained away, as if Johnny had pulled the plug.

"I hope I've done some good in the world. The ATF gave me a way to help stop gun violence, and I'm good at what I do. But you're good at what you do, too, Tessa. I've seen the smiles on the faces of customers leaving Patty Cakes. You make people happy. That's an amazing gift." He tried for a smile. "God knows I've never been particularly good at it."

If part of him hoped Tessa would contradict him, protest that he'd made her happy during their marriage, he was doomed to disappointment. Instead she sucked in a breath and twisted her hands together nervously into the silence.

Dr. Voss clapped once, startling both of them. "Okay! It sounds like you two are ready to get started. I'm hearing that there are some logistical issues to be sorted through, but in my experience, logistics are the rational mind's way of providing a reason for emotional behaviors. Meaning what you already know, deep down: you're living apart because your relationship is in crisis. If we can weather that storm together, chances are good that the issue of where to live and how to deal with your respective careers will seem much less impossible to solve."

Johnny looked at Tessa, who was biting her lip. The plump flesh was caught between her teeth, going a deep, tempting pink, and suddenly all Johnny could think about was biting that lip for her.

"Sorry, Dr. Voss," she said, cheeks flushing.

"No need to apologize at all." The therapist smiled, another one of those calm, accepting smiles as if nothing either of them could say or do would shock her. "This is exactly what we're here for. To get things out into the open and work through them. I'm here to facilitate that process, not to take sides or write a prescription for what you should do."

Then what the hell good are you? Johnny thought grumpily as Dr. Voss directed them out of the barn and down the hill to the back paddock while she wrangled the horse they'd be using for their exercises.

"I should apologize to you, too," Tessa said abruptly, stopping in her tracks at the edge of the paddock fence. "I didn't mean to pick a fight back there."

Weariness dragged at Johnny's bones. "You don't have to apologize. The doc was right. If we don't talk about this stuff, we're never going to move past it."

Not that he was happy about that. Going along not talking about stuff had worked for him for years. But if this was the way to keep Tessa in his life, he was willing to give it a try. At least it had the added benefit of getting her to open up about what was going on in that mysterious mind of hers.

"It's just that where we live feels like one of those insurmountable problems that no amount of talking will solve." Tessa's mouth pulled into an unhappy curve. "Honestly, Johnny, I love it here. I'm doing fine. Better than fine! I really think you could leave me here and go on with your life, with a clear conscience."

"Damn it to hell, I'm not worried about my conscience, Tessa." God knew, there was an ancient stain on Johnny's soul that nothing could ever remove. He shook his head forcefully, unsettled and stirred up.

"Please don't snap at me. I'm trying to do the right thing, here."

"By leaving me?" Johnny ran agitated fingers through his hair. "That's not the right thing, Tessa. Not for me, anyway."

Tessa's flashing eyes softened. "Tell me what you need. I'll do my best to give it to you."

Because she thought she owed him. Johnny looked away, grinding his back teeth. "All I need is for you to try this with me, just for a few weeks. That's it."

Tessa was silent for a long moment. "And at the end of four weeks, if nothing has changed between us— you'll go back to your life, and leave me to live mine."

Could he agree to that? What was he doing here? Johnny's chest felt hollow, an aching cavern that echoed with his own selfish needs.

Maybe he should let her go right now. He could head back to D.C., submit to talk therapy with the departmental doctor, whatever it took to get fully reinstated. He could sell their house, get an apartment that would be easy to take care of and hold no memories. He could volunteer for the next dangerous undercover assignment that came up, and the next, and the next, until his luck finally ran out.

Tessa would be fine without him. Better off, probably. She'd proven that in the year since she moved to Sanctuary Island.

Maybe these four weeks were a waste of time, a pointless exercise in torturing himself with what he could never have: Tessa as his wife. But before Johnny could unstick his tongue from the roof of his mouth to tell her so, he heard the clop of hooves behind them.

"Well, hello again!" A sunny voice sang out, making Johnny shoot a swift glance over his shoulder.

Sure enough, leading Clover down the hill with her hand on his leather halter lead, was the cheerful young woman he'd met earlier at the bakery.

Distracted and off balance, Johnny fell back on charm. "Quinn, right? This is my wife, Tessa. How did those cupcakes go over?"

Quinn's big blue eyes sparkled. "Hey, good memory! And they went over like gangbusters, only not with Marcus Beckett. He's not a sweets person, I don't think. Unlike the ladies here! I brought the cupcakes along for my volunteer session and they were very well received, so they didn't go to waste. Or to *my* waist, either! Which, let's be honest, was more likely than me throwing them out, once Marcus didn't want them."

"You two know each other?" Tessa asked, frowning slightly. "I didn't think you knew anyone on Sanctuary Island, Johnny."

"We just met this morning," Quinn explained as she unlatched the paddock fence and led the placid horse inside. "Johnny gave me some advice about baked goods and job hunting, although some of the advice was better than the rest."

Faint relief loosened some of Johnny's tension. "Sorry the job didn't work out, but I think you're probably better off. Marcus Beckett is—"

"My new boss!" Quinn bounced on the balls of her brown leather paddock boots, clearly tickled pink. "He totally hired me and I have you to thank, because you sort of warned me that he might need some buttering up, and then I wore him down and got the job! So thank you!"

In one lightning-fast move, she looped the lead rope high over the horse's neck, turning him loose in the fenced-in ring, and threw her arms around Johnny.

Nearly bowled over by the exuberant hug, Johnny managed to keep his feet and his cool. But inside, all he could think was, "That's it. I have to stick around. There's no way a man like Marcus Beckett hired an innocent like this just because she knows how to pour a beer."

Quinn Harper, with her freckles and bright, strawberry-blond hair and wide, guileless blue eyes . . . she tugged at every one of Johnny's protective instincts. When she planted a loud, smacking kiss against his cheek before pulling away and running after the wandering horse, she reminded him so strongly of Angie, it hurt.

Stop it, he ordered himself harshly. *Quinn is not your little sister. But she might need your help, all the same. And if that means sucking it up and enduring the hell of being around your wife without actually having her . . . so be it.*

He'd lived through worse and come out the other side, stronger than before. He'd be fine.

Turning, he caught the hint of a frown on Tessa's expressive face, an unhappiness that tore at his gut and made him want to promise whatever it took to fix it.

Maybe "fine" was pushing it. He'd better shoot for simple survival.

Chapter 10

Tessa watched as the pretty redhead cheerfully handed Clover's lead rope to Dr. Voss before walking out of the ring, waving to Johnny over her shoulder.

"She seems very sweet," she murmured to her husband, whose eyes were still tracking the young woman's retreat.

Overhearing, Dr. Voss smiled pleasantly and said, "Quinn is wonderful. She's one of our very best volunteers—great with the horses, even better with the clients, especially the children. I don't know what we'd do without her."

"She sounds valuable enough to hire on full-time," Johnny observed, transferring his laser focus to the doctor, who sighed a little.

"I wish we could. I've talked to the board about it but there's just no wiggle room in the budget since hiring, well, me. Also, the fact is that I'm not sure Quinn would take the job if we offered it. She seems to really enjoy making her own schedule and keeping odd hours."

Johnny's frown made Tessa's stomach tighten into a knot. "I know she's been looking for paying work. This place seems a lot more suitable for someone like her than working in a bar."

Dr. Voss tilted her head, studying Johnny's expression as if she were learning something new about him. "It's kind of you to take an interest in someone you've only just met."

"Johnny is nothing if not kind," Tessa said, trying to tamp down her sudden, irrational jealousy and failing miserably. "But Quinn is an adult, and she seemed perfectly capable of making her own decisions."

The way Johnny blinked as he stared down at her made Tessa wonder if he'd forgotten she was there. "You haven't met Marcus Beckett. If you had, you'd understand why I'm concerned."

Tessa was afraid she understood all too well. Johnny had kind of a thing for saving people. It was, after all, how they'd met. And why they'd gotten married, and stayed married for so long. It stood to reason that now Tessa had finally grown up and started looking out for herself, Johnny might be looking around for someone new to save.

She was being unfair. Tessa pressed her lips together, sickened by her own bitterness. She needed to let go of this, if she was serious about working on their marriage.

With the near-magical sense of timing she'd displayed already, Dr. Voss gently drew them back to the purpose of their visit to Windy Corner.

"Today is about me getting to know the two of you, individually and as a couple, so I can be your mirror. My job, as I see it, is to reflect your relationship back to you, allowing you to see how you interact and hopefully gain insights into your dynamic as a couple that will help you interact in healthy and productive ways."

At Tessa's side, Johnny shifted his weight slightly, as if suppressing a sigh. This must be hard for him. For her part, Tessa was glad of Dr. Voss's friendly, straightforward approach. She seemed less like a doctor and more like one of the older women from the commune, who'd seen it all and had the faith in their own experiences to prove it. Those women gave great advice, if one cared to listen, but they didn't like to offer a step-by-step how-to for solving problems.

Every person, every relationship, every problem was different. There was no one-size-fits-all solution for a happy life. Tessa's parents hadn't wanted to believe that—they'd lived their lives according to the idea that if everyone in the world would follow the same philosophy, the entire world would be a better place.

Maybe they were right about some of it, but Tessa had understood before she knew how to talk that following her parents' one-size-fits-all lifestyle would never make her happy.

Baking sinfully delicious pastries made her happy. Drinking wine with Patty made her happy. Being independent made her happy.

The rest of her life was a work in progress, but for the first time ever, Tessa was pretty sure she was on the right track. Even if the person who made her happiest—and saddest—in her entire life was both right beside her . . . and feeling further away than ever.

She tuned back in to Dr. Voss's speech in time to see her slip the halter off Clover and hide it behind her back. Clover stood politely still, as if this were all old hat to her, while Dr. Voss showed them the halter that she had now unhooked until it looked like a random bundle of worn brown leather strips attached to each other with flat metal circles.

Holding it out between them, Dr. Voss said, "Go ahead, take it. I want you to put it back on Clover."

Johnny's lips twitched, and Tessa knew he was holding back a comment about how if Dr. Voss wanted the halter on the horse, she shouldn't have taken it off in the first place.

As if to show he was willing to be a good sport about it, though, he reached for the halter.

The minute he'd grasped it, though, he held it out to Tessa with a smile that was only slightly forced. "Here, honey. You try it first."

Tessa fought not to melt at the smallest hint that Johnny was trying, but it was tough. She'd been conditioned to hunt and gather those tiny signs of affection and respect from Johnny. Not that he'd ever been cold or deliberately cruel—never that. But he'd been distant. Unreachable.

No matter how much she'd loved him, no matter how much she'd wanted to read into his absentminded good-night kisses and his sincere thanks for the dinners she put on the table, Tessa had never truly been able to fool herself into believing it was enough.

But as she gazed into his brown eyes and read the

sincerity there, she began to wonder if maybe, just maybe, Johnny had never been as far out of reach as she'd thought.

Pushing the halter back toward his chest, Tessa quirked a grin and said, "You just want me to get it going for you."

"I should have mentioned," Dr. Voss broke in, "this exercise is partly about cooperation and teamwork. So feel free to work together, or not, as you choose."

If Johnny didn't let himself roll his eyes soon, Tessa was afraid he'd strain a muscle.

"So what the doc is saying is that she's making a note of everything we do, and judging us based on whether we work together or not," Johnny muttered under his breath. "I, for one, don't intend to give her the satisfaction. How about you?"

Tessa grabbed the halter from him, jingling it gamely. She wished she'd been paying better attention when the thing was on the horse. Did this strap go behind the horse's ears? Or under its nose?

"Okay, fine." She turned the halter over and over in her hands. "Give me a crack at it."

Johnny held up his hands as if to say "It's all yours," but Tessa caught the slight lift at the corners of his full, kissable lips. He didn't think she could do it on her own. Sending him a narrow stare, she went back to the halter with renewed determination to figure it out by herself.

In the end, it took both Johnny and Tessa working together about twelve minutes to get the halter put together and on the horse's head correctly. Hot-cheeked and sheepish, Tessa crossed her arms over her chest and waited to hear Dr. Voss's diagnosis.

Johnny, who'd been quiet since she snapped at him over the placement of the last clasp, stood at her side with a hard jaw and a blank look on his face. Unhappily aware of what a mess they must look like as a couple, Tessa lifted her chin and forced herself to stand tall.

But Dr. Voss didn't seem upset.

"Well done," she said calmly, tucking her pen behind her ear and flipping to a new page in her clipboard.

Well done? What exercise was she watching? Tessa bit her lip against saying anything, but she should have known the doctor would notice.

"You don't feel you did well, Tessa?" Dr. Voss asked, all unflustered interest.

"It took us a long time," she pointed out. "And we weren't exactly the model of good communication while we worked it out."

"But you did work it out," Dr. Voss countered. "And you could have moved much more quickly, considering that Johnny knew exactly how to put the halter together before you even began."

Johnny winced, unable to wipe the guilty look off his face in time to hide it from his wife.

"Is that true, Johnny?" she demanded, aghast. "You could have put the halter together right off the bat?"

"I grew up on a farm," he reminded her helplessly. Tessa looked away, her shoulders hunching in a way that was so familiar it made his gut clench. "Oh, right. Of course. Lord, you must think I'm such an idiot."

"I have never thought that." Johnny couldn't let that stand. "You're not an idiot."

She shrugged but wouldn't say anything else. Johnny's hands tightened into impotent fists at his sides.

"As it happens," Dr. Voss said gently, "your communication as a couple is pretty good. The reason Johnny held back was because you'd asked him to let you try. From my observations, that was difficult for him, but he did it. He only jumped in when it became clear that you were becoming frustrated and upset, Tessa. Would you like to talk about why this exercise may have brought up emotions you weren't expecting?"

Tessa's shoulders hunched further, and Johnny couldn't stand it. He stepped forward to wrap his arm around her while giving the doc a look. "Maybe not today, okay?"

Something flickered in Dr. Voss's deep brown eyes. "My other observation from your interactions is that Johnny is quite protective."

He stiffened. "Nothing wrong with that."

Dr. Voss inclined her head. "Not at all, especially given that you seemed willing to allow Tessa space to be independent when she asked . . . up to a point. But I wonder if you've considered that Protector is your default setting with your wife."

Part of Johnny wanted to drop his arm and step away from Tessa, but he didn't. It clearly wouldn't fool anyone at this point, anyway. "Protecting people is what I do for a living. And the first person I'm committed to protecting is my wife."

"The issue I see here is that you may have become more protector than husband," she said quietly.

"Are you saying I can't be both?" Johnny demanded. "A husband and wife should take care of each other. That's the way it's supposed to be, right?"

He didn't know much about what made a good marriage—God knew his parents were no shining example—but he knew that.

And Dr. Voss apparently didn't disagree. She nodded easily. "Absolutely. It's a question of balance, give and take. And in the conflict Tessa obviously feels toward your protectiveness, I'm seeing a potential imbalance in that aspect of your relationship."

Screw this. Johnny clamped his jaw shut, unwilling to say more. He knew this song and dance. The patient stillness, the expectant pause, letting the silence stretch until the other person broke and filled it. Johnny had played that game himself, many times, and won.

You're going to have to do better than that if you want to see me crack.

What Johnny wasn't counting on was that he hadn't been Dr. Voss's target. At his side, Tessa straightened and shook off his encircling arm. There went that chin, those slender shoulders pulling back as if she were facing a firing squad.

"Johnny is very protective. Not just of me, but it's always been a big part of our relationship. When we met, I needed his help very much, and I continued to rely on him for longer than I should have. It's not his fault—he's not trying to smother me, or anything."

Dr. Voss gave Tessa a grave nod. "I never imagined that was the case."

Tessa relaxed a bit, and Johnny had to hand it to the doc. She was a pro. Using misdirection, she'd pushed Tessa into opening up. He stared at Dr. Voss with new respect, but the woman's entire focus was on Tessa.

"Good. Johnny isn't the problem here. I'm the one who demanded to be allowed to try the exercise on my own, even after you told us it was about teamwork, and I'm the one who get all hot and bothered when it turned out to be harder than I thought." Tessa shook her head in dismay and Johnny ached with the need to reach out to her, to pull her back from the brink of herself. But when she turned to him, the clear resolve in her eyes told him a hug wasn't what she needed just then.

Johnny's mouth went dry. God, she was gorgeous. And stronger than she even knew. They locked eyes for a long, heated instant that brought a flush of beautiful color to her pale cheeks.

Tessa glanced back to their therapist. "You asked why I got so frustrated. I'm not sure what the answer is, but I guess it probably has to do with the way I was raised."

In a few brief, dispassionate words, Tessa outlined her past for Dr. Voss. The commune, the back-to-nature philosophy, the home-schooling . . . her parents. "They were very dedicated to their way of life. Well, are, I suppose. I assume they're still on the commune. I'm no longer welcome there, and I've never gotten a response from any of the letters I've sent my mother over the years."

Johnny's eyebrows went up. He hadn't been aware that Tessa had reached out to her mother, or that she'd endured the heartache of getting only silence in return.

"I got my GED after I married Johnny," Tessa was saying to Dr. Voss, the pride in her tone a bare echo of how proud he'd felt the day he'd come home from work to find Terri clutching the official certificate in her trembling hand.

He hadn't even known she was studying for the test, he remembered now, grimacing at the memory of how he'd picked her up and swung her around in celebration . . . then told her she should have let him know so he could help.

Talk about a hard habit to break.

"After I got my GED, I took a few classes at the community college," Tessa continued. "That was my first experience in a classroom with other students."

Johnny blinked. He'd never thought that through, and she'd never mentioned it. "Was it weird?"

"Yes, very." Tessa reached up to tuck a lock of hair behind her ear, a nervous gesture left over from her Terri days. "Home-schooling with my mother—she did her best, but let's just say that questions were not encouraged. There wasn't a lot of discussion, different interpretations of what things might mean, different readings and opinions. Those community college classes were nothing *but* different opinions! And the questions, not just clarifying facts, but actually questioning the professor's findings or arguing with the textbook! I couldn't believe it. And I definitely didn't know how to handle it."

"That must have been frustrating," Dr. Voss said.

Tessa smiled faintly. "And upsetting. I nearly stopped after the first semester. I do my best not to think about how hard things were for me back then. But it was the first thing that popped into my head when you asked why I hated this exercise so much. It was because it felt exactly like sitting in that classroom with everyone around me talking over each other, debating with each other, while I had no idea how to join in."

And then she'd discovered that Johnny had known the answer all along, just like those college kids who hadn't included her.

"So when I turn away your help and get frustrated because I can't do something," she concluded, "it taps into all the pain I felt after I left home."

"I had no idea you were going through all that."

"You were busy, and I hid it well," Tessa said with a rueful smile. "I wanted you to think I was strong, mature, capable . . . You know, it's funny; now that I actually feel stronger and more capable, it's less scary for me to show it when I'm frustrated. Maybe that's progress."

"If it matters," Johnny said, chest tight, "I think you're amazing for accomplishing what you did back then—and I think you're amazing now, for how far you've come."

Tessa flushed and ducked her head, and Johnny felt warmth spread through him at the pleased look on her face.

Johnny was still staring at his wife, caught in the undertow of an emotion he couldn't name, when

Dr. Voss tucked her clipboard back under her arm and said, "I think we've done excellent work today. See you again on Friday?"

Walking Clover out of the ring, she left Tessa and Johnny gazing at one another in a moment of hushed intimacy, with new information and the start of a new understanding filling the empty air between them.

Chapter 11

Marcus looked both ways before peering through the bakery window. The coast was clear. He seized his moment and pushed open the door.

"It's been a week," the old lady who owned the place was yelling over her shoulder. "I can't believe you still haven't told him I want to sell this place to you."

He paused with one hand on the door handle. Marcus had zero interest in getting in the middle of some personal conversation between the bakery ladies. But before he could make up his mind to ditch, Miss Patty turned back to pin him with a narrow stare.

"You again," she said, mouth twisting into a smirking half smile. "What is this, the fifth day in a row? If you're not careful, you'll get to be a regular."

Marcus stiffened at the idea that his movements were becoming predictable, but he forced himself to relax. He was home now. Even if it didn't feel like it, most of the time.

Even if he hadn't actually gone back to the house where he grew up, yet. The house where his father still lived.

"I'll have a couple of the sticky buns," he said, reaching for his wallet.

"Not much for small talk, are you? Well, too bad. Tessa's too busy kneading dough to chat with me, *not to mention she wants to avoid having this conversation again*," Patty said, raising her voice on the last bit before cocking her head at Marcus. "So you can stand here and shoot the poop with me for a quick minute while I bag up your breakfast, m'kay?"

"Sounds like I don't have much of a choice." Reluctantly amused, Marcus tapped the edge of his wallet on the counter and regarded the bakery owner thoughtfully. He'd developed a soft spot for Patty over the past few days since he gave in to the curiosity about the treats Quinn had brought to her unscheduled job interview.

Patty was about five foot nothing, with the final few inches made up by the height of her short gray curls. She wore no makeup—probably it was too hot for it back by the ovens—but she still somehow smelled like the inside of a woman's cosmetic case, waxy and powdery. That scent, plus the fact that she was as sharp as the business end of a broken bottle, with a dry, unexpectedly twisted sense of humor combined to remind Marcus of things he'd prefer to forget.

"That's right," she said with a decisive bob of her salt-and-pepper curls. "No choice at all. So what's shakin', bacon? I hear you've got some help over at that den of iniquity you're building."

Right, of course. His pushy new tenant's wife—ex-wife? Marcus didn't know and wasn't planning to ask—worked at Patty Cakes. And, of course, his pushy new employee, Quinn, also frequented the shop, but he hadn't seen her since she tricked him into hiring her.

He absolutely wasn't hoping to run into her, but if he did, he'd take the opportunity to let her know she didn't need to come in to work for him, if she'd changed her mind.

Miss Patty was most likely talking about Johnny, though. Marcus nodded once.

Luckily, Patty didn't seem to need much more conversation participation from him than that. "That's real good. I bet things are moving along a lot faster with four hands instead of two. And it's nice to have some company. I couldn't believe what a difference it made, when Tessa came to work with me."

Marcus couldn't say he had noticed a huge difference, beyond the annoyance of having another person around all the time. A slight uptick in the speed of repairs and renovations, maybe, although half the time it probably would've been faster to do them alone than to take the time to explain what he wanted. He grunted noncommittally.

"Of course, very few partnerships click instantly," Miss Patty said, peering at him keenly. "It can be hard to get used to relying on someone else."

Marcus had the uncomfortable feeling that the old lady was reading his mind and responding to his thoughts rather than his—admittedly terse—words.

He cleared his throat and wished she'd bag up the

sticky buns already. Talking to her, or rather, listening to her, was tough. The cadence of Miss Patty's voice and the Southern twang were all her own, but there was a sarcastic edge to her words and an abruptness that was sharply familiar to Marcus. Miss Patty was a woman who took no bull and tolerated no fools. Marcus could respect that quality, even as it broke open the jagged wound of his past.

But a wound hidden away and covered up never healed, so Marcus made an effort.

"So." The words stuck at the back of his tongue, but he coughed and pushed them out. "You're thinking about selling this place?"

"Heard that, did you?" Miss Patty sent a shifty look over her shoulder, jerking a thumb in the direction of her baking assistant. "Well, don't go spreading it around, because I'm not sure it's going to work out. I'm not looking to sell to just anyone, and that one isn't sure she can scrape up the cash. I wish I could afford to give it to her outright, but not only would she not accept it— which I respect, a woman needs to know she can make her own way in this world—but the main reason I'm even contemplating selling out is on doctor's orders. With my health and medical bills being what they are, I need a nest egg. Or a rich husband, one or the other."

Miss Patty leered cheerfully at him, clearly relishing the chance to make him uncomfortable.

Marcus's innate contrary streak reasserted itself for the first time in months. He leaned on the counter and gave Miss Patty a slow, filthy smile. "I'm not the marrying kind, but would you settle for a rich, young sugar daddy?"

Cackling with delight, Miss Patty yelled into the back, "Tessa, get out here, we're changing the name of the bakery!"

"What?" The younger baker appeared, holding her hands clear of her sides to avoid getting wet, sticky dough everywhere. "Oh! Hello."

"Call up Noah Hackley and get him out here to change our sign," Miss Patty chortled, slapping her thighs. "Patty Cakes is no more! From now on, this place will be known as Sugar Daddy's."

The ruggedly handsome man smiling at Patty over the pastry case didn't look much like the taciturn, dangerous loner Johnny had described. Sure, there might be a slight burn of red over his cheekbones and across the back of his neck, he might be shaking his head in bemusement, but that was a fairly typical reaction to Patty's shameless flirting.

For the past week, Tessa had seen Johnny every single day. They'd continued their meetings with Dr. Voss, who had encouraged them to work on communicating even when she wasn't around. It wasn't always easy, but it was addictive. Tessa was learning more about the man she'd married than she'd ever known.

Tessa was horribly afraid she was in danger of falling in love with her husband all over again. Thank goodness she'd managed to keep from kissing him anymore, in spite of heavy temptation in the form of walks along the beach, quiet moments over glasses of wine, and, well, basically every time she looked into Johnny's dark, shadowed eyes.

It was possible Tessa was in a bit of a pickle. Because in all the sharing and discussing and *communicating,* she hadn't managed to tell Johnny about Patty's offer to sell her the bakery.

Oh, and also, Johnny had still never once said, "I love you."

So basically Tessa was treading water; not sinking, but not exactly floating, either. And in the meantime, one of the things they *had* managed to talk about was the man Johnny was living with.

According to her husband, Marcus Beckett was bad news. Looking at Marcus now, waggling his brows and flexing while Patty gleefully upped the ante by batting her lashes and squeezing his formidable biceps, Tessa had a hard time seeing Marcus as a villain.

As she'd finally exclaimed to Johnny when he was walking her home the night before, it felt as though Johnny were searching for a reason to be on his guard.

"You sound like Dr. Voss," Johnny had said, scowling.

Tessa would not be derailed. "I obviously don't know Marcus Beckett well, but it seems to me that you don't, either. You've spent a week sharing space with the man, working side by side, and you've barely got more information than the gut instinct you started out with!"

"One, my gut instinct is nothing to sneeze at," Johnny'd replied. "And two, I know a bit more than that. Like for instance that his family is from here, but this whole week I haven't seen him visit or call them one single time."

"Not being in touch with your family is hardly evidence of criminal behavior," Tessa had said, a bit stiffly, thinking of the last time she'd written to her mother and gotten the envelope back, unopened and marked "Return to Sender."

On bad days, Tessa tortured herself by wondering if her mother wanted to read the letters, but her father wouldn't allow it. She wasn't under any illusions about how angry he'd been that Tessa left home and escaped his control. On worse days, she wondered if her mother was dead, and no one had bothered to let her only daughter know.

The uncertainty, along with the ache of regrets and unresolved anger, would eat a hole through Tessa's heart if she let it.

"You're right," Johnny said immediately. "Of course there are plenty of reasons for families to grow apart."

Tessa could tell he'd made the connection to her situation, and he was sorry he'd brought it up. That, and the stroke of his hand up the back of her neck, let her breathe out the pain on a sigh of acceptance.

Johnny's fingers lingered at her nape. He seemed fascinated by the newly bared skin there, his fingertips returning again and again, sensitizing the tender patch of skin unbearably. Tessa had yet to ask him to stop.

"Anyway, that's not all," he'd gone on, doggedly determined to make his point. "There's also the fact that he hired Quinn Harper."

"Oh, here we go." Tessa pulled away from his touch. Johnny's brow wrinkled. He honestly seemed to have no idea why Tessa was irked. "What do you mean?"

"Forget about it." Tessa sighed, wished she'd kept her mouth shut.

"No, you've got something to say about this situation. I want to hear it."

"I'm pretty sure you don't."

"I know you don't seem to like Quinn, for some reason, but if you'd spent any time with Marcus Beckett, you'd be worried about her, too."

Tessa averted her gaze from Johnny's disappointed scowl. "Honestly? I like Quinn a lot—from what I know of her, she seems like a caring, warm, funny young woman. But my feelings about her are irrelevant," she said quietly. "*Your* feelings are what concern me."

He'd reared back like she'd slapped him, shock widening his eyes. "I don't have feelings for her! I'm married to you—I'm only here on this island to fight for our marriage. You honestly think I'd waste my time chasing after a kid like Quinn when it would put our marriage at risk?"

Tessa couldn't help but notice that it was their marriage he cited as a reason for his loyalty—not his overwhelming, undeniable love for his wife. Shaking her head to dispel the thoughts, she'd said, "Of course I'm not saying you're falling for her, or trying to seduce her or something. But you can't deny she presses your buttons. She seems like maybe she needs help. And you can't resist that."

"Helping people is my job!"

"Quinn isn't one of your assignments. She's just a

nice woman who's making a choice you don't happen
to agree with. But it's her choice, and you can't save
her from it. You're a good man, Johnny, but you can't
save everyone."

Real pain tightened his features for a moment. His
eyes were inky black pools of anguish. "Believe me,
I know that. No one knows it better."

Confused, Tessa had paused, unsure what he meant.
She had the sudden feeling that she was fumbling
through a pitch-dark room and her splayed fingers had
just found a light switch. "Johnny?"

He'd shaken his head like a horse resisting the bri-
dle, then taken a step back, his dark eyes shuttering
once more. "You know there's nothing going on between Quinn and me. This is an excuse not to com-
mit to our marriage, and I won't accept it. I'm a lot of
things, Tessa, but you can't accuse me of disloyalty."

That had been the end of the fight, because Johnny
had stalked off and left Tessa standing in front of her
door with a bruised heart and a sense that there were
still huge parts of her husband's soul that were completely hidden from her.

"Yoo-hoo, earth to Tessa!"

She jolted, blinking to realize Marcus and Patty
were both staring at her. Embarrassed, Tessa rubbed
her sticky hands together with a grimace. "Sorry! I'm
still waking up, I guess. Is there coffee in the carafe?"

"There was," Patty admitted, looking shifty. "But
it's gone now. I'll brew a new pot."

She grabbed the empty carafe they kept out front
to sell by the cup and sauntered toward the back
kitchen, leaving Tessa alone with Marcus. Who had

his wallet out on the counter and an unhappy glower on his face.

"Gosh, I'm sorry, Mr. Beckett. What did you order? I'll bag it up while Patty gets the coffee going. Did you want a cup to go with your . . . ?"

"Sticky buns," he said, still frowning distractedly in the direction Patty had disappeared. "Did she drink that whole carafe of coffee herself?"

Tessa whipped out a piece of wax paper and grabbed the biggest sticky bun on the tray. "What? Oh, probably. She's terribly addicted."

"She shouldn't drink that much caffeine." Marcus pinned Tessa with a glare. "It's not good for her heart. She has a heart condition, doesn't she."

It didn't sound like a question, the way he said it, but Tessa nodded slowly in affirmation. "How did you know?"

His gaze turned inward, unhappy and distant. "I recognize the signs. And she told me about the deal she wants to make you."

Feeling awkward discussing her personal affairs with a man she hardly knew, Tessa focused on wrapping the sticky buns up and sliding them into a brown paper bag with the bakery's logo stamped on the front. "Well. We're still talking about it."

She looked up and was instantly caught in the intensity of Marcus's shadowed eyes. "I knew someone like your Miss Patty, once. Someone who should have taken better care of herself. Someone I wish I'd done a better job of caring for."

His voice sounded like sand being ground down to glass. Tessa bit her lip in sympathy. "I try to take care of Patty, but she's stubborn. There are things she won't let me do for her."

A brief smile creased his face, sharp and commiserating. "I know how that goes. But there's something she will let you do, a way you can help her right now, if you want."

Tessa paused in the act of handing over his bag of breakfast rolls. She glanced up at him questioningly, her heart beating a rough, rapid rhythm.

Staring into her eyes, Marcus Beckett took the bag from her hand and said, "I'd like to help you."

Chapter 12

Johnny cast a sidelong glance at Tessa. For the hundredth time that morning, he wondered what she was thinking about.

He'd worried that she might ditch their next appointment with Dr. Voss after their conversation the day before. Johnny refused to call it a fight—it was a difference of opinion. That was all. And he wasn't angry about it. Tessa didn't have all the facts. She didn't understand that protecting the innocent was the way Johnny balanced out the darkness in his soul.

She didn't understand that Johnny knew in his bones that Marcus Beckett had the capacity for violence and destruction because Johnny had it, too. Like recognized like.

Tessa didn't understand, but he should've known she wouldn't quit on him. Of course she'd showed up to their appointment and they'd gotten through today's exercise of coaxing an indifferent Clover through an obstacle course of poles on the ground and barrels to walk through.

Now they were winding down the session by grooming Clover together, although so far Tessa was doing most of the work. Johnny watched the flick of her delicate hands over Clover's dappled gray haunches, the puff of dust as she dragged an oval currycomb through the short hairs.

Her attention wasn't on the grooming, though. Johnny would bet his life on it. There was something on Tessa's mind, something she hadn't shared with him.

Well, that was fair enough. A muscle jumped in Johnny's jaw and he clenched down hard to quiet it. There was plenty he hadn't shared with Tessa, after all.

Maybe it was time that changed. Tessa didn't understand—and it was hurting her. He didn't know if he could change who he was at this point in his life—not even to make Tessa happy. But maybe if she knew where that part of him came from, she would start to see why Johnny did what he did.

The idea of opening up the secret box where he kept those memories made Johnny feel like razor blades were burrowing under his skin. But Tessa deserved to know the truth.

Even if it meant that she'd never look at him with her heart soft and sweet in her eyes again. Even if it meant she backed away from him and demanded he go through with the divorce. The longer he spent on this island with his newly confident and happy wife, the more Johnny realized he couldn't hope to keep her confident and happy in their marriage without giving her more than he'd given in the past.

Without giving her more than he'd given *of* his past.

"So, listen—"

"I was thinking—"

Johnny stopped, gesturing for Tessa to go ahead. He couldn't deny a spasm of relief at getting to delay this conversation even for a few minutes.

"Sorry." Tessa bit her lip, sending a shot of lust to Johnny's extremities. He tamped it down and focused on what she was hesitantly saying.

"I have this opportunity. It's not something I went looking for, and I'm not a hundred percent sure I should take it, but it's not just about me."

She twined her fingers into a knot, twisting and untwisting restlessly. Concerned, Johnny reached across Clover's back to cover her nervous hands with his. "Hey, honey. Whatever it is, you can tell me. We'll work it out."

Her lips trembled into a smile. "Have I ever told you how much I love it when you call me that?"

"What? Honey?"

The fingers trapped in Johnny's grasp twitched. Tessa glanced aside, as if she felt shy. "Yeah. It used to make me feel so . . . married."

The weight of his regrets was suffocating. "Because most of the time, you didn't feel married. Not for real."

That got Tessa to look at him. "I'm not complaining. I know you didn't marry me for love, and to be honest, when we were first married I wasn't at all ready for anything more than the companionship and support you offered. But after a while, I started to want more."

Physical awareness flickered to life between them. Johnny felt the heavy beat of his blood, the sudden tightness in his jeans. Turning her hand under his, he stroked his thumb over the thin, tender skin at the inside of her wrist where her pulse fluttered. She filled his mind, his entire consciousness. There was nothing but Tessa.

"You want more, honey? All you have to do is ask."

She shivered, her eyes darkening as desire blew her pupils wide. Lips parting, Tessa stretched up on her toes over the horse's back and Johnny didn't care about the thousand-pound animal between them—he had to get his mouth on her, right now.

Spearing his hands into the short wisps of hair at the back of her neck, Johnny leaned in and kissed her.

The rest of the world fell away, leaving nothing behind but Tessa's sugar-sweet mouth, the high, surprised noises she made in the back of her throat, the clutch of her fingers in the collar of his jacket as she pulled him closer.

He hadn't kissed her since that first day. He hadn't wanted to push her, or to make her think all he was interested in was sex.

That was a mistake. He should have been kissing her every day. Every minute.

Clover took a step forward, jolting them out of their embrace. The horse looked curiously over his shoulder as Tessa started to laugh. It was the laugh Johnny had seen for the first time through the bakery window, full throated and joyous, with Tessa's head thrown back in abandon.

Overcome with the need to seize this moment, Johnny grabbed the currycomb and threw it in the bucket before rounding the horse to snag his wife by the hand. Tessa looked up at him, breath coming in fast pants and eyes glazed, pliantly following where he led. It was all Johnny could do not to take her down to the sawdust-covered floor and hope Clover was smart enough not to step on them.

No. Tessa was untouched. She'd been waiting for this for a long time—and her first time wasn't going to be a literal roll in the hay. But that didn't mean either of them could stand to wait until they found a bed.

He reached for enough patience to get out of the stall and latch the door behind them. Dumping the bucket of grooming tools by the stall door, Johnny tugged Tessa by the wrist down the barn corridor to an empty stall he'd noticed earlier. It was unoccupied, completely clear of hay except for a few pieces strewn here and there, and Johnny backed Tessa into it for a little privacy. She went willingly enough, although he could see her brain starting to come back online, awareness of what they were doing starting to show in her eyes.

If he were a good man, he'd back off and let the sexual tension clear from the air between them. Tessa, who'd had so few choices in her life, deserved to make a real choice about this, one not clouded by overwhelming sensations. Johnny was at least a good enough man to vow not to take her here and now. He was relieved to find that he still had limits.

But that didn't mean he could stop himself from providing Tessa with a damn good argument for why she should choose him.

Why she should choose them.

One smooth step forward had Tessa pressed up against the rough wood of the wall, his hand coming up to cup the back of her head and keep her from hurting herself. He never wanted her to feel a moment's pain, not if he could help it.

A soft smile pulled at her mouth. She turned her head far enough to nuzzle his arm, her gaze steady on his even as her cheeks flushed deep pink. She was irresistible. Johnny dipped his head, sipping kisses from her lips, small and sweet and playful to make her sigh. Her neck stretched, so vulnerably naked without the covering of her long, brown hair. The fingers of his free hand had to pet down the pale, slender length of it.

Tessa sighed into his lips, a breath with a hint of moan underneath—enough to vibrate through her throat against the sensitive tips of his fingers and reverberate through Johnny's own chest. Hunger throbbed and ached between his legs, heavily undeniable, but he ignored it for the moment. This was about Tessa. Tessa's pleasure, Tessa's awakening, Tessa's beautiful, beloved, familiar-but-new body.

With a last swipe of his tongue across her plush lower lip, Johnny dragged his mouth from hers to nip his way down her throat to the juncture of her shoulder. He paused there to suckle at the soft skin, pulling up a mark that sent a heated pulse of possession through him. Satisfaction rumbled in his chest as he trailed his hand from her neck to follow the path of his mouth lower, and then lower still. She shuddered when he reached the full roundness of her breasts.

Hungry for more but unwilling to expose her in this semipublic place, Johnny's fingers shaped her through her thin sweater. He loved the way she shivered and peaked up, tightening into a bud he could feel . . . and needed to taste.

Johnny contented himself with wetting the fabric over the hard tip of her breasts, rubbing the knit weave of her sweater over the sensitive skin before enclosing her in warmth and pulling strongly enough to make her moan. High-pitched and shocked, the sounds Tessa let loose made Johnny groan with the need to restrain himself.

He knelt on the hard-packed dirt floor in front of her, forehead pressed to her softly rounded belly as he panted and worked to get control of the passion that wanted to run away with them both.

"Don't stop," she begged in a heated whisper he felt in every fiber of his body.

Johnny tilted his head up to meet her stare. Red-cheeked and wide-eyed, Tessa stared down at him. She looked nervous, excited, turned on—but she didn't look as if she were too overwhelmed to make a real choice. Her eyes were clear.

He still didn't want her first time to be in a barn. She deserved better than that. But there were many firsts for Tessa to enjoy, and Johnny could give her one right here.

Keeping his gaze on hers, hot and direct, Johnny

licked his lips and reached for the button on her khaki
pants.

Tessa couldn't believe this was happening. It felt like
a dream, one of the many dreams that had kept her
company in her lonely bed down the hall from Johnny.
But when his long, strong fingers delved into her open
pants to lay that first, shivery-good stroke over the ten-
derest part of her, Tessa knew she wasn't dreaming.

No dream could ever feel this good.

She moaned, the noise sounding loud in the quiet
barn. Johnny's eyes flicked up to her and he whispered
a breathy "Shhh," as he peeled her pants down her hips.

Tessa brought a hand up to cover her own mouth. It
was the only way to keep quiet when even the air
brushing against her underwear felt like too much
stimulation. This was really happening. Johnny wanted
to—and she was letting him—

Letting him. The thought broke through Tessa's
brain like a hysterical giggle. She would let Johnny
do anything he wanted with her. That had always been
true, from the very first moment she met him. The
surreal part was that he finally wanted to.

Part of her, the sensible part, whispered that there
were plenty of potential reasons for Johnny's sudden
interest. Reasons that made a lot more sense than that
after years of living together, she'd become attractive
to him basically overnight.

But the larger part of Tessa didn't care what the reasons were. This might be her only chance to experience making love with the man she loved.

Her body ached, empty and unfulfilled. Her skin was too tight, responsive to the lightest brush of Johnny's hands. His lips.

Oh, God, his tongue.

Dimly, Tessa realized she was whimpering and straining to spread her thighs wider for him. But her pants and underwear were tangled at her knees, restricting her movement in a way that shouldn't have been sexy, but was. The grip of Johnny's warm hands on her hips didn't hurt, either.

Johnny made an incoherent sound in his chest, the hum of it devastating against Tessa's wet, burning core. Every slow, thorough swipe of his tongue soothed her craving . . . and stoked the fire even higher.

One hand left Tessa's hip, leaving her off balance enough to scrabble at the wall behind her. Without ceasing his insatiable devouring, Johnny's hand worked its way between her taut, quivering thighs to find the place where much of Tessa's longing was centered.

The pleasure screwed tighter and tighter, coiling irresistibly at the base of her spine. His fingers were gentle but sure as they explored her folds, his gaze hot on her face and studying her helpless reactions.

Tessa's cheeks burned. She was shocked by her own utter abandon, but what Johnny was doing to her felt too good. She couldn't pretend to be indifferent, not with her thigh muscles jumping, her belly clenching, and Johnny rub, rub, rubbing insistently against the part of her that was starving for his touch.

It broke over her in a spangled burst of light, aftershocks hitting her like tiny explosions and forcing the air from her lungs. Her legs wobbled and only Johnny's steady grasp kept her upright.

She was still shuddering and squirming through the aftermath when Johnny shot to his feet and buried his face in the side of her neck. He smelled like a hot day at the beach, salty and musky. Tessa reached up with both hands to hold him to her as he shook and muffled curses against her skin.

The moment pierced Tessa with tenderness. The man in her arms had given her pleasure beyond her wildest dreams, but he'd taken none for himself. His arms were like iron bars, straight and corded with muscle where they barricaded her against the wall. Johnny held his lower body carefully away from her, but his breath was warm and steady against her neck.

She'd never felt closer to him.

"I didn't know," Tessa whispered, heart swollen and hurting. "I didn't know it would be like that. That it would make me feel like this."

His lips brushed the side of her throat in a brief kiss. "I'm sorry it took me this long to show you."

Tessa's head hit the wall with a muted thump and Johnny looked up to meet her gaze. His eyes were still dark with unsatisfied lust, but his mouth was curved in a small smile. He looked happy. Maybe happier than she'd ever seen him.

Which made this all the harder, but she had to do it. Letting it go on wasn't fair, to either of them.

"No," she said gently. "Not the . . . pleasure, although it was wonderful. I mean, I didn't know that making love would tie my heart to yours this way. Everywhere you look these days, people seem to be having sex with no emotional repercussions, just two consenting adults doing what comes naturally. I thought I could be like that. Maybe I could, with someone else. But not with you."

Hope ignited in his gaze. His hands left the wall to cradle her jaw, so gently that Tessa wanted to cry. "You still love me."

She held back the tears because she couldn't afford to be misunderstood. Not about this.

"Of course I still love you," she said, throat tight and painful. "That's why we can't do this again."

"You're not making any sense." Johnny shook his head, petting lightly at her hair and rubbing circles into her jaw with his thumbs. "What we have together is good. You don't even know how good—you have nothing to compare it to. But it's not always like this. We're lucky."

Tessa's eyes burned. "Maybe we could have been, once. But we missed our chance, Johnny."

"No, Tessa, come on."

She cut off his alarmed denials before they could weaken her. "I'm sorry. I should've had the guts to tell you this before, but I promised to take the therapy seriously, and if I'm honest, I loved doing those exercises with you, finding out more about you . . . but it's no use. I have a chance here on Sanctuary Island, a chance to be my own woman, and I have to take it."

"I want that for you," he argued. "I'm not expecting

things to go back to the way they were before I left for my undercover assignment."

"I know," she assured him. "And that means so much to me. You don't even know. But God, Johnny . . . don't you see that it *would* be the same? No matter how much we both want to change, the essentials haven't changed at all. Maybe now you want to sleep with me, which is great, but I *love* you."

The words hurt as they choked their way out of her. The look on Johnny's face hurt worse, the way his eyes went bleak, but she had to finish. "I love you. And you . . . you're fond of me. You care about me, but you aren't in love with me. I can't live like that. And thanks to Patty and my friends here on Sanctuary Island, I don't have to."

Tessa held her breath, searching Johnny's desolate expression for a hint of answering emotion, something that would prove her wrong about how he felt—but in the next instant, he straightened and stepped away from her. Chill air rushed in, raising goose bumps everywhere Johnny had been touching her, but it was her heart that felt frozen.

"You've decided," Johnny said flatly. "You're staying here."

It felt wrong, everything about this felt wrong, as if Tessa were driving down a busy highway in reverse, full throttle. Heading for a crash. But she forced her voice steady. "Patty needs to sell the bakery, and she wants me to buy it. I'm taking a loan and I'm doing it."

Johnny stilled, his muscles going loose and ready like a predator's. "Taking a loan," he repeated quietly.

"Not taking out a loan, like from a bank. So this would be a personal loan, then."

Swallowing hard enough to make her throat click, Tessa nodded. "Marcus Beckett offered me the money. And I'm taking it, Johnny."

Chapter 13

The trees along the winding country lane showed the brilliant green of new leaves tipping their sheltering branches. Redbuds and forsythia splashed dots of pink and yellow among the green. Spring was beautiful on Sanctuary Island as the midday sun began to warm the sand and salt marshes.

But inside Johnny's rented sedan, the atmosphere was as cold and barren as the depths of winter.

Johnny, who'd offered to drive because he would have offered to do anything for Tessa and it was the first thing that sprang to mind, gripped the steering wheel with grim focus. All he wanted was to jerk it to the right and pull them off the road, lean over the gear column and convince Tessa she was wrong with his hands, his mouth, whatever he could . . . but she didn't want those things.

She wanted his heart. And that would be fine, except Johnny was pretty sure he didn't have one.

His heart and soul—his ability to love the way Tessa wanted—had been burned out of him years ago, long before he ever met her.

So Johnny kept driving and he kept breathing, even though the loss of hope felt like having his ribs prized open with a bone spreader. Looking at Tessa only made it worse, but he couldn't stop himself. His gaze moved from front windshield to side mirrors to rearview to the woman staring out the passenger side window on a ceaseless rotation.

"Can you please drop me off at the bakery?"

Her quiet voice broke the silence that had gripped them since his offer to drive her home had been awkwardly accepted. Johnny battled the hot spurt of resentment at the mention of the shop that was taking his wife from him.

It was so much more complicated than that, he knew. But still. He didn't think he'd ever be able to look a sticky bun in the face again.

"Sure. No problem," he said, working to keep his tone even and free of blame. They were still about fifteen minutes out from the center of town, where the bakery was. If these were some of his last moments with Tessa as his wife, Johnny wanted to savor them. Even if it hurt.

He was casting around for something to say, some topic that would allow him to hear Tessa's sweet, husky voice without starting World War III all over again, when a truck in his rearview mirror caught his attention.

Big and covered in enough rusty patches that it looked almost more brown than black, the truck's engine roared as the vehicle sped up behind the smaller car too quickly for him to make out more than a vague impression of the driver as a burly man with a knitted cap pulled low over his brow.

"What's this jackass up to?" Johnny wondered aloud, firming his grip on the wheel and keeping a steady pace despite the way the truck was riding his tail.

"That's weird." Tessa frowned at her side mirror. "People on the island are pretty considerate drivers, usually. They have to be—the sheriff's department hands out tickets like candy, trying to keep speeding down. For the wild horses, you know."

Johnny did know. The bands of wild horses that roamed Sanctuary Island stayed away from the roads, for the most part, but it wasn't uncommon to see them grazing alongside the verge. They were wild creatures and Johnny didn't trust them not to leap out in front of his vehicle, which was why he'd been driving so slowly and carefully.

Definitely not to prolong this alone time with Tessa. That would be pathetic.

A sharp tap against his rear bumper jolted Johnny into cursing. He steadied the car and spared a glance to show him that Tessa was fine, if a little pale. "Maybe pull off to the side of the road and let him go around you," she suggested.

No way was Johnny stopping and risking getting into an altercation with a driver as aggressive as this guy while Tessa was in the car. Not wanting to alarm Tessa any further, though, all he said was, "Here, I'll pull as far right as I can."

Johnny slowed even further as he did so, rolling his window down far enough to stick his arm out and wave the guy around him. The truck's engine revved threateningly, huge wheels grinding on the dirt road as the truck zoomed alongside Johnny. Jaw clenched, he glared over at the other driver, but the height of the cab put him at an angle where Johnny couldn't see more than the knit cap on top of the guy's head.

"Jerk," Johnny muttered as the truck pulled past them. His grip on the wheel was just about to relax when the truck driver cut his wheel to the right and clipped the front bumper of the sedan hard enough to send the smaller car into a spin.

The rental car's tires skidded on the icy slush lining the sides of the road. Pulse thundering and adrenaline churning, Johnny breathed out slow and forced the steering wheel to turn steadily in the direction of the skid when all he wanted to do was stomp on the brakes.

Beside him, Tessa was gasping with fear and clutching at her seat belt where it had locked tight against her chest, but Johnny zeroed every inch of his focus on bringing the car to a controlled stop.

The whole thing was over in seconds. Their car shuddered to a standstill with its nose buried in the scrubby, brown shrubs at the side of the road while the truck roared away in a cloud of dust and gravel.

Johnny dropped his hands from the wheel, his fingers cramped and stiff. His pulse thundered in his ears, blood high and pumping with the terror he hadn't let himself feel before. He practically lunged sideways in his eagerness to get his hands on Tessa, to check her over and make sure she was unmarked, unharmed by the last few minutes of dangerous driving.

Sweeping his palms up her arms and over her shoulders, tracing her neck and up into her hair to feel for bumps or knots or cuts . . . the litany of potential injuries running through his head drowned out everything else for long, breathless moments. Finally a firm grip on Johnny's wrists brought his frantic gaze down to meet Tessa's.

"I'm okay," she was saying, over and over. Her tone was urgent, thin with the dregs of shock, but steady. "Johnny, look at me. I'm fine. I'm okay. We're okay."

"That truck," he gasped, fury roaring up to burn away everything else. "What the hell was that guy doing, I've got to go after him . . ."

Tessa's slim fingers tightened around his wrists. "You do not," she said emphatically. "You need to stay here with me."

He framed her face with shaking hands, noting the chilly pallor of her skin and the trembling of her mouth. "You said you were okay."

It came out harsh, accusing, but Tessa didn't flinch away. Instead, she gave him a tremulous smile and said, "I am, because you kept me safe. Like you always do."

Johnny couldn't resist the temptation to kiss her. He didn't even try. For all he knew, this was his last chance to taste his wife's sweetness and imprint the memory on his tongue.

Once she recovered from this near miss, she'd go back to being through with him. He had no doubts about that. What Johnny doubted now was whether he could bring himself to leave Sanctuary Island, knowing that he might be leaving Tessa in danger.

Because whoever that truck driver was, he'd just deliberately tried to run them off the road. And this car? It had been sitting out back, behind the Buttercup Inn for the past few weeks. Long enough for anyone on the island to see it there and start associating it with Marcus Beckett.

Everything came back to Marcus Beckett. And this was more than a gut feeling—this was Tessa's life in danger.

Panic, pure and mind-altering as a hit of heroin, gripped Johnny by the throat and throttled his rational mind to a standstill. Johnny breathed in the powdered-sugar-and-vanilla scent of Tessa's hair and struggled to rein himself in. But then she pulled away, cheeks pink and eyes darting away from his, and Johnny was left with no anchor in a rough sea. Without Tessa in his arms, he had nothing.

Nothing but the animal instinct to protect his mate. At all costs.

The front door of the Buttercup Inn opened with a bang, startling Marcus into cracking his head on the underside of the bar.

Cursing fluently, he threw down the power drill he was using to attach hooks to the front of the bar and came to his feet in a snarling rush of bad temper, only to stop in his tracks when he saw who was there.

"Oh," he said rudely. "It's you."

"It's me," Quinn replied. She looked unforgivably perky in a bright orange softball jersey, which should have looked weird with her red-gold hair, but somehow didn't. "I'm here to help out."

What is it with people thinking I need help? Marcus wondered grumpily. Used to be, he exuded an air of competence ruthless enough to keep him an island unto himself. Well, for the most part. Burying the memory of the one person who'd never let him get away with being strong, silent, and surly, Marcus pulled the handkerchief from his back pocket and swiped it over his forehead. "Don't need any help. Come back when there are customers to serve. Or feel free not to come back at all."

Quinn dumped the backpack she was carrying onto the floor, rolling her eyes. "Oh, stop. We already had this conversation. And I won! I'm hired. And my class was canceled today, I volunteered at the barn yesterday, so . . . I'm all yours. Where should I start?"

Backpack. Class. How young was she, exactly? "Go do your homework someplace else. I'm busy here."

"I see that." Tucking her hands into the pockets of her cutoff shorts, Quinn wandered closer to squat down and peer at the hooks. "What are these for?"

"Jackets, scarves, ladies' purses. Whatever."

"That's smart. And convenient for your customers." Her eyebrows went up, as if she hadn't expected Marcus to have any interest in creating a pleasant experience for his bar's guests. Which, okay. Fair enough.

"Keeps their crap out of my way." Marcus picked up the drill and went back to work, intensely conscious of the lithe young figure of the girl at his back.

The *schoolgirl* at his back. *Get her out of your head, you dirty old man.*

"How did you think of that detail?"

Her genuine interest was hard to resist, but Marcus did his best. "It's a pretty common feature at a lot of bars. You're probably too young to know about that."

"I'm twenty-five!"

With his back to her, Marcus allowed his eyes to slip closed on a silent curse. Ten years. He had ten years on this girl. And they were ten hard years. He shouldn't look twice at her. Hell, he shouldn't look once at her— she shouldn't be anywhere near a man like Marcus.

"Congratulations," he grunted. "Now get out of here."

Before I do something we'll both regret.

Her feet retreated without another word, and Marcus told himself he was glad. It was good he'd run her off. He was still struggling to believe it when the sound of hammering startled him into dropping the silver hook he was about to install.

With a sense of inevitability, he looked over his shoulder to see Quinn teetering, perched on a stepladder to reach high enough to hang the set of antlers he'd found at the antique store down the block over the door to the bar. As he watched in disbelief, she leaned back as if to get a better view while straightening the mounted rack, and overbalanced.

Faster than thought, Marcus was on his feet and across the bar, ready to pluck her from the air as she tipped backward with a cry of alarm.

"I've got you," he said into the cloud of red hair behind her ear.

"Thanks." She sounded breathless with surprise and the lingering fear of falling, her heart rabbiting away against his forearm where he'd grabbed her to pull her into his chest. But when she turned in his arms, it wasn't fear flushing her cheeks that delicate pink color.

They were pressed together from shoulder to knee. For the first time, Marcus realized she was taller than average for a woman. He was a couple inches over six feet, and the top of her head came to about his nose.

Which meant all it took to line up their mouths was a slight tilt of her pert, dimpled chin.

Temptation bit hard, clenching Marcus's guts and sending his blood flooding south in a thick, heavy pulse. Her eyelids lowered to half-mast, cornflower-blue eyes gleaming as her hands stole around his shoulders to dig into the muscle there. The prick of her kitten claws sent a chill of heat racing down Marcus's back, but it was the pleased smile tipping up the corners of her strawberry mouth that made him push her away.

Okay, he pushed her out to arms' length. That was as far as he could manage, apparently. His hands refused to let go of her completely.

"We're not doing this," he told her. He wished his resolve were as firm and steady as his voice sounded.

She had the audacity to link her fingers at the nape of his neck, as if refusing to be pushed away. "Why not?"

Too many reasons to name. They jammed in Marcus's throat, fighting to get out. Unfortunately, the first one to untangle itself was, "I'm too old for you."

Her lashes swept down, long and darker than he'd expect for a redhead. "Maybe I like older men."

The throaty purr went straight to Marcus's head like a shot of Irish. His hands flexed on her shoulders, aching to reel her in, but he resisted with a halfhearted sneer. "I'm not interested in helping you work out your daddy issues."

He saw her reaction to that burn across her nose and cheekbones. *Angry flush is different from sex flush,* he catalogued automatically.

But instead of jerking out of his grasp and telling him where he could get off, Quinn shoved in closer. The front of her denim-clad thighs rubbed against Marcus's, the tiny bit of friction producing enough heat to start a fire in the giant, empty fireplace at the end of the bar.

"You're not *that* old. Maybe a little crotchety, but I can work with that."

Marcus stared down into her face. It was a surprise to find the stubborn set to her lips such a turn-on. He was cracking up, after everything that had happened. That was the only explanation.

Lost for words, Marcus could always count on his body to act. He relaxed his grasp on her shoulders, finger by finger, and let her go without allowing himself to shiver at the drift of silky, red-gold hair over the backs of his hands.

She cocked her head to one side, scrutinizing him with a level of piercing intensity that made Marcus feel like he was on the wrong end of a sniper rifle's scope.

"How about if I promise not to fall in love with you?" Quinn asked, her tone all bright inquisitiveness.

The floor beneath Marcus's boots felt as if it had a slight slope to it that he'd never noticed before. He ought to get a level in there, check it out, he thought vaguely as Quinn's question reverberated through his head.

He crossed his arms over his chest to hide the way his hands shook with wanting to reach out for her once more. "Love isn't on the table."

"Right. Like I just said." She arched a brow, a knowing smirk at the corner of her sexy mouth. Marcus experienced something uncomfortably like whiplash . . . but in his pants, not his neck.

"I'm absolutely not looking to settle down anytime soon," Quinn scoffed. "My life is just getting started. Why would I want to tie myself down by getting married or something?"

The M-word raised every red flag Marcus had. He instinctively backed up, raising his hands as if warding off a feral cat, only to see Quinn roll her eyes.

"Oh, stop it. I'm saying I have no idea if I ever want to get married," she protested. "Much less right now. You might not have noticed, but I like to keep my options open. What I do know, though, is that you're hot. Even hotter than I remember—and believe me, broody teenaged you made a big impression on the girl next door."

Talk about hot. Marcus tugged at the frayed collar of his battered cotton T-shirt. He hadn't worried about fixing the air conditioner yet, since it was still spring, but now he was regretting it.

"I want you," Quinn said boldly, stalking forward to curl an arm behind his neck as if it were the easiest, most natural thing in the world. Her words puffed warm against his cheek as she nuzzled in to whisper, "Every way I can have you, over and over, until it's not fun anymore. No strings, no expectations, and definitely no falling in love."

Marcus shook his head like a man waking up from a dream. He fisted one hand in the waves at the back of her head and pulled, lightly enough not to hurt, but rough enough to drag a heated moan from Quinn's throat. Glaring down into blue eyes gone smoky and slumberous with desire, Marcus felt himself backslide.

A good guy would pat Quinn on the head and send her away to find a bright, happy, uncomplicated boy her own age to play with. A good guy would fire her and ban her from the bar to keep from ever being tempted to slip. Hell, a good guy probably wouldn't be tempted in the first place.

So much for being a good guy.

Quinn's lower lip pouted open gently, her breath coming in sharp and fast, as if she knew she was about to get her way. But if they were doing this thing, if Marcus was giving up on his bid to straighten up and fly right, they were going to do it his way.

She wanted a kiss, he knew, and he gave her one—but not on the lips. Dropping his head, he closed careful teeth over the soft skin of her neck, just above the collar of that stupid sweater. Instead of biting, he scraped his teeth lightly. Triumph and satisfaction rocketed through him at the high-pitched sound of shock she let loose. Her hips nudged forward, blindly seeking. Marcus dropped his hands to keep her still, but she was impossible to control. One endless leg lifted and curved around his backside, notching them together, hard to soft.

Without warning, Marcus slid his hands around her hips to cup the perfect round apple of her bottom. She squeaked when he picked her up and moaned when her back hit the doorjamb, but she locked her ankles behind his back without hesitation. Propping her elbows on his shoulders, Quinn got her hands on his head and angled his face up to hers.

Frank lust, straightforward and simple, stared back at him from Quinn's eyes. She knew what she wanted, Marcus understood. He wasn't going to push her past some invisible boundary. She wanted whatever he wanted to give her.

Marcus had known plenty of women. Beautiful, elegant, worldly women. Women who were his equal in age and experience, women who knew how the game was played.

And yet nothing in Marcus's life had prepared him for the punch of lust he got from seeing that look on Quinn Harper's bright, open face.

It was official. Marcus was a bad, bad man.

But as he finally gave in and savaged her mouth, he couldn't find it in himself to care.

Chapter 14

Tessa is in danger. Tessa is in danger. Tessa is in danger.

The words beat in Johnny's blood, sharp and incessant and undeniable. As long as Marcus Beckett roamed the island, with his shady past and his volatile temper acting like a magnet for trouble, Johnny could never feel right about leaving Tessa alone here.

Johnny felt like he was losing his grip on reality, actually feeling it slip from his fingers. The worst of the darkness that had covered him during his undercover assignment was back. But it was even more consuming, now, because it wasn't his life or even his sanity that was on the line here—it was Tessa. And there was nothing that mattered more. Nothing Johnny wouldn't do to protect her.

Including giving himself over to the violence and ugliness he knew dwelled within him.

That need to protect drove him after he dropped

her off at the bakery, making sure Patty was there and doing a quick perimeter check of the building. Part of him wanted to stand guard at the door with his gun drawn and his most forbidding expression in place, but he knew Tessa wouldn't stand for that. At least, not without a damn good reason . . . and Johnny couldn't bring himself to share his fears with her.

He didn't want her scared. He wanted her happy. And safe.

Which meant he had to figure this out. After retrieving his rental sedan, he spent a couple of hours driving the length and breadth of Sanctuary Island looking for the rusted-out truck, but he found nothing. Johnny finally gave up and went back to the Buttercup Inn.

Okay, first he did a drive-by check of the bakery where he could see Tessa smiling and joking with a customer through the front window. He stayed parked across the street for half an hour or so, but when Tessa had a break in her steady stream of customers, he could see her narrowing her gaze through the glass as if trying to see who was staking out her shop. Sighing, Johnny rolled his window down and waved at her, so she'd know it was him.

When her only response was a deeply concerned frown, Johnny tightened his jaw and drove back to the tiny parking lot behind the Buttercup Inn.

He had to think. Work it like a case. Fear for Tessa's safety was a handicap—he couldn't avoid that. It clouded his brain and overwhelmed his thoughts, kept his adrenaline flowing and his heart rate cranked high. But he had to push through it.

Slamming out of the car and up the front steps of the bar, Johnny shoved the door open to find Marcus Beckett obsessively polishing the same six-inch circle of his zinc-topped bar while watching Quinn Harper out of the corner of his eye.

Quinn's cheeks were red and her eyes were shining as she hummed happily and stacked bottles on the glass shelves behind the bar. Her hair was in a messy braid down the back of her jersey, strands poking out here and there as the braid swayed over her last name picked out in white letters. When she turned and said, "Hey! You're back!" Johnny noticed that her shirt was buttoned wrong.

Shooting an assessing glance at Marcus, Johnny found the man glaring down at the rag in his hand as if it had personally offended him.

"About damn time," Marcus muttered.

Quinn laughed, bright and mischievous. "Oh, I think his timing is pretty perfect. You don't?"

Johnny's hackles went up. It didn't take a trained investigative agent to read the signs here. Marcus was taking advantage of Quinn's innocence. She was too young and sweet to see it. He hoped like hell that she hadn't convinced herself she was in love with the jerk. "Sorry, I didn't realize you were starting work here today. As an employee," he said pointedly, staring at Marcus.

The older man only grunted and threw down the rag in favor of grabbing a box cutter and going to town on the shipping boxes stacked by the bar.

"I haven't officially punched the clock for my first day yet," Quinn replied sunnily, as if oblivious to the undercurrent of tension between the two men. "I came to see if Marcus needed any help and found him about to set up the bottles completely wrong."

"My uncle always put the Irish whiskey down front on the right, easiest to get to," Marcus surprised Johnny by saying. "I don't see what's so wrong about that."

"That makes sense in an Irish pub." Quinn grinned, holding up a bottle of Jameson by the neck. "But you're back down South now, not in your uncle's pub in New York, and I guarantee you're going to have a lot more requests for bourbon than for Irish. Plus, I have some ideas for featured cocktails and I need to have everything handy so I can test my mixology recipes."

"We're not serving any damn cocktails. I told you before, this isn't that kind of bar." Marcus turned his thunderous frown on Johnny next. "And not that I need the help, but since you offered and you're staying here rent-free, it wouldn't kill you to pitch in a little more."

Since that was undeniably true, Johnny shrugged and said, "Fine. Where do you want me?"

He pretended he didn't hear Marcus's mumbled "Somewhere else, out of my hair." Johnny chose to pay attention to the nod of Marcus's head in the direction of the back office.

"New file cabinet got delivered," Marcus said. "Set it up with folders and dividers, yeah?"

"Sure." Johnny dredged up a smile from someplace and sauntered out of the bar with his hands in his pockets as Quinn piped up to argue the merits of serving fancy cocktails.

The back office was as good a place as any to

search for clues about Marcus Beckett's past. He let himself into the small room that smelled like dust and old paper. A small window high in the wall provided the only natural light.

The fading afternoon sun beamed down on a battered metal desk and the latest model laptop sitting on top of it. Ignoring the file cabinet and its empty drawers for the moment, Johnny moved swiftly to open the laptop, but it was password protected. That would take a while to crack, and maybe some help from the bureau. If he could convince them there was something here that merited investigation . . . special agents with the ATF had a lot of latitude to pursue inquiries on their own, but in order to requisition bureau resources like one of their cybersecurity specialists, Johnny would need more than a gut feeling.

Closing the laptop, he rifled through the desk drawers quickly, finding nothing but pencils with chewed-up erasers and a box of staples, unopened. A plastic inbox sat next to the laptop, overflowing with papers that turned out to be mostly invoices for construction supplies and a copy of the bar's application for a license to serve alcohol. Which was all in order, Johnny noted with irritation. At this point, he was desperate enough to get Marcus on serving liquor without a license, but there was no reason he could see why the license wouldn't come through in time for the opening next week. Marcus Beckett had done everything right.

Johnny threw himself down in the rolling chair behind the desk and winced as a wire coil poked him in the small of the back. He brooded thoughtfully at the file cabinet he was supposed to be setting up. The edges and corners of the thing were all banged up, scuff marks dark along the left side. One of the handles was clearly loose, hanging at an odd diagonal. Marcus had found a secondhand file cabinet to go with his crappy desk and ancient desk chair, then he'd spent thousands on the newest laptop to hit the market?

As he glanced around the depressing little room, the laptop was the only new thing Johnny saw, the only thing that was in better than decent condition . . . except for that picture on the wall.

Brows drawing together, Johnny stared at the shiny, black metal frame and the brilliant white of the matting that set off a vintage-looking photograph of a city block. The photo centered on a lit sign pointing down a set of stairs to a couple of golden-lit windows set below street level. The sign said BECKETT'S. It was the family bar Marcus had talked about. Had to be. So the photo was actually old, but the frame was brand-new.

Working on a hunch, Johnny rose from the desk chair and crossed to stand in front of the picture. The matting was so wide, it almost dwarfed the photo, making the footprint of the entire framed thing more than twice as large as if Marcus had framed the photo itself, with no matting. It seemed like an oddly fussy decorating choice for a man who clearly didn't care about having more than the bare necessities for his office.

Palms prickling with sweat, Johnny reached up and lifted the frame off the wall, revealing a black safe hidden behind it.

He smiled grimly. He might need help cracking a computer password, but the day he needed help cracking a basic combination lock like this was the day he hung up his badge. He took the precaution of wheeling the desk chair over and hooking it under the doorknob to give him a few seconds' warning if anyone came along to check on him, and got to work.

"I call it a Devil's Punch," Quinn announced, holding a glass full of shocking red liquid triumphantly aloft. "Here, try it. You like spicy things, right?"

Marcus eyed the vile brew suspiciously. He wasn't drinking anything that was fifty percent melted cinnamon candies. "You're not serving that."

"Why not? You don't even know if it's good! People might love it. It could be our signature cocktail."

"Because it looks like it would burn the lining right out of my customers' stomachs, and then they won't come back and spend more money here." Impatience clipped his words short, but it was still more explaining than Marcus normally liked to do. Somehow this slip of a girl was always getting him to act in ways that were so out of character, he hardly recognized himself.

"Don't be such a baby." Quinn waved the glass under his nose and taking it as an opportunity to get all up in his space.

Marcus flexed his hands around the beer glasses he was stacking in the sink to be washed and reminded himself that they weren't alone anymore. He couldn't grab her hips and lift her onto the bar, bury himself between her thighs and devour her whole.

No matter how good that sounded. Marcus gave his unruly erection a stern look.

He wasn't ashamed of having sex with Quinn. She was legal and consent had been enthusiastically given. Several times. But his personal life was no one else's business. Especially not the weird guy who'd somehow conned his way into staying in the studio next door.

The weird guy who suddenly burst into the bar with a wild look in his eyes and his dark hair standing on end like he'd stuck his finger in a socket. Marcus straightened, instinctively putting his body between Quinn and the guy with crazy eyes.

"Who the hell are you?" Johnny demanded, guttural and urgent.

Marcus didn't blink. He wouldn't take his gaze off Johnny at this moment any more than he'd glance away from a striking cobra. "You know who I am. Just a man who came back to his hometown to open a bar."

Johnny shook his head, fists clenched at his sides. "No. That's not the whole story. Because there's no reason for a simple bartender to keep a bag of cash and an entire freaking *arsenal* in a hidden wall safe."

Marcus stiffened, but it was the hesitant voice of the woman behind him that put him on high alert. "Marcus? What is he talking about?"

He had to get Quinn out of here, before the violence and panic he saw percolating in Johnny's gaze boiled over. But he already knew that just asking her to go would never do the trick. So he pulled out his harshest voice and said, "None of your damned business.

Now get out of my bar and take your crappy cocktail recipes with you."

The sharp intake of her breath was like a spike to the back of Marcus's head, noticeable even through the mounting tension as Johnny said, "He's right, Quinn, you should go. Marcus and I have things to discuss."

Without another word, Quinn slipped away and grabbed her coat. Marcus could hardly believe she was going so easily, but he shoved down the wave of gratitude in order to keep an eye on Johnny. The younger man had started pacing, flexing and stretching his fingers as if he couldn't wait to get them around Marcus's neck.

He was welcome to try. Marcus waited until Quinn was out the door with one last, searching glance over her shoulder before baring his teeth at Johnny.

"You had no right to go snooping through my things. You need to get your stuff and get the hell out of my building."

"That's right, you own the whole building." Johnny shook his head. "But where did you get the money? And exactly how much do you have left? I saw rolls and rolls of fifties in there, man—too many to count. But I counted the guns, all right."

Marcus stood stone-faced and loose, ready for a fight. He certainly didn't wince, even though he knew exactly what Johnny had found in his lockbox.

"Six weapons," Johnny said, his voice going grim. "Enough ammo to take out every cop from here to New York, much less the sheriff's department on a tiny island."

For some reason, that actually surprised Marcus. This guy thought he was stockpiling guns and bullets for some kind of last-stand shootout with the police? He shook his head, letting the idea rattle around a little, but ultimately it didn't matter what Johnny thought was going on. "It's none of your business. You've got five seconds to hit the stairs and grab your crap before I throw you out of here headfirst."

Johnny stalked closer, every line of his body tensed with aggression. "I'm not leaving without answers. Who was driving the truck?"

"What truck?" Every other idiot in this town owned a pickup.

"Don't give me that bull." Johnny jerked a fist in the collar of Marcus's flannel shirt, hauling him in close. "I know you know what's going on. Someone is after you, and my wife almost got caught in the crossfire!"

Marcus felt a twinge of concern. Whatever went down with this phantom truck, what was for sure was that Johnny was wigging out. First things first, though.

Taking advantage of his height and reach, Marcus stiff-armed Johnny back out of his personal space. "Is Tessa okay?"

"No thanks to you," Johnny growled, straining against Marcus's hold for only a second before tearing himself free and bouncing backward on the balls of his feet. He moved like a fighter, like someone who knew how to inflict damage, and Marcus felt some of what had been bugging him about his tenant all along finally slot into place.

"Tell me what I need to know," Johnny insisted. "Or I'll beat it out of you."

Marcus appraised the situation with a glance. Johnny was wound up, a coiled wire waiting to spring. That energy had to go someplace; might as well be directed at Marcus. At least he knew he could take it.

"So, does whatever agency you're with know that you're going through a paranoid break with reality?" he asked, casual. But there was nothing casual about the deliberate step he took into Johnny's space.

With an incoherent sound of anger, Johnny swung hard at Marcus's jaw. Marcus took the blow on the chin and turned with it, letting half the force dissipate in the shock of sudden pain. A better hit than he'd been expecting, Marcus decided dispassionately. Even in mid-breakdown, Johnny was a formidable opponent.

Too bad for him that Marcus was extensively, exhaustively trained in the art of taking down formidable opponents.

Johnny followed up his advantage with a left hook, but Marcus blocked the blow with his forearm. Grunting and shoving, they grappled uselessly for endless, sweaty minutes, too evenly matched—especially when Marcus was defending himself but not throwing any punches.

Finally, after the third time Marcus ducked a blow, he tried to restrain Johnny in a chokehold, which Johnny easily dodged. "You're not fighting to win," he panted, head lowered like a confused bull unsure of whether to charge. "Why aren't you fighting to win?"

Marcus relaxed out of battle stance but didn't take his wary gaze off Johnny. He shrugged one shoulder. "Got nothing to prove to you. I'm not a criminal. I've got a license for every one of those guns. And I came by my money the old-fashioned way."

"Yeah, but *how* did you earn it? That's what worries me." Suspicion tightened the corners of Johnny's eyes.

Old regrets and tired pain twisted at Marcus's gut, but he knew none of it showed in his blank expression. "I never said I earned it. I said the old-fashioned way. I inherited it."

"From who?"

From whom. Marcus heard the irritated correction, the kind of comment he'd grown so used to over the last couple of years. The kind of comment he never would've thought he'd miss—but damn, he sure did miss it. Setting his jaw stubbornly, he only stared at Johnny in response.

He'd said all he planned to. Johnny didn't get to know more about Marcus's past than that.

Some sort of struggle was going on behind Johnny's shuttered gaze. Winded and rubbing at his knuckles, his shoulders slumped. He dragged a hand down a face that suddenly looked gray with exhaustion. "I believe you. Man, I am sorry. I don't know what to say, except Tessa could've gotten badly hurt and I flipped my lid. I shouldn't have gone off on you like that."

He held out a hand and Marcus shook it. Marcus wasn't above squeezing a little too hard around Johnny's sore knuckles—knuckles he'd bruised on Marcus's *face*—but Johnny only grimaced and wrung out his hand with a wry grin.

"Thanks. I feel like an ass. I don't have any excuse, except that I recently finished a job where it was a matter of life and death to be suspicious of everyone I came in contact with. I guess I'm having a harder time coming home from that than I thought."

Marcus studied Johnny's shadowed eyes and the bleak twist of his lips. Not entirely true, Marcus decided. Johnny knew he was having a rough time of it. But as Marcus could attest, knowing you were in trouble didn't always make it easier to get the help you needed to get yourself out of trouble.

Which didn't make what he had to say any easier, but it still needed to be said. "I don't know anything about a truck," he clarified slowly. Johnny's gaze flew to him, intense and interested. "But as far as I know, there's zero reason anyone would be after me."

He waited, hoping Johnny would put the pieces together himself. The guy was kind of a mess. Marcus had been there, and he didn't especially want to be the guy who made things worse for Johnny.

But when all Johnny said was, "Okay, thanks for telling me," Marcus had to hold back a sigh.

Sometimes, his life sucked beyond the telling of it.

Kindness didn't come easily to Marcus. He didn't have a ton of experience with it. Still, he tried to gentle his normally gruff tone into something resembling compassion as he said, "Johnny. I don't know your life or what kind of shit you've been in. But nobody who can crack a safe and fights like you do has lived squeaky clean. You need to consider that if there really is something going on, someone on the island who's deliberately looking to cause trouble—it might be someone from *your* past, not mine."

And for the second time in his life, Marcus Beckett got to watch the life drain out of someone's stare as their world turned to ashes and dust around them.

Chapter 15

Kneading bread always put Tessa into something like a trance. As far as she was concerned, kneading was better than yoga, better than meditation, better than anything except prayer for getting into a state where she could let her mind drift through the problems of her day, and find some peace.

She'd probably be praying later, but for now, there were the ten loaves of sourdough the Firefly Café had ordered for their weekend sandwich special. Tessa let Patty wipe down the counters and lock up while she checked the rise.

Prying back the corner of the big plastic tub, she pressed a satisfied fingertip to the puffy, white dough. The indentation lingered in the sticky surface for a second, then sprang back. With a practiced eye, Tessa judged that the dough had roughly doubled in size since she first covered it and left it to do its thing. Perfect.

She dumped the dough out on her lightly floured workstation and used a metal scraper to neatly portion out a dozen lumps. Tessa liked to do a second rise with sourdough, and this time, she'd form each loaf into the round shape it would be baked in. Scooping the first mound of dough to the middle of the counter, Tessa floured her hands and got to work.

What was she going to do about Johnny? The incoherent scraps of worry, guilt, fear, and doubt wove themselves into a dark patchwork as her hands and arms worked on autopilot.

He was so protective of her. He always had been, since the first night they met, but while it used to comfort Tessa and make her feel cherished and cared for, now it felt smothering. She breathed in the sharp smell of the yeast and savored it. This was the scent of independence, to Tessa.

A woman who's conquered sourdough can beat anything, Patty had told her when she first started teaching Tessa the intricacies of maintaining a starter. And in a very real way, Tessa knew it was true.

She'd learned a skill here, a marketable skill that could get her work almost anywhere. She hadn't just learned to bake bread. She'd learned how to support herself, how to stand on her own two feet.

The fact that Johnny still treated her like the shaking, traumatized teenager she'd been when he found her . . . Tessa sighed and used the edge of her wrist to dab at her damp brow.

Kneading was hard work. Satisfying on every level. But somehow today, the usual calm serenity escaped her.

Still, by the time she heard voices out front and looked up from her dough with a frown, half an hour had passed without her awareness. She'd gone through eight of the loaves and stacked them on rimmed baking sheets spread with parchment paper, each pan nestled into a tall, wheeled rack.

It was after closing time. Patty shouldn't be letting any customers in, she should be totaling up the cash drawer . . . Tessa frowned, nerves tingling. Even as she told herself she was being paranoid, letting Johnny's overprotectiveness get to her, she called out, "Patty? Everything okay out there?"

But it wasn't Patty who appeared in the doorway to the back kitchen. It was Johnny.

"I sent Patty to the bank, told her I'd walk you home when you were done here," Johnny said, without preamble.

"Okay." Tessa took a moment to stare at the man who was her husband. Maybe it was because she'd been thinking so much about the night they met, but there was a look about Johnny that reminded her of the boy he'd been. A little older than she was, more confident, sure of where he was going in life—but wounded, too. She hadn't been able to see it as clearly when she was barely more than a child herself, but now?

Johnny was hurting. And it made Tessa's own heart ache as if a rough hand had reached into her chest and squeezed it tight.

"Thanks. But I don't need an escort," she said gently. "I'm fine to walk home on my own. I've been doing it for more than a year now."

A muscle ticked in Johnny's jaw. "Things have changed."

"Why?" Tessa slammed the dough down a little harder than necessary. It felt good. "Because now you're here to see me do it? I'm sorry, Johnny, I know this is hard for you but that's not a good enough reason."

"The man driving that truck—"

"Was an ass," Tessa said bluntly, without looking up from her knuckles buried in the soft dough. "A reckless driver who definitely ought to have his license revoked. But Johnny, come on! I can't hide in the bakery or Patty's house and never go out on the street again in case that guy happens to be driving by!"

She could practically hear Johnny's teeth grinding. "I think there's more to it than that. I can't prove anything, but I believe we were targeted. On purpose. And I want you to come with me to an ATF safe house right now, and stay there while I figure this out."

Shock shuddered down Tessa's spine, along with a healthy dose of dread. Turning slowly, she stared at her husband across the tidy kitchen.

"Johnny," she started, then paused, unsure what to say. "Do you hear yourself? I mean, do you get what this sounds like to me?"

There went that muscle in his jaw again, and oh, look, there was a throbbing vein at his temple now, too. "I know it sounds like the ravings of a paranoid lunatic," Johnny ground out. "I can't help that. You just have to trust me."

"I've trusted you with my life since the moment we met," Tessa said softly, watching his eyes close in relief. She almost hated to shatter the moment, but she had to. Or they were doomed to play out the same unequal, stilted pattern that had marked their entire relationship so far. "The problem isn't whether I trust you. It's the fact that you don't trust me. You never have."

Johnny's eyes flew open. "That's not true."

Even Tessa was surprised by the bitter edge to her laugh. She went back to her dough, deftly shaping the loaf into a mounded circle and setting it on the waiting parchment-papered pan. "Oh, I think it is. When was the last time you told me . . . anything, really?"

"I couldn't tell you about my assignment," he said instantly. "The details were classified."

"That's not what I'm talking about. I understood about the assignment, and about your missions for the army before that. But you shut me out in other ways, too."

Johnny made a frustrated sound and paced closer, as if he were contemplating throwing her over his shoulder and dragging her to the safe house by force. "We don't have time for this conversation, Tessa. We need to go."

"I'm not going anywhere. You're free to leave, obviously. But if you stay, we're having this conversation, because it's long overdue."

The sound of the next lump of dough hitting the countertop punctuated Johnny's low, vicious curse. Then he sighed and said, "Fine. Say what you need to say. But then you have to hear me out about this situation."

Tessa thought it over. "It's a deal. But I'm not promising to drop everything and scurry off to some undisclosed location."

"No," Johnny agreed dryly. "That would be entirely too easy."

Shrugging, Tessa punched down the dough and flipped it over, relishing the silky feel of the flour and the elasticity of the sourdough. "If you want easy, you don't want marriage."

"When did you get to be such a hard-ass?"

Tessa shot him a glare, but there was a smile pulling up the corner of his mouth. She tilted her chin at the waiting piles of dough. "Can't afford to be soft when there's this much work to do."

"I could help. If you give me some tips."

Tessa thought it over. She remembered the way Dr. Voss worked things during their sessions out at Windy Corner so that there was always an activity, something physical to do with the horses while they talked. She thought about the way those sessions had shown her more about Johnny in a few weeks than she'd learned in years of marriage—and she thought about the way Johnny closed up tighter than a fist during one-on-one conversations, with both people just sitting and staring at one another.

"Go wash your hands," she instructed, jerking her head at the sink in the corner. "Then come back here and I'll show you what to do."

The impromptu bread-baking lesson only took a few minutes. Johnny was tense beside her, clearly humoring her and wishing they were putting Sanctuary Island in their rearview mirror, but he listened attentively. She wasn't surprised when he got the knack of kneading on the first try.

Johnny had always had good hands. Long, lean fingers, strong but sensitive. Tessa shivered, riding out the rush of heat that prickled across her skin at his nearness. The close, solid, unmistakably male presence.

When they were both in the rhythm, pushing and pulling at the dough, Tessa forced her mind back to the topic at hand. "We were talking about trust. And the way you don't trust me, not just to take care of myself like a competent adult, but with any part of you."

"I don't think of you as incompetent, or a child," Johnny argued. "How could I, when you're clearly doing fine here without me. Better than fine. You're actually happy. God knows, that was something I never managed to do for you. You had to do it for yourself."

The regret in his tone tore at Tessa's defenses. "I was happy with you. Sometimes. But I always wanted more than you could give me, and that's not exactly a recipe for happiness."

To her relief, he didn't ask what she'd wanted that he didn't provide. The fact of her unrequited love sat on the table between them, as sad and misshapen as Johnny's first attempt at shaping a round loaf.

She stepped in to tidy up the boule, leaning in front of him to mold the dough into the desired, uniform shape. Behind her, close enough that his breath stirred the fine hairs at the back of her neck, Johnny said, "I wish I could give you . . . everything. You deserve it."

Drawing back hastily, Tessa suppressed the tremor of longing and tried to stick to her guns. "You gave me a lot, and I don't mean to sound ungrateful. But I know you don't want my gratitude, and the fact is, there were things you could've done, things you could've said, that would have made a difference. Even if you didn't . . . even if you couldn't love me back the way I wanted."

Drowning a bit in the humiliation of that last sentence, Tessa started when Johnny grasped her shoulder and turned her to face him. His intent, dark eyes searched her face avidly. "What things? Tell me, whatever it is, and I'll do it."

A thrill sang down her spine. It was always heady to be the focus of Johnny's undivided attention. Add in the warmth of his hands on her shoulders and the new knowledge her body carried of the ways they could bring each other pleasure, and Tessa had a hard time thinking of anything she wanted more than Johnny's kiss.

But he was asking, really asking, and she couldn't waste this chance to fix what was wrong between them. Maybe even to start fixing whatever it was that haunted Johnny.

"I want to know you," she told him simply, reaching up to brush the floury back of her hand over his sharp cheekbone. "You know everything there is to know about me. My parents, my past, where I came from. I don't know anything about you except that you grew up on a farm, that you don't have any brothers or sisters, and that you're the kind of man who can't resist trying to save everyone around him."

The hands on her shoulders went tight for an instant as a shadow darker than pain crossed his rigid face. Tessa caught her breath at the sight of it and his grip instantly loosened, his hands dropping away to hang at his sides.

"That's not entirely true," he finally said, voice sharper than the serrated blade of Tessa's bread knife.

Her mouth dropped open in confusion. "What part?"

His jaw worked silently for a moment before he cranked it open and said, "The part about me being an only child. I grew up with . . . I had a sister."

It had come to this. Johnny was about to rip himself open and spill his guts on the countertop to convince Tessa . . . what? That she mattered? That he trusted her, so she should do the same and go with him to the safe house?

Urgency still beat through Johnny's bloodstream, pushing and shoving to get them moving, but it had dimmed somewhat in the face of Tessa's stolid refusal to believe there was any danger.

First Marcus, then Tessa—Johnny wasn't an idiot. He could see the way they looked at him, the caution mixed with pity as they tried to figure out how to tell him he was acting like a crazy person.

Well, maybe Johnny was messed up in the head. But as the saying went, it wasn't paranoia if people actually were coming after you.

But that wasn't going to be enough for Tessa. Nothing he could say would be. Johnny was under no delusions about that. Unless he could open his mouth and force out a lie about love, he and Tessa were through.

So maybe it was stupid of him to go through with this painful bloodletting, but Johnny didn't care. He owed it to the woman he'd married, but never really let in. She was right about that. And what did it matter now? One way or another, he wasn't going to be seeing much more of Tessa after tonight.

The pain of that realization was crushing enough that it almost overshadowed the deeper, older ache of his memories of Angie.

"Johnny?" Tessa bit her lip, obviously unaware of the way it dragged his attention to that spot. "You don't have to talk about this if you don't want to."

There she went, giving him the easy out. Johnny wasn't the only one with protective instincts. The thought warmed him and gave him courage.

"I don't want to talk about it," he admitted roughly. "But I think I need you to hear about it, if that makes any sense."

She leaned one hip against the counter, heedless of the flour and sticky bits of dough smearing her jeans. "I'm listening."

This was harder than Johnny expected. He swallowed hard and reached for another lump of dough, needing something to do with his hands. Prodding it restlessly, he said, "My little sister, Angie, was the kind of kid everyone instantly falls in love with. She had this way about her, a curiosity about the world and a smile that made you want to smile back. I was five when she was born. I guess my parents had been trying for a second child for a while, and I remember how thrilled they were. She was a miracle baby, and I was excited to be a big brother."

At his side, Tessa drew a shaky breath as though she had some inkling of what was coming.

Doggedly determined to get through it, Johnny ducked his head and pressed the dough down with his fists. "Angie followed me everywhere, and you'd think it would be annoying but it just . . . wasn't. She was my best friend before she could walk or talk, and I was so proud of the way she looked up to me. She wanted to do everything I did, even though she was five years younger. By the time we were eleven and six, Mom trusted me to look after her while she worked the farm."

Heat prickled behind his eyes, a spike of pain gathering at his temples where Johnny realized he had clenched his jaw hard enough to grind his molars. He made a conscious effort to relax, to stop his hands from shaking. But they wouldn't, so he hid them in the dough and pressed on.

"I don't know if you remember from that night you wandered onto our property, but we had a pond out back of the barn. It wasn't very big, but Dad had stocked it with trout and I liked to take the rowboat out and fish when the weather was nice. Ange was allowed to go with me, but she had to wear a life jacket. She was too little to handle the oars, which made her mad, but I didn't mind rowing us around."

The memory of those days on the pond were a poisoned apple, bitter and sweet all at once. If he closed his eyes, he could see the head of dark curls leaning out over the murky water, chattering loud enough to scare away the fish.

"One night while Mom was cooking dinner, I came downstairs from doing my homework and asked where Angie was. Mom said she thought she was with me, and we got worried when we realized neither of us had seen her in a while. She was going through this phase where she loved hide-and-seek, but she'd forget that she was supposed to let us know she was playing. We started combing the house, looking in all her favorite spots like behind the dining room curtains and under Mom's bed, but she wasn't there. Finally I checked the hall closet and saw her life jacket hanging there, and suddenly, I knew."

Johnny bent over the counter, hands flat and bracing him up as his stomach swooped down to his knees the way it had that awful night.

"Oh, Johnny." Tessa's voice was wrecked. "Oh, no."

He nodded once, chin to his chest, and forced out the rest of the story. "Like I said, she was curious and impatient to grow up and be big enough to do everything her big brother did. I tore down the stairs and out to the back porch. From there, I could make out part of the pond. It was still as glass, no wind to ripple the water. I stood there for a second trying to calm down and convince myself I was wrong—when the tip of the rowboat drifted into view from behind the edge of the barn. I nearly threw up. I don't remember running down to the pond, or falling down and getting back up, although I must have because later there was a hole in the knee of my jeans and my hands were badly scraped. I don't remember any of it. All I remember is coming to the end of the dock and seeing the rowboat floating in the middle of the pond, right where it got deepest . . . completely empty."

He paused, chilled and clammy with the horror of the memory, only to tense when Tessa wrapped her arms around him from behind. She held on anyway, pressing her forehead between his shoulder blades. Johnny felt himself grow calmer, his body reclaimed and anchored in the present instead of caught in the waterlogged weeds of the past.

"I swam out to the boat," he said dully, "but Angie was gone. One of the oars was floating in the water beside the boat. Maybe she fell over the side trying to reach it. Maybe she got stuck drifting out there and couldn't work the oars to come back in, so she tried to swim for it. I don't know. I'll never know. They had to drag the pond to find her body, but my mother wouldn't let me see her. I know why, now, and I don't blame her, but at the time, it was like Angie simply vanished from the world. And all I could think was that if I'd been paying attention, if I'd been protecting her the way I was supposed to, she would still be with us."

The back of his shirt felt damp. Tessa was crying. He couldn't take that. Feeling creaky and old, Johnny reached back to pull her against his chest, where she immediately buried her face against his neck and sighed wetly. "Johnny, I'm so sorry. What a tragedy, to lose your sister so young—I can't even imagine the pain of it. Your poor parents."

"My dad was long gone by then. But Mom never

really recovered. She tried to pull it together for me, but I didn't make it easy for her. I was a pretty angry kid, for a long time. Anger to cover up the guilt, I guess."

"You were angry because you were grieving, and anger is a part of it," Tessa pointed out, lifting her head to give his face a searching look. "But you had nothing to be guilty over, Johnny. I hope your mother made that clear."

Johnny shrugged, his shoulders as tight and sore as if he'd been hefting five-hundred-pound sacks of flour all day. "That's what she said, but it didn't change how I felt."

How I feel.

As if she'd heard the silent confession, Tessa's brows lowered. With her eyes red and swollen and her cheeks as pale as the dough rising behind her, she should have looked awful. Instead, Johnny thought he'd never seen anything more beautiful.

"It was a terrible accident," Tessa argued. "No one was at fault. Certainly not you—no matter how much your parents trusted you to watch over your sister, you were only a child yourself. And you had your own life, your own responsibilities, your school work . . ."

Johnny's chest ached. "None of that mattered, none of it was more important than keeping Angie safe. I would give everything I am, sacrifice everything I have, for one more day with her."

Pulling back and placing her palms gently against his chest, Tessa stared up into his eyes. "So you grew up and sacrificed your future for a girl you didn't even know. And you found a job where you would be asked to sacrifice your very identity for a chance to make the world a safer place."

"This isn't one of our therapy sessions." Johnny glanced away, feeling the burn of Tessa's stare like fire against his cheek. "I didn't tell you this so you could psychoanalyze me. You said I never let you in, well, this is it. You wanted in, you're in. This is all that's inside me. A gaping, black hole full of my failure to protect the people who depend on me."

Chapter 16

The devastation in Johnny's beautiful, coffee-dark
eyes tore a jagged wound in Tessa's heart. Part of her
wished she hadn't pushed this, hadn't made Johnny
dredge all of this up—but most of Tessa was aware
that she and Johnny had never been closer than they
were in this moment . . . not even when he'd propelled
her to ecstasy with his passionate, intimate kiss.

"Not what you were hoping for, I know." Johnny's
profile was stern and imposing, but Tessa could see
the throb of his pulse in his strong, tanned throat.

She picked her words like she was picking tiny
shards of eggshell out of a bowl of yolks. "I hate that
your family went through that. I hate that you have to
live with the loss of your sister. But I could never, ever
be disappointed by the man you are inside, John Alexander. My husband."

That brought his eyes back to hers. A wry smile
touched his lips. "For a little while longer, at least."

Tessa stared at him, her heart swelling until it crowded her lungs and made breathing a chore. He'd given her so much, shown her so much. Was it enough? Did she truly have the right to ask for more?

The moment held, like a strand of spun sugar pulled taut between their bodies, stretching thinner and thinner until it finally snapped. Johnny glanced down and wiped his hands on a damp kitchen towel before digging in his pocket for his phone. He thumbed it on and swore softly. "Come on, Brad. Call me back."

Tessa frowned. "What do you need to talk to your boss at the ATF about?"

"Something Marcus said," Johnny replied vaguely, slipping the phone back into his pocket. "Not important. But I'm going to head out tonight, drop into the office and see if I can't catch him there."

"You're leaving?" Tessa's swollen heart shrank, shriveling up hard and wrinkled like a raisin. "And you've given up on trying to get me to a safe house."

He pressed his lips together in a flat line. "Maybe I'm blowing things out of proportion. And maybe there's some slight connection between my tendency to get overprotective, and my past. Either way, you have the right to make decisions about your own safety, and if you don't want to leave Sanctuary Island, I won't force you."

Tessa tried for a smile even though she felt as if she'd never have a reason to smile again. "Good. There was a minute there where I was afraid you were planning to knock me out and kidnap me."

Embarrassment shaded his cheekbones brick red. "Maybe Brad was a little right, too. I probably need a break from the job. I'm starting to see bad guys and evil plots everywhere I look."

Tessa caught her breath. It was a huge admission from Johnny, and a huge step toward him getting some help dealing with the incredible stress he'd lived with while undercover.

"Why not stay here and finish out the sessions at Windy Corner?" Tessa said, hating the slight pleading note in her own voice. "I mean, you do need a break. You deserve one. Do you really have to go back to the office?"

A strange expression tensed Johnny's handsome features. Stepping close, he cradled her face in his large palms, thumbs stroking her cheeks in the way that always sent shivers through Tessa's core. "Yes. Because I can't stay here with you any longer, knowing that I'll never have you."

Tessa's stomach clenched, emotion swamping her in a shocking flood. "You could have me. Just tell me you love me. Lie to me, I don't even care."

Tenderly, slowly, Johnny swiped at the tears that spilled from her eyes. "I'll never lie to you, Tessa. Not even to keep you."

She choked on a sob and grabbed at his hands when he went to pull away. Desperate and fevered, she cried out, "Wait! Don't go."

"I have to." Johnny's wrists were iron-hard with tension, straining in her grasp. "I'm a mess, Tessa. I need to get my head on straight, and that's not your responsibility. Not anymore. Besides, if leaving you here to fend for yourself is the only way I can convince you that I trust you—that I see you for the astonishing, intelligent, skilled, beautiful woman that you are . . . well, I'd say that's the least I can do for you."

With every word, Tessa felt the chains of love twine more strongly through her soul, tying her to this man she'd given her heart to so long ago. Maybe he didn't love her; maybe he never would. But that didn't change the fact that she was so in love with him, she could barely breathe.

And she would be damned before she let him walk out of her life without trying every weapon in her arsenal to get him to stay.

"I'll let you go," she said slowly as her breathing calmed and her heart began to thump a steady beat. "But first, I want one night in your arms."

His eyes went molten black, full of heat and desire. But his body was stiff. He held himself away as if he didn't trust himself to touch her. "I don't know, Tessa. I'm not sure what good it would do."

That almost cracked her in two, but she didn't falter. "I want the memories. I want to know what other brides found out on their wedding nights, and I want it with you. Please, Johnny. Don't make me leave this marriage as untouched as I came into it."

She'd barely finished speaking before Johnny was kissing the words from her lips, sucking and nipping and stealing her breath and her sanity. Tessa retained just enough of her rational mind to gasp out, "Not here! Patty would kill me if I defiled her kitchen."

"Mmm." Johnny nuzzled into her neck, his restless hands shaping her ribs before sneaking up to cup her breasts. "Not to mention what the health inspector would say. Because I plan to do things to you that are definitely not sanitary."

Tessa laughed at the same time that a hard shudder of lust shook her. Gripping tight to Johnny's shoulders, she said, "That's one way you made me happy. You could always make me laugh."

"That's because I like making you feel good. Hopefully tonight, I'll discover some new ways."

The whispered words, heated and rough against her skin, made Tessa go boneless in his arms. Everything seemed to add to her desire—the rub of her thighs together, the texture of Johnny's hair between her fingers, the brush of hot air from the cooling oven . . . shoot. They were in the bakery.

"Yes," she gasped, stiffening her trembling arms and trying to push away. "Tonight. I'll come to you at the bar."

"We could go right now," Johnny suggested, resisting her attempts to separate their bodies.

"I want to, believe me. But unfortunately, these sourdough loaves aren't going to bake themselves." Tessa managed to step back a pace, one self-conscious hand going up to straighten her top and fix her ruffled hair. "And . . . I want to have a little time to get ready for you. For our wedding night."

Johnny's eyes went soft and dark like melted chocolate. "Our wedding night. Only slightly delayed."

"Better late than never." Was that really her voice? Tessa wondered. Husky and low . . . she sounded more confident than she felt.

As if Johnny could hear the nerves underneath her

attempt at seductive flirting, he ran his fingers through her hair one last time before letting go of her completely. "Go. Bake. Do whatever you have to do to get ready, then come find me. But for the record? All you ever need to do is smile at me."

The sweetness of that stayed with her through Johnny helping her knead the last few loaves and set the trays on the rolling cart for their second rise overnight. That sweetness stuck around through his lingering kiss before they parted ways after locking up the bakery. It carried her down the street as if she were floating, her feet barely touching the pavement.

But by the time Tessa was in her room at Patty's house trying on different bras and nightgowns, that sweet, floaty feeling was long gone.

A knock on the door startled her out of her sad contemplation of herself in the mirror.

"Can I come in, sugar?" Patty called.

Taking one last, discouraging look at her favorite nightgown—a light pink satin shift with skinny straps and a ruffled hem—Tessa went to let her friend in.

The older lady's brows lifted toward her salt-and-pepper hairline. "I thought you were going back out. Change your mind?"

Tessa debated being embarrassed and decided Patty would only scoff if she blushed. "No, I'm still going. I'm trying to find something to wear that might entice my husband to finally help me get rid of my stupid virginity."

"And you think that little pink number is your ticket to Orgasm City?"

"Patty!" Tessa laughed and gave up trying not to blush.

"Pshh." Patty waved that away with a crepe-papery hand. "I'm old, not dead. And even though I've never been married, I've lived what you might call an adventurous life. Trust me, you and your pink nightie aren't going to shock me."

"I'm afraid they're not going to shock Johnny, either," Tessa said glumly. "I thought this nightgown was so pretty and sexy when I bought it. Now it looks more like something a little girl would wear playing dress up."

Patty wandered over to the guest room closet and started flipping through the hanging clothes. "Tell me what you want your outfit to do."

"I want it to make Johnny want me," Tessa said baldly. "I want it to make me irresistible, so irresistible that he can't do anything but kiss me and take me to bed. And stay there with me forever."

Casting an amused glance over her shoulder, Patty said, "That's a lot of pressure to put on a scrap of satin, sugar."

"I know. Especially when the woman inside the satin is more of a girl next door than a femme fatale."

"Fiddlesticks. Any woman can be a femme fatale, if that's what she wants to be. But don't underestimate the appeal of that girl next door, either. Listen up, sugar. I've got a secret for you."

Tessa looped her arm around Patty's frail shoulders, her heart full of love and gratitude for this spitfire of a woman, with her years of experience and wisdom, even as part of her ached for her mother.

What would Tessa's mother have said in this situation? She'd never know.

Setting aside that well-worn longing, Tessa said, "I would love to hear your secret."

"Well, sugar, it's this. We act like sexy underthings and skimpy nighties are for the man's benefit, to get him in the mood." Patty held up a shirt Tessa had buried at the back of the closet—a man's white button-down shirt, worn at the cuffs and collar, all starch long gone. "But men are already in the mood. They're always in the mood. The truth is, the point of a woman wearing lacy undies or silky lingerie is to make *herself* feel sexy. Desirable. Sensual. It's not about what will turn him on. It's about you feeling confident and ready to be loved."

Tessa touched a trembling finger to the collar of the shirt Patty held. "That's Johnny's shirt. It's one of the only things I took from our house when I left."

"I had a feeling."

"It smelled like him," Tessa whispered. "I wore it every night for the first year after he went on that undercover assignment."

"And how did you feel when you put it on?" Patty pressed.

"Safe. Warm." Tessa swallowed. "Loved."

Even the illusion of Johnny's arms around her had been better than nothing.

When Patty tossed aside the hanger and held the shirt out, Tessa shrugged into it. It was like wrapping herself in the best memories of her life with Johnny. She glanced in the mirror, surprised at the small, secretive smile that curved her lips as she settled the plain cotton on her shoulders. The sleeves reached past her fingertips, but she'd long ago rolled them to bare her wrists.

Breathing in, Tessa still caught a whiff of Johnny's clean, masculine musk. She felt her muscles loosen, tension releasing, even as something deep inside her coiled taut with the expectation of pleasure.

"How did you get to be so wise, Miss Patty?"

A nostalgic smile flickered across the wrinkled visage. "My mother was a wonderful woman. Ahead of her time in many ways, and one of those ways was that she hated how many of her women friends didn't enjoy sex. She told me that I deserved to someday have 'a healthy marital relation,' as she called it. I know she hoped I'd find it with a husband, but well, that's another story."

Unexpected and unwelcome, tears threatened at the corners of Tessa's eyes. "I miss my mother," she admitted. "I know she wasn't perfect, but I also know she loved me. And sometimes I feel sort of . . . I don't know. Incomplete, not knowing how she is or even if she's still alive."

"Oh, sugar." Patty's eyes misted over. "It's been decades since my mother passed on, and I could stand here and bawl right now talking about her. The bond between mother and daughter is complicated. Good or bad, there's nothing quite like it."

Sniffling, Tessa gave their reflection a watery grin. "I can't be too sad when I have you in my life. I hope you know how much I love you, Patty Cuthbert."

"I never had any children of my own, so I missed

out on grandkids, too, but if I'd had a granddaughter, I would have wanted her to be just like you, sugar."

"Stop it!" Tessa wailed, tipping her head down to Patty's frail shoulder. Laughter through tears, what a weird and wonderful feeling.

"All right, all right, that's enough of that." Patty dabbed at her eyes briskly, then took Tessa by the arms and squared her up to face the mirror.

Tessa blinked at herself wrapped in Johnny's old shirt, the color high in her cheeks and her eyes bright with unshed tears and overflowing emotion. She looked . . . ready.

"You're beautiful, young, and in love," Patty declared. "Don't squander it! Go get 'im, girl."

Chapter 17

Tessa stood outside of the Buttercup Inn, the hand-painted sign swaying gently above her head in the night air. The door was locked, of course. She was just debating whether or not to call Johnny to come down and get her, or to throw pebbles against his window or something, when a sudden chill lifted the hairs along her arms.

She wasn't alone in the alley.

Holding her breath, Tessa dropped her car keys casually into her palm, one key sticking out between her knuckles the way she'd learned in the self-defense class the Sanctuary Island Sheriff's Department had put on last fall.

Normally she wouldn't have thought twice about it, she realized distractedly, listening for footsteps or movement behind her. Some of Johnny's worries must have rubbed off on her after all, even though she didn't truly believe she was in any danger.

A glass bottle clinked against the pavement, kicked by a careless foot, and Tessa spun with her fists raised and ready to strike out . . . at a wide-eyed Quinn Harper.

"I surrender!" Quinn held her hands up, her dimpled chin quivering with the effort of suppressing a laugh.

Tessa rolled her eyes at herself and blew out a breath. "Sorry, you just startled me, is all."

"Here to see Johnny?"

Finally noticing the nervous anticipation jittering through the younger woman, Tessa raised her brows. "I am. Are you here to see Marcus?"

She tried to keep her tone completely free of judgment, but from the way Quinn stiffened, she didn't quite succeed. That dimpled chin stuck out obstinately. "Yep. And I've already heard what a bad idea that is from everyone in town, it seems like, including Marcus himself. But I don't care. I want to be here."

For the first time since Tessa met Quinn, she glimpsed something beneath the bright, carefree mask the girl wore like a second skin. Quinn wasn't just having fun, sowing her wild oats with a sexy older man. She was in deeper than that.

Tessa recognized the signs; she'd just spent an hour staring at them in her own mirror.

"Sometimes that's enough." Tessa smiled and watched Quinn relax enough to smile back. "Do you have a key?"

"I do, as it happens." Producing her key with a flourish, Quinn let them in and led the way through the darkened bar to the back staircase. She navigated around piles of cardboard boxes and tables stacked with upside-down chairs as if she'd been there plenty of times in the dark.

Tessa followed her quietly, musing on the ways she and Quinn were different—the married virgin and the free-spirited single girl—and the ways they were the same. Both of them were laying their hearts on the line when they lay down with the men they loved . . . and both of them were likely to wake up one day with those hearts broken into a million pieces.

But wasn't that true of everyone who took a chance on love? And wasn't the hope of a happy ending enough of a reason to take the chance?

Tessa had already spent too much of her life cowering in the shadows and hoping the world would pass her by. And guess what? It did pass her by, but staying safe hadn't kept her from heartbreak. Here, on Sanctuary Island, she had taken more risks and exposed her vulnerabilities and basically invited the world to take its best shot—and she was closer to getting what she wanted now, tonight, than she ever had been before.

At the landing at the top of the stairs, Quinn turned to the door on the left. Pausing with her hand on the doorknob, she gave Tessa a smile that looked brave in the dim light of the moon streaming in the window. "Have a good night," she whispered.

Tessa's heart began to gallop as she stared at the door on the right. Johnny was behind that door, waiting for her. "You, too," she said absently, reaching for the doorknob.

"We'll try to keep it down," Quinn said, the sparkle and mischief returning to her laughing voice. "But no promises!"

She whisked away into the front apartment, leaving Tessa blushing on the landing. Did she have the guts to be like Quinn, to throw open the door to what she wanted and walk right in as if she belonged there?

Not really.

Sighing, Tessa lifted her hand to knock but before it connected, the door swung open to reveal Johnny's lean, muscled form silhouetted in the moonlight.

Tessa clutched her coat around herself and swallowed dryly, her throat clicking in the silence of the hallway. Every cell of her body vibrated like a struck tuning fork, reverberating with Johnny's nearness and pulling her in closer to him.

Johnny's eyes glittered, nearly black with hunger. Without a single word, he reached out and drew her inside.

His heat scorched her skin, pouring off him in waves that made her gasp. The gasp turned to a moan when his arms clutched her to his chest and his mouth crashed down on hers. They surged together, ravenous and shaking with it.

"How did I wait this long?" Johnny muttered against the sensitive skin over her jawline. His roving hands combed through her hair and down her back, molding her more closely to him. Tessa's breasts crushed against his chest, naked under her clothes, and even that rough caress turned her on.

She didn't want to talk about why they'd gone

years—years!—without this when they could have
been . . . when all along, she'd wanted . . .

Dazed and in need of oxygen, Tessa tore her mouth
from Johnny's and pulled back far enough to kick off
her shoes and shrug out of her coat.

"Don't—"

Whatever protest Johnny was about to make
died on his lips when his stare dropped to her body.
His shirt hung on her slender frame, unbuttoned far
enough to show the pale skin of her sternum. Her
legs were bare, and he couldn't see it, but she'd decided against underwear.

What was the point? she'd reasoned. They'd only
slow her down.

The point was, she realized now as she fought not
to squirm under Johnny's intense gaze, that underwear
made you feel more covered. Less bare.

Somehow, wearing Johnny's shirt and nothing
else, Tessa felt more bare than if she'd actually been
naked.

"You're wearing my shirt." Johnny's dark brown
eyes lifted to scrutinize Tessa's face. "You kept it. All
this time. And you're wearing it. Do you have any idea
what that does to me?"

Tessa couldn't hold back a smile. Maybe wearing
sexy things wasn't only about pleasing herself. Maybe
it was about pleasing both of them.

"Do you like it?" she asked, sending a coy glance
up through her lashes to check his reaction.

His reaction did not disappoint. Chest flexing,
Johnny brought one hand down to palm the hard ridge

of his erection, solid and obvious in his jeans. He made a sound like he couldn't believe his eyes.

"I can't believe you can ask me that. Yes," he said definitely. "I like it. A lot."

"I'm nervous," Tessa explained with a breathless laugh. "I'm sorry, I wish I weren't."

"Don't be sorry. I'm nervous, too." Johnny's mouth twisted in a rueful grin. "I'm not a virgin, but it's been a while."

Struck, Tessa said, "Wait. How long has it been for you?"

Johnny frowned. "Since before we got married."

The ground shifted beneath Tessa's bare feet, her entire life and everything she thought she knew rearranging itself around her. "You haven't . . . you never slept with anyone else while we were married? I assumed you did."

Crossing his arms over his chest, Johnny said, "No way. We made vows, Tessa. That means something to me. It means a damn sight more than getting my rocks off, I can tell you that."

"But . . . it wouldn't have been a betrayal." Tessa was still reeling. She couldn't wrap her mind around it. "Not really. Our marriage was in name only. I would have understood."

She would've hated it, but she would have understood. And on some level, she'd been glad to think that even if Johnny wouldn't touch her, he could be happy with someone else even briefly.

But apparently not.

Johnny's jaw looked as hard and uncompromising

as the marble of her favorite pastry board. "What, you think I couldn't keep it in my pants? I'm so ruled by my dick that I'd break our vows, betray your trust, abandon my family . . ."

He choked off the words, but Tessa made the connection. "Your father was long gone by the time you lost Angie," she said slowly. "You told me that earlier, but I didn't put together what you meant. I was too focused on the tragedy of your sister's death. But that wasn't the first tragedy your family suffered, was it?"

Johnny's lip curled in something like a sneer. "A tragedy is a horrible accident, a loss that haunts you every day. My father leaving my mother for the woman he was cheating on her with wasn't a tragedy. It was just your average, everyday garden-variety faithless loser running out on his family. Happens all the time. We were better off without him."

Thinking back to the details of Johnny's story about his past, the things Tessa had missed in the first flush of horror and sympathy, she remembered that the pond where Angie drowned had been a favorite fishing hole of Johnny's. Stocked with fish by Johnny's long-gone father. Who had been thrilled when Angie, their "miracle baby," was born.

At some point, the Alexander family had been whole and happy. Johnny could deny those memories all he wanted, but on some level, he was still grieving the loss of that unbroken family as much as he was the loss of his sister.

"A man doesn't cheat." Johnny met her gaze, direct and serious. "A man keeps his word and he stands by his family. To do anything else . . ."

He shook his head, disgust twisting his mouth down, and for the first time Tessa got an inkling of what she'd been asking when she asked Johnny for a divorce.

To Johnny, who had learned the pain of his father's abandonment down to his bones, their "marriage in name only" was sacred. Something to be protected and cherished, even if it wasn't exactly the kind of marriage most people had.

She understood him so much better now than she ever had before. He might not be driven to stay with her out of love, but as far as Johnny was concerned, love was irrelevant.

He would stay because that was what a man did— the kind of man he wanted to be. The kind of man his father wasn't.

To be asked to break those vows must have felt like a blow against everything Johnny had worked to become. And he'd fought back, heroically, by following her to Sanctuary Island, by agreeing to couples therapy in spite of his discomfort, by kissing her . . . and now that he was finally willing to admit defeat, Tessa didn't know if she could bear to let him go.

"You're a good man, John Alexander."

The words weren't enough. They were too small to encompass the way she felt about Johnny, the awe and fierce love and desperate longing that filled Tessa at the thought of the life she could have with this man.

They were so close. Closer and more connected than they'd ever been, and so heartbreakingly close to being a real married couple.

Maybe a night of passion would help them move

forward together; maybe it wouldn't. Tessa wouldn't know unless she tried.

"I'm only a man," Johnny said, every atom of his attention focused on Tessa. "Better than some, worse than others. But I'll make you this promise, Theresa Mulligan Alexander. No man has ever wanted to touch any woman more than I want to touch you at this moment."

With a silent prayer for the night to come and a vow to spend the morning begging Johnny to stay and try, Tessa threw herself into his arms. He stumbled back before taking her weight, kicking aside his packed duffel bag to lay her down on the soft, faded white sheets of his bed.

Tessa opened her heart and her body to the man she loved, reveling in the closeness, the almost unbearable intimacy of sliding skin to skin, mouth to mouth.

They rocked together, limbs entwined and heartbeats synced, on the too narrow bed in the corner of the studio. Tessa could see the moon through the window over Johnny's shoulder. It silvered his silky-hot skin, limning his shoulders with a white glow. He moved inside her, gently at first but then with more urgency, and the moon blurred and spangled into a thousand pinpricks of light as Tessa gasped and shot into the stars.

Johnny's breath was harsh in her ear. He sank atop her, his warm, heavily muscled frame so welcome even as she struggled to draw a deep breath. Breathing was overrated, Tessa decided, delirious with the pleasure still sending aftershocks through her newly awakened body.

"I thought I would feel different," she whispered. "When I wasn't a virgin anymore. I thought it would change me. But I feel more *myself*—the person I'm meant to be, deep down—than I ever have in my life."

Johnny slid to the side, taking most of his weight off her but keeping her tucked close against his chest. He was silent for so long that Tessa's eyelids began to slip closed, weighted with exhaustion.

"I know exactly what you mean."

Johnny's low voice reached into Tessa's sleepy, sated half-dream. She woke up just long enough to smile at the kiss Johnny pressed to her temple— the same good-night kiss he'd given her every night they were together, and it did feel different now— before sinking happily into sleep wrapped in her husband's strong, steadfast arms.

Chapter 18

Tessa blinked awake, disoriented for a moment by the unfamiliar slanted ceiling over her head. Her body ached pleasantly in places she'd never been aware of before.

The night before spilled back into her mind on a cascade of hopeful joy. She and Johnny had connected like never before. She knew things about him now, things she'd never known. Not only the taste of his skin and the sound he made when he came deep inside her, but the pain of his past and the scars on his soul.

She was finally getting to know Johnny, in every sense of the word. And Tessa would do anything to hold on to this second chance at happiness.

Turning over in bed to tell him so, Tessa's reaching hand encountered only emptiness. Her heart spasmed.

She sat up, clutching the sheets to her naked chest,

and stared around the apartment. But it was only one room. There was nowhere else for Johnny to be. He was gone. And when she searched the floor with desperate eyes, she saw that the duffel bag they'd nearly tripped over the night before was gone, too.

When she sank back against the pillows, defeated and winded, something crackled. Tessa was up like a shot to grope among the pillows. Her hands shook as she drew a folded piece of paper out from between Johnny's pillow and the headboard.

A sense of déjà vu—or was it karma?—settled over her as she opened it and began to read.

Dear Tessa,

Thank you for last night. You gave me a gift I'll never forget, and I will cherish the memories. I'm sorry you're waking up alone, but I had to leave. Partly because I wasn't sure I'd be able to if I waited until morning—and partly because I got a call back from Brad, finally. One of the men who was arrested as a result of my undercover op escaped from custody. There is no reason to think he can track me, or that he knows anything about you or where you live now. I've never been so grateful that you picked up and left without a trace. You should be safe, and I'm heading back to D.C. to make sure of it.

Tessa's stomach cramped with fear for him. She wasn't an idiot. She knew he was leaving to draw the danger away, whatever danger there was. But she also knew that it wasn't easy for him to leave her unprotected when any danger threatened.

This note was truly a message to her, one that she had to be smart enough to read.

You'll be fine, Johnny wrote. *You are a survivor. I believe you would have landed on your feet all those years ago, with or without my help. And if that's true, then we never needed to be married at all.*

Tessa's breath caught in her chest as her eyes devoured the rest of the note.

You were right about me hanging on to our marriage because, selfishly, I didn't want to be like my father. Maybe you were even right that I'm too protective, because of what happened to my sister. You were right about everything except this: I'm not a good man, Tessa. Because I would do all of it again, everything the same, just to be able to end up where we were last night.

Take your independence and your brave new life, and be happy. No one deserves it more. And maybe one day soon, you'll let me come visit you and see how you're doing. Not because I think you'll need my help by then—but because I can't wait to see what you accomplish on your own.

Your husband, for a little longer,
Johnny

Tessa leaped out of bed, her hands shaking as she dropped her very own "Dear John" letter on the nightstand. It landed on a stack of paper she didn't remember seeing there the night before—and when she moved the letter aside, the top page looked horribly familiar.

Oh, no.

Heart shriveling like a fig left out in the sun, Tessa picked up the divorce papers she'd had drawn up. She flipped to the last page and had to shut her eyes briefly at the sight of Johnny's black, slashing signature underneath her own lighter script.

He'd signed them. Last night, after the most amazing experience of Tessa's life while Tessa was dreaming of new beginnings . . . Johnny was saying good-bye.

As Tessa stood there, alone with the wreckage of her hopes, she realized exactly how far she'd come from the scared girl who'd accepted the first helping hand ever to reach out to her. Because as gutted as she was, her first instinct wasn't to cry or hide or look for someone else to fix this for her.

No, all Tessa wanted to do was find Johnny and tell him exactly how wrong he was. About everything.

Scrambling for her clothes, she hurried into them on her way to the door. She stuffed the signature page from the packet of divorce papers into her pocket as she raced down the stairs. She had to hurry if she was going to find Johnny and tell him if he thought she'd thank him for finally agreeing to this divorce, he could think again.

Not to mention the fact that the stubbornly hopeful part of her heart was shouting that the man who wrote that letter was not incapable of love. He was one of the most incredibly loving, self-sacrificing, dear, darling idiots she'd ever heard of, and she couldn't wait to tell him so.

But first she had to catch up to him. It was the only thought in her mind as she shoved open the back door and rushed out into the alleyway. After the dark interior of the bar, the morning light was bright enough to make her eyes water.

She ran toward the bakery, where her car was

parked, but before she'd made it five steps, she felt a hand clamp down on her shoulder.

"Johnny?"

Whirling, she had time for joy to transform into confusion and shock before a dark cloth dropped over her head and she was being dragged, struggling, and thrown into a waiting vehicle. Before she could draw breath to scream, her head hit the side of the door frame and everything went black.

The phone in Johnny's pocket vibrated at the exact instant he was fumbling to find the ticket to hand to the ferry captain.

It was his boss at the ATF, Brad Garner. Johnny's exhausted brain went sharp in an instant, the edges of his vision going overbright.

Stepping aside rather than hold up the line, Johnny tightened his grip on his duffel and held the phone to his ear.

"Alexander," he said tersely. "Tell me you've got a lead on this guy, Brad."

"I've got better than a lead . . . I've got the guy."

The quiet satisfaction in his old friend's voice made the tense ball of dread in Johnny's gut dissolve. "You got him. Are you kidding me? That's great news, man."

As Brad recounted the swiftly unfolding series of events that had led to recapturing their fugitive, Johnny staggered down off the gangplank and away from the crush of people waiting to board the ferry.

From the moment he got Brad's middle-of-the-night code red, Johnny's pulse had never jumped once. He'd actually felt himself going into Ice Man mode, switching off and shutting down every part of himself that might get him killed in an armed showdown. And the fact was, he'd almost welcomed the deep freeze because it came with a bona fide enemy to engage and destroy.

Not to mention that it was easier to deal with the deep freeze than with the shocking chaos of emotion he'd felt with his arms and his bed full of a warm, naked, enthusiastically sensual Tessa.

But now, as he thawed, those feelings started coming back. Along with the metallic tang of receding adrenaline came the flood of memories—Tessa's short, silky spikes of hair against his throat, her long thighs clasping his hips, her body gripping him tighter than a fist and twice as sweet.

Johnny "Mm-hmm"-ed into the phone and reached out to grab the dock railing with his free hand before the force of his emotions shoved him right over the edge and into the drink.

Whoever said women were the only ones who got sex and feelings mixed up was a hundred percent wrong. Johnny had never been more mixed up in his life. He didn't know whether he was coming or going.

Did this change anything he'd written in the note he left for Tessa?

"Johnny, are you there?" Brad's voice in his ear was impatient, as if he'd repeated the question already more than once.

Lifting his head, Johnny hesitated at the sight of the ferry captain waving to him with a questioning scowl on his wind-chapped face. "You coming aboard or what, mister?"

He held up one finger in the universal gesture for "hold on a minute," and said into the phone, "I'm here, Brad. Good work. I want to hear more details, but I need to call Tessa and let her know. Not that she was ever afraid."

"Of course not," Brad bragged. "We're the ATF. We always get our man."

Johnny grinned, relief finally distinguishing itself as the strongest emotion currently firing his blood. "Damn straight. You're one of the good ones, Brad. Talk to you later."

Without pausing to ask himself if he was calling instead of texting because he already missed the sound of Tessa's voice, Johnny dialed her number and let it ring.

And ring. And ring and ring and ring.

Frowning, Johnny stared down at the phone in his hand. He hadn't hit the wrong number. Maybe she was screening his calls, didn't want to talk to him after he'd left her this morning without saying good-bye.

But if he'd said good-bye, he wouldn't have found the strength to leave.

Waving off the impatient ferry captain, Johnny called her again. No one picked up. Then he tried Patty's landline with no response . . . but it wasn't until he phoned the bakery and listened to the endless repetition of the ring that he started to get worried.

It was after six. The bakery would open in less than an hour. Both Tessa and Patty should be there by now, Patty prepping the display counter and Tessa pulling freshly baked scones and muffins from the hot oven. Patty would be listening for the phone, ready to take call-in orders for takeout. There was no way they'd just let it ring.

The relief Johnny had been enjoying fizzled out as if an ocean wave had doused a single candle.

Ice began to trickle down his back. He turned to the ferry and yelled, "Go ahead without me. Sorry to keep you waiting."

Something in his voice or expression made the ferry captain squint down at him with concern. "You okay, mister?"

It only took a moment's debate between looking like a paranoid idiot and having backup for Johnny to shake his head. The man in the field had to make the call, and he was calling it. There was something wrong here.

"I'm worried my wife might be hurt or in trouble. Can you call—"

Crap. Who? The sheriff's department? What could he possibly say that would make them take him seriously? So his wife wasn't picking up her phone after he walked out on her that very morning. Shocker.

Johnny needed someone who knew what he was doing in a fight, someone Johnny could count on to have his back. He paused for a moment, struck by a sudden inspiration.

Might be a crazy idea, but then again, he was low on options.

With a decisive nod, Johnny rattled off a set of instructions to the grim-faced ferry captain, who nodded back. Johnny ran for his car. He tossed his duffel in the backseat and peeled out of the dockside parking lot as if he were on his way to defuse a bomb.

Maybe he was. If anything had happened to Tessa, his life would implode, never to be the same again.

Uncaring of the speed but keeping a sharp eye out for pedestrians and wild horses crossing the road, Johnny drove with controlled aggression and his heart beating at a sluggish, subzero temperature. His brain felt as if it were emitting white noise, a buzzing static where thoughts should be, where he should be making plans and calculating contingencies . . . except he had no information yet.

All he knew was that this wasn't something from Marcus Beckett's past, and it had nothing to do with his own most recent bust. Maybe one of his older cases, come back to bite him and deciding to take a tasty chunk out of Tessa instead?

He pushed the crappy little rental car to its limits, pulling up in front of Patty's house on the town square in less than ten minutes. No lights were on that he could see as he ripped himself free of his seat belt and bolted up the front porch steps, taking them two at a time.

Raising his hand to knock on the front door, the hairs on the back of his neck lifted when the first rap nudged the door ajar. The creak of its hinges shuddered down his spine with chill terror, because this door shouldn't be open. He knew Sanctuary Island was a place where people knew their neighbors and felt safe, but that meant leaving doors unlocked—not leaving them unlatched for the wind to blow open.

Johnny had never wished more intensely for the gun and badge he'd left in Brad's office when he went on leave. Forcing himself to breathe slowly and evenly, he slowly cracked the door open further and peered inside. A quick sweep of the corners and blind spots showed no danger, but he was unarmed. It wouldn't help Tessa if he ran shouting into this house and got himself picked off like a trout in a barrel. He was going to go slowly and carefully if it killed him.

But every thought of slow and careful flew out of his brain when he caught sight of the bare foot, vulnerable and pale and terribly still, poking out from behind the corner of the staircase.

Breath too frozen to allow a curse, Johnny rushed into the foyer and scrambled around the stairs, every beat of his heart thumping out, "Please don't be Tessa, please don't be Tessa, please don't be Tessa lying here on the floor."

It wasn't.

Johnny dropped to his knees next to Miss Patty's unmoving form. A sickening blend of relief and grim understanding coiled through his guts, but he kept his hands moving, checking for injuries without disturbing the older woman's neck or spine. His questing fingers found a sticky lump behind her left ear, and when he pulled them away, they glinted scarlet with blood.

Blood had been spilled, violently, in the house where his wife lived. Where he'd left her unprotected.

Stop it, he told himself viciously. *No time for that now.*

Johnny shrugged out of the flannel shirt he'd thrown on over his T-shirt that morning as he dragged himself away from his sleeping wife. Balling it up, he pressed it to Patty's head wound, but the bleeding had slowed considerably.

Thank God for his investigative training. Even in this awful moment, his mind was quietly calculating that based on the amount the blood that had clotted, he could estimate that the wound was inflicted several hours ago. Whoever did it was likely long gone from here before Johnny had even managed to extricate himself from Tessa's arms in the cold, predawn light.

Which meant Tessa wasn't here, because there was no way she could have missed seeing her friend's unconscious body lying on the hall floor. Just to be sure, Johnny called her name a few times, pausing to listen intently, but there was no response.

The cold reality settled over him like a mantle of snow. Patty was hurt, assailant unknown. And Tessa?

He had no idea where Tessa was, or if she was okay. For all he knew, she could be hurt worse than Patty.

She could be dead.

Johnny's heart gave a painful thump, shattering the ice that had grown around it. Fire and agony raced through him, banishing every trace of the cold, competent operative who'd subsumed his very identity in order to carry out his mission.

He bowed his head over Patty's chest and shook with the realization that there was nothing left behind but a man in danger of losing everything that mattered most to him.

Chapter 19

The first thing Marcus saw when he ran in the door of Miss Patty's house was Johnny on his knees on the floor, one hand holding one of Patty's and the other pressing his cell phone to his ear.

"Yeah, and hurry. She's coming around, but I'm concerned she lost a lot of blood before I found her."

Ugly déjà vu whipped around Marcus's head for a dizzy second, but he muscled through it with the ease of practice. "Ambulance on its way?" he demanded when Johnny ended the call.

The younger man nodded, face stern but eyes wild with an emotion so raw, Marcus had to force himself to meet Johnny's stare. "They're coming, and I think Patty is going to be okay. At least, she started coming to a few seconds ago. What did you find at the bakery?"

Marcus didn't shock easily. He'd seen and done enough in his life that nothing much surprised him anymore. The call this morning from a guy calling himself "Captain Buddy" and saying Johnny needed his help?

That had been a surprise.

"We couldn't get in at first," Quinn said from behind him, her voice tight with nerves and urgency. "It was all locked up. Marcus had to break in."

Now it was Johnny's turn to look surprised. He raised his brows at Quinn and Marcus knew what he was seeing. The messy coil of strawberry-blond curls hastily pulled up and out of her way, the way her slim fingers were tangled in the hem of Marcus's black sweater. The way Marcus wasn't shoving her off him.

She'd still been in his bed when the call came in, all his good intentions about keeping her from spending the night no match for the pounding, insatiable hunger of his body for hers.

He hadn't paused to argue when she refused to go home after the ferry captain's call. Partly because there wasn't time, and partly because until they'd clocked this unknown threat and neutralized it, he didn't particularly want to let her out of his sight.

So Marcus towed Quinn along in his wake as he moved farther into the house. A quick glance at Johnny, who dipped his chin and gave him a subtle thumbs-up, had Marcus shrugging his jacket back over his shoulder holster. The coast was clear. He took a knee by Miss Patty's wan face, observing the wrinkle between her eyes and the quivering eyelashes.

The older lady moaned, weak and thready, but the sound sent a wave of relief through Marcus. It was worse when they didn't move, didn't respond. Didn't make a sound.

"Hey, Miss Patty," he said, reaching down to capture the wrinkled hand she was lifting weakly toward her head. He squeezed her fingers reassuringly. "Don't touch, I know it hurts. There's an ambulance on its way and they're going to fix you right up."

Her lips moved soundlessly for a second, stopping Marcus's heart, but Patty coughed a little and managed to say, "Quit talking like . . . I'm dumb. Turn you over . . . m'knee."

Marcus grinned. If she was feeling well enough to sass him, she was going to be okay. "You don't know, I might enjoy that."

Scandalized delight lit the older woman's faded eyes briefly before a grimace of pain crossed her face.

"Don't try to sit up," Marcus cautioned. "The EMTs are going to want to check your spine."

"Did I fall?" The feebleness of her voice and the confusion betrayed by her own question seemed to annoy her. She scowled while Marcus and Johnny exchanged a look over her head.

As much to calm Johnny's sudden alarm as to reassure Patty, Marcus said, "It's okay if you don't remember what happened. Short-term memory loss is common with a head injury."

"Head injury," Patty echoed, the irritation in her expression shifting to something like dread. Marcus hated to see a woman like Patty, so vibrant and vital, reduced to a helpless old lady prostrate on the floor.

"And you came to so fast," Marcus complained teasingly, "I didn't even get a chance to perform CPR."

He waggled his brows to make Patty smile. "Missed

opportunity," she agreed smugly, some of the fear clearing from her eyes.

On her other side, Johnny was practically vibrating with impatience. "Miss Patty, I hate to ask—"

"So don't," Marcus growled. "Give her a minute. She already said she doesn't remember how she got hurt."

"But she might remember something from earlier in the day," Quinn pointed out from behind him, making Marcus stiffen. He'd almost forgotten she was there. "She still knows her name and vital stats, right?"

"Patricia Catherine Cuthbert." Patty sighed. "Two dozen sticky buns, four dozen cinnamon buns, and five dozen cinnamon streusel muffins."

Alarmed, Marcus shot a questioning look over his shoulder. Quinn was smiling, though. "That's her morning list for the bakery. The stock they need to open. I'd bet anything. Her memory is just fine."

"Then Patty, please think back," Johnny begged, leaning over her. "What's the last thing you remember?"

Marcus held his tongue, even as the lines fanning from Patty's eyes deepened with pain. "I don't . . . Oh. I came downstairs and Tessa wasn't here. I was surprised, but . . . I thought she must be with you. Which made me glad. But then I heard the front door open and I thought maybe she'd come home. It wasn't Tessa, though. It was—"

She stopped and Johnny leaned forward. "Who was it?"

Patty's breath came faster, shallow little sips of air that couldn't possibly be enough. "That's enough," Marcus snarled.

"Damn it," Johnny burst out, his face set like stone. "I need to know. If there's any way she can help me find Tessa . . ."

"Tessa," Patty gasped. "Tessa. Oh, my God, she's in trouble."

"Yes! And I need your help."

Patty stared up at him, a single tear running down her temple and into her blood-matted hair. "Anything."

With a muttered curse, Marcus shot to his feet and stalked to the front window to watch for the ambulance. It was too much, all of a sudden, watching the injured old woman push herself past her own limits in her attempt to help someone else. It was hard to watch.

"Are you okay?"

Quinn's voice was as gentle as he'd ever heard it, and even that put him on edge. "This entire island could fit inside Yankee Stadium. What the hell is taking that ambulance so long to get here?"

"She's going to be fine," Quinn replied. Her hand settled on his shoulder, tentative and light as a dragonfly landing on the surface of a lake. "You were wonderful with her."

Practice makes perfect. Marcus stared out the window at the breaking dawn and said nothing, while behind them, Johnny and Patty carried on a slow, halting conversation he couldn't really hear.

"Is someone after Tessa?" Quinn asked. Her voice was carefully casual, as if she were working hard to sound unafraid. "I didn't think things like that could happen here."

She was so painfully young sometimes. "Bad things happen everywhere."

"But everyone here knows everyone else," she argued. "I mean, how could a bad guy hope to get away with anything on Sanctuary Island? We all know each other's business!"

Before Marcus could respond, Johnny was rushing past him to scoop Quinn off the ground and into his arms. He twirled her around and said, "You're a genius!" before opening the front door and rushing down the steps, nearly crashing into the paramedics on their way up.

"What did I say?" Quinn laughed, flushed to the roots of her strawberry-blond hair.

Marcus stomped over to let the paramedics in, but first he had to uncramp his fingers from the fist they'd instinctively made when Johnny put his hands on Quinn.

Opening the door wider, Marcus let his training come to the fore as he directed the EMTs toward the patient and filled them in on her known condition. He watched them work, staying close to Patty because his presence seemed to soothe her, and the whole time he carefully didn't look at Quinn.

And he carefully didn't think about the fact that in the instant when he'd seen her in Johnny's arms, Marcus had wanted to rip the guy's head clear off his shoulders.

Which was ridiculous, because Johnny was stupid in love with his own wife. He wasn't after Quinn, and even if he were . . . so what? Marcus had never been the jealous type before.

There was nothing to be jealous of anyway. Quinn

was a fun girl, a beautiful girl, with a smile that lit up a room and a body that wouldn't quit. She was the girl-next-door fantasy come to life, literally.

So what if she'd started looking at Marcus like she saw something in him? So what if Quinn had stars in her eyes when she stared his way? So what if her entranced expression did something to Marcus, deep inside—something that made him covet every moment when Quinn's focus slipped away from him to someone else?

So what if they'd spent hours the night before, sharing a pillow and talking about Quinn's dreams and plans for her future, and Marcus hadn't been bored or annoyed even for an instant?

Damn it to hell. Tessa wasn't the only one who was in trouble.

Johnny raced down the sidewalk, the soles of his shoes slapping loudly in the early morning quiet. Would they be there this early? Or would they still be asleep?

Please, please, be there, Johnny pleaded silently. *You're my only hope for a lead and the clock is ticking. I don't want to have to track you down.*

The moment he'd overheard Quinn say that crime was impossible on Sanctuary Island because everyone was in each other's business, it had clicked. He'd stared wildly down at Patty, who must have read the look in his eyes because she'd gripped his fingers with surprising strength and said, "Go! I'll be fine. Go get our girl and bring her home."

Johnny ran past the bakery, not even wanting to

look at the darkened windows. Tessa should be in there, safe and sound and baking up a batch of crazy-delicious scones. But she wasn't.

The hardware store came into view and Johnny's breath seized in his lungs when he caught sight of the two old men in their rocking chairs out front.

They were there. The guys he'd met his first day in town, almost a month ago, who'd interrogated him as to his purpose in visiting the island more thoroughly than any customs officer ever had.

The younger one, wearing a red knit cap with a pom-pom on top underneath his beat-up old costume crown, beamed down at Johnny with friendly curiosity. "Look, it's Mr. Tessa! Maybe he knows why the bakery is closed. Is Miss Patty taking a vacation?"

"That old cat wouldn't know a vacation if it bit her in the Acapulco," the other man scoffed, eyeing Johnny as if appraising him as a potential source for good gossip. "She hasn't taken a day off in thirty years. What gives?"

"Patty was attacked in her home early this morning." Johnny didn't see any point in beating around the bush. They were going to see the ambulance coming from her house in a minute anyway, plus they might as well spread the word that there was someone dangerous in town. Maybe it would encourage the townspeople to be more alert and cautious than usual.

The man wearing the crown, the one Johnny remembered was called King, cried out in dismay. "Oh, no! Is she okay?"

"We should go see if there's anything we can do to help," the other man suggested, hauling himself out of his rocker and thumbing his dangling suspenders back up over his shoulders.

Johnny held up a hand to stop them. "The paramedics are with her now, and I think she's going to make a full recovery. But my wife, Tessa, is missing. Did you see her this morning?"

Alarm widened the older man's eyes while King's face just crumpled in pained confusion. "We only got here a few minutes ago," he said regretfully. "And you're the first person we've seen all morning."

So they hadn't been at their posts when Marcus and Quinn ran over from the Buttercup Inn. They hadn't seen the abduction, or the person who attacked Patty. Struggling against the wave of disappointment, Johnny forged ahead with his questions.

"What about yesterday?" he demanded. "Anything odd or unusual happen in town? Any strangers?"

Johnny was braced for another disappointment, but King nodded vigorously. "The big black truck," he said urgently to his friend. "Remember? I said it was new but you said no, it was old and in bad shape, just listen to that engine, and I said I just meant it was new to me."

Johnny's heart was in his throat. "Did you get a glimpse of the driver?"

The two men shared a glance then shook their heads regretfully. But King perked up and said, "But I saw a red plastic tank in the back of the truck, looked like marine fuel. Does that help?"

Pulse quickening, Johnny said, "It doesn't necessarily tell me who has my wife, or why, but it gives me some ideas about where to search. Thank you."

He turned to go, but the fretful voice of one of the older men stopped him. "Shouldn't we call the police?"

"Please do," Johnny replied. "But I'm not waiting around for them. If you call, let them know I'll be scouring the perimeter of the island, starting with the docks. Is there any place else you know where people tie up boats?"

"Not in a big group like down at the docks," King said, shrugging. "But almost every house on the water has its own dock."

Johnny's resolve hardened. That was potentially a lot of boats, a lot of private docks to check, but he would find her. He had to.

"Listen, maybe call the Coast Guard, too," Johnny suggested over his shoulder. "If you're right about what you saw in the truck, I think I know how he plans to get Tessa off the island—and it isn't by ferry."

"He who?" King yelled after him as Johnny loped off down the street, setting up a steady, ground-covering pace. "Who could it be? Who has Tessa?"

Johnny wished to God he knew.

Chapter 20

Tessa came to as she was being dragged from the cab of the truck. Her left temple ached with a vicious throb, and when she fluttered her eyes open, even the gray light of dawn scared her retinas.

Dazed and disoriented, she stumbled at another rough tug on her wrist and blinked down at the coarse-haired, masculine hand clamped around it. She twisted her arm and gasped when the hand tightened bruisingly hard. Shaking her head, Tessa squinted up just as an image—a memory? A hallucination?—flickered behind her eyes.

It couldn't be. She thought she'd seen . . . but that didn't make sense.

Another stumble brought Tessa's weight down wrong on her ankle. The stabbing pain made her whimper but it also cleared her head.

She was outside. There were maritime pines all around, growing shorter and shorter like the ones at the water's edge, and she could hear the *shush-shush* of the ocean close by. A big barrel of a man with iron-gray hair straggling down to his shoulders was pulling her along behind him, his hand rough and calloused around her sore wrist.

Panic rolled through her, only heightened by the wild memory emblazoned on her brain, because Tessa thought, she couldn't tell, it had been so many years and so many miles since she'd seen him, but she was almost certain that the man who'd pulled her off the street and driven her here was . . .

"Dad!" she gasped when he turned his head, exposing the sharp, bladelike profile that had frightened her when she was little.

Abe Mulligan glared back at her, steely eyes dark under his bushy, graying brows. "Hurry up, Terri, quit dragging your feet. We need to go."

There was an edge in his gruff voice and a wildness in his eyes that scared adult Tessa as much as his scowl had scared her younger self. "Where are we going? What are you doing here?"

She kept putting up resistance, trying to pull free of him, but her father held her arm tightly and muscled her forward inexorably. "I'm here to get you. You need to come home, so Naomi will finally come home."

Naomi. Tessa's mother. Pulse thundering louder than the waves against the shoreline, Tessa said, "Dad, please, stop and talk to me. What happened to Mom? Where did she go?"

But her father didn't stop. He just kept hauling her through the dew-damp cord grass, not even seeming to notice the thorny shrubs that scratched at his arms and whipped toward Tessa's face. "Naomi will come back to the community when you're back home. She only left because you did, it was all your fault. It was never the same after you left. I looked for you for a long time, to make her come home, but I didn't know where you went. And then Harry Cartwright brought me a newspaper from town with your picture in it, from winning some contest, and I knew what I had to do."

Tessa's breath left her as her head spun. Her father had been looking for her? And not for a happy family reunion, no matter what he said about her mother. Hysterical laughter bubbled up her throat at the irony of the fact that one of the proudest moments of her new life—winning that blue ribbon at the county fair for her scone recipe—had led to this painful, shambling run through the woods in the grip of a nightmare version of her father.

Her father had always been a hard man, rigid and uncompromising, but the man who stopped dead and loomed over her now was something else altogether. Years of loneliness, resentment, and hatred glittered in his accusing glare. She shrank back, old and instinctive fears kicking in.

"You're living wrong," her father said fiercely. "We taught you better. You know better. But here you are, living this decadent, wasteful, immoral modern life and probably loving every minute of it."

"Tell me more about Mom." Tessa couldn't allow herself to get drawn off topic. "When did she leave? Did she know I wrote to her? Did you tell her about my letters?"

"Bragging about your new life." He sneered, jerking her harshly into motion again so that she was forced to scramble after him. They came to the edge of the tall cord grass and started slip-sliding down the gravelly dirt that became sandier the closer they got to the water.

At the water's edge lay a small boat with an outboard motor. All at once, Tessa realized that her father wasn't just dragging her around with no goal—he was trying to get her to the boat. He was trying to take her off the island, and back to the commune with him so that her mother would come home again, and *that was a crazy plan.*

As in, it was the plan of a crazy person who wasn't thinking or behaving rationally. Which meant her father, who had always been unpredictable in terms of his moods, was scarier than he'd ever been before.

And Johnny was long gone by now. Tessa was on her own.

Struggling against the chill of that thought and the drag on her aching arm, Tessa tried again, but this time she tried playing along. "Please, Father. Let go, and I'll come with you. I'd love to see the house, and be there when Mom comes home."

He paused, suspicion in every line of his haggard face. It hurt Tessa's heart to look at him. Abe Mulligan wasn't a kind man, but he was her father. And he looked at least twenty years older than he should. Life on the commune was hard, but Tessa didn't think that was what had aged him.

"No," he decided gruffly, retightening his hold even when Tessa winced. "You're lying. They taught you to lie out here, away from the community. But I know you don't want to go back, or you would've come to see me sometime in the last eight years."

"I didn't think I'd be welcome," Tessa explained, desperation seeping into her tone as they reached the boat.

"Get in."

He threw her arm toward the boat, nearly jerking her off her feet. Tessa caught herself against the side of the small craft and gagged on the scent of rotting fish guts. "Where did you find this thing? Are you sure it's seaworthy?"

"It'll do," her father said tersely. "Get in. Now."

Looking up at him where he stood by the back of the boat, ready to shove it into the water and push away from the shore, Tessa experienced a moment of disbelief. This couldn't be happening. He couldn't be serious. She had to snap him out of it.

"Daddy, no. I know you don't approve but this is my life now, and I'm happy here. I'm not going with you, and I'm sorry, but it sounds to me as if Mom left a long time ago. If she's been gone that long, maybe something happened to her, or maybe there was more than one reason she left—but either way, I don't think she's coming back. Even if you drag me home."

A frightening anger built and built in her father's eyes as she spoke, the lines of his big, farmer's body going tense with rage. "Your mother is coming home, even if I have to hold you hostage there forever to make her come."

Chilled by the certainty in his voice, Tessa burrowed her hands into her jacket pockets and discovered he hadn't taken her cell phone while she was out cold. It took everything she had not to allow her sudden hope to register on her face as her fingers moved over the familiar buttons. She could dial 911 without looking, she was pretty sure, so long as her father didn't notice what she was doing.

Keep him talking. "Why would you do that to me? What did I ever do that was so awful, except be determined to survive my childhood?"

"You deserve to be punished for destroying our family!" He pointed at her, accusatory finger trembling with rage. "Now get in the damn boat, before I knock you out and throw you in like a sack of cornmeal."

That couldn't happen. She needed to be awake and aware to assist with her own rescue. Stepping gingerly over the side of the boat, Tessa picked her way among the stained tarps and dirty, tangled ropes and netting to huddle on the bench seat stretched across the middle of the boat. "Fine, you win. I'll go with you. Just don't hurt me."

She stealthily removed her hand from her pocket, praying that the line was open and Ivy Dawson, the dispatcher, could hear them through the layers of fabric.

"Can you at least tell me where you're taking me?" she said a little loudly.

"I told you," her father grunted, shoving the beached boat into deeper water with a splash. "Home. To the community."

"Are we going to take this boat the whole way?"

"Living in the world has made you stupid, girl." Abe climbed into the boat, kicking aside a red plastic fuel container and planting himself by the outboard motor. "Or maybe you worked too hard to forget where you came from. The community is inland. We're using this boat to get back to the mainland; from there we'll drive."

He sounded proud of his plans, and for the first time, Tessa thought about what a stretch all of this must be for him. When she was a kid, he'd refused to drive even the few miles into the nearest small town. He'd tilled the earth with a hand plow, choosing back-breaking labor over the convenience of modern farming techniques and modern farming equipment. He hated to leave home, and he hated being forced to use modern technology even more.

Yet somehow, he'd gotten himself all the way here from the foothills of the Blue Ridge Mountains, to kidnap his own daughter. If nothing else, that told her how determined he was to see this through.

"This boat is so small," Tessa said, thinking furiously about how to give more clues to the sheriff's department. "I hope we don't have far to go in it. But I'm sure you thought of that."

Abe scowled at her, but underneath, Tessa thought he seemed pleased. "I couldn't stash the boat at the docks—too many nosy people—but we're not that far up the coast from it."

Tessa's heart pounded in her ears, loud enough to nearly drown out the roar of the motor. "So we're on the western side of the island, heading toward Winter Harbor on the mainland," she yelled, struggling to be heard as their speed increased and the wind seemed to tear the words from her lips and scatter them.

She had no idea if any of that got through to the sheriff's department. Her father hadn't seemed to hear her—all his attention was focused on the distant Virginia shore and the continuation of his plans to win back his wife. Or to blackmail her into coming home, whichever worked. Grimacing, Tessa glanced over his shoulder toward Sanctuary Island.

They must be about a thousand feet out already, and the island was growing smaller and smaller behind them. Tessa felt jittery and her head still throbbed with a deep ache, but she had to choose her moment.

Could she afford to wait and hope for the sheriff to show up and save her? Or should she jump ship now and swim for it before they got any deeper into the open water of the Atlantic Ocean? If she jumped, what would stop her father from turning the boat around and coming to scoop her back up? And the water splashing up the sides of the boat to wet her hands was extremely cold—how long could she last in that temperature?

As she sat in an agony of indecision, she saw the glimmer of red and blue lights flashing through the trees at the shoreline behind them. Her heart gave a great thump and Tessa gripped the sides of the boat with chilled fingers. It was the sheriff. It had to be. Her phone call must have gone through!

In that case, she had to try. Now. She'd have backup once she was close enough to signal for help and let them know where she was. And she was a decent swimmer. She could stay afloat long enough for someone to get to her, even if she couldn't make it all the way to shore.

Ignoring the insistent dizziness and the pounding headache, Tessa cast a wary look at her father. He seemed to have forgotten about her already, lost in his fantasy of reuniting with his wife. For a moment, Tessa let herself experience the full weight of crushing sadness that she would never be the son her father had always wanted—and he would never be the loving father she'd longed for.

Then she forced herself to wobble up to a half crouch, holding on to the side of the boat, and said a quick prayer. Then she took a deep breath and dove into the water.

Chapter 21

Johnny scrambled down the hill above the shore, his boots skidding on the loose gravelly sand. He'd never seen any sight so welcome as the sheriff's department SUV parked at an angle behind the abandoned black truck just off Shoreline Drive.

As he'd quartered the island, searching desperately for some sign of the truck that had tried to run Tessa and him off the road, the thought that haunted Johnny's mind was . . . what if he was looking in the wrong place?

When he'd noticed Angie missing, all those years ago, he'd wasted precious minutes tearing the house apart from top to bottom, and it had cost him his sister. The most precious thing in his life . . . until now.

So when he'd pulled in next to the sheriff's car and followed the tracks down toward the water, Johnny had been filled with relief. Not only had he managed to find the truck, but now he'd have backup with whatever went down.

He thought he was prepared, but nothing could have prepared him for what he saw when he reached the muddy edge of the shore and stared out across the water.

There was a boat floating in the ocean, rocked by the movement of the water, and completely empty of human life. Tessa was gone.

His heart stopped. It was his worst nightmare come to life. He staggered a few paces into the water, barely registering the frigid temperature, but a hand on his shoulder pulled him back.

"Coast Guard is coming." A tall, serious-faced woman in a tan uniform with a gold star clipped to the belt pointed past him to the large boat steaming toward the smaller craft. "She called from her phone, let us know exactly where to send them."

"My wife," Johnny gasped, the words tasting like ashes and brine. "Tessa. I think she was in that boat. Did you see what happened to her?"

"She jumped in, and the man jumped in after her. No, sir— Wait!"

But Johnny couldn't wait. He'd caught a glimpse, only a flash, of movement on the far side of the empty boat. Tessa was out there. And she wasn't alone. She needed his help.

Tearing off his jacket and shoes, Johnny waded into the water and started slicing his way toward the boat with fast, clean strokes. His shoulder muscles warmed up, loosening and propelling him through water so cold, it felt like knives against his skin. Tessa was in this water, trying to stay afloat, trying to stay warm. He pushed himself harder until he was close enough to pause, treading water, to scan the water around him.

The Coast Guard had beaten him to the boat, and they were loading a gray-haired man in sodden flannels onto their deck, but Tessa was nowhere in sight. Johnny's vision dimmed, history repeating itself in the most sickening, soul-killing way possible, but he kept looking.

And there! A flash of pale, chilled skin, a waving hand behind him, closer to shore. Johnny threw himself toward the person he'd spotted. When he got to where he thought she'd been, he searched the murky depths with frantic eyes but saw nothing.

Swirling his hands through the water, he dove once, twice, three times, forcing his burning eyes open . . . and on the fourth dive, his fingers caught on rough fabric.

He clamped down and hauled upward with all his strength, using great, scissoring kicks to shoot them up toward the sun-dappled waves above. Breaking the surface of the water, he dragged in a breath and pulled the sodden, limp form of his wife into his arms.

Tessa's head sagged toward him, her lips a terrifying shade of blue. He kissed her, shocked at the chill of her skin.

"Come on, honey, come on," Johnny chanted as his fingers sought out her pulse. There—distinct and strong enough to make Johnny's legs momentarily go numb with relief.

He kicked them awake in time to keep him and Tessa from sinking.

"Johnny." Her lashes tickled his cheek. "You're here. What are you doing here?"

"I came to rescue you," he said, unable to stop himself from nuzzling her cheek. "But that turned out to be unnecessary, since you'd already rescued yourself. And called out the Coast Guard to capture your abductor."

"My father!" She stiffened in his arms, trying to raise her head to peer around and simultaneously nearly drowning them both.

Once Johnny got both their mouths above water once more, he said, "Your father? It was your dad who's been following us?"

She nodded miserably, tufts of wet hair sticking up all over her head and making her look like an angry owl. "He said . . . Oh, Johnny, it was awful. I guess after I ran away, my mom left him? And it seemed like he blamed me for it, even though from my memories of growing up in that house, I can tell you that Mom was never happy. But still, he wanted her back. And I guess he thought that if I came home, she would, too."

"And he was willing to take you by force, if you wouldn't go with him willingly." The rage filling Johnny's chest was more buoyant than a life jacket.

She shivered against him, her legs tangling briefly with his before floating away. "I thought I was on my own, that you were gone and wouldn't be riding to the rescue this time."

"And you got yourself free and called for help." A pang shot through Johnny's belly but he forced himself to smile at her. "You're an amazing woman, Tessa Alexander. You don't need me to save you. Maybe you never did."

"I'm still glad you're here." She whispered it like a secret, like a confession torn from the depths of her soul, and Johnny wasn't too proud to clutch her close. He savored the cold rub of her nose under his ear, the hot wash of her breath against his neck.

She was alive. She was safe. And she was no longer his.

Where the hell did they go from here?

Tessa shivered in his arms, her teeth chattering lightly, and Johnny snapped out of it. He knew exactly where Tessa was going from here—to the hospital, to get checked out.

"Sheriff," he called over Tessa's shoulder. "Can you call the paramedics?"

"Already done," the uniformed woman assured him. "They're dropping Miss Patty off at the docks to get water-taxied over to Winter Harbor General, then they're on their way here."

Tessa's fingers clutched at Johnny's shoulders. "Miss Patty! What happened?"

Johnny glared at the sheriff, who grimaced and mouthed "Sorry" before striding away to supervise her deputies as they cuffed Tessa's father and read him his rights.

"Miss Patty is going to be fine," Johnny said soothingly. "But she had a little run-in with your father while he was looking for you, and she got a bump on the head."

As if unconsciously, Tessa's hand lifted to the side

of her own head, just behind her left ear. "Oh, no," she moaned, swaying against him. "This is all my fault."

Alarmed, Johnny brushed her fingers aside to explore the spot behind her ear. He found some swelling, but no blood, and said a quick silent prayer to hurry the paramedics in their direction.

"It's not your fault," he told Tessa firmly.

"How can you say that? If I had never come here, my father would never have followed me. He and Patty would never have even met, and he never would have done anything to her. Now she's hurt, maybe hurt really badly, and it's all because of me."

"First of all, Miss Patty is a tough old bird, and it's going to take more than this to slow her down. And secondly, take it from someone who's spent a lot of his life shouldering the blame for every damn thing that happens in his vicinity—it's no way to live, honey."

"But if I'd just been home, with Patty," Tessa fretted.

"He might have hurt her anyway," Johnny pointed out. "I can't see Miss Patty sitting quietly by and letting him haul you off. Can you?"

That brought a watery smile to Tessa's face. "No. I guess not. But—"

"But nothing," Johnny said firmly. "The only person to blame for what happened today is that man in the back of the cop car. You couldn't control his choices or his actions. I hope you can accept that, and find some peace with all this."

A stubborn look glittered in Tessa's blue eyes. "I'll work on accepting that I'm not responsible for every bad thing my father did, if you'll do the same."

Johnny opened his mouth to argue that it *wasn't* the same, not for him, but he shut it with a snap. Maybe . . . Tessa had a point. Maybe it was time for Johnny to give himself a break and look for the kind of peace he wanted for Tessa.

Maybe he'd never get over his sister's death. It wasn't the kind of thing a man could move on from, and he wouldn't want to—it would be too much like forgetting her. But somehow, in that moment when he pulled his wife from the freezing waters of the Atlantic, something inside Johnny shifted. Lightened.

As if a hand had reached down from above, showed him where to find Tessa, and lifted away a burden he'd been carrying for so long, he hardly knew it was there until it was gone.

"Maybe you're right," he finally said, and had the satisfaction of watching Tessa's eyes go round with surprise. "It's a deal. I'll work on it if you will."

"Deal." Tessa pulled away to put her hand out and shake on it, but Johnny's hands closed reflexively over her hips to keep her close. His tight clasp squeezed water from her pockets, drenching their legs.

Tessa gasped and laughed, then stopped suddenly. "Oh! That reminds me. I'm mad at you."

Johnny's heart lurched sideways as she reached her hand into one pocket. She pulled out a sodden mass of paper, and wrung it out like a dirty dishtowel.

She shook it out and Johnny recognized the page from their divorce papers. The page with his signature at the bottom, the ink running down the paper like dark blue tears. Tessa met his eyes, arched a brow . . . and tore the soggy paper cleanly in half.

Blood pounding, Johnny stared at her. What did that mean?

"You divorced me!" Tessa's brows drew together, aggrieved. "How could you do that?"

Hope was a sharp knot in Johnny's throat. "You . . . you asked me to. Several times."

"And you chose the morning after we first made love to finally listen to me?" Tessa whispered fiercely, cheeks reddening beneath the pallor of her damp, chilled skin.

"I thought it was what you wanted." Johnny felt the half-truth burn like a coal in his chest, forcing him to add, "And I thought you'd be better off. Without me. I'm dangerous."

The furrow between Tessa's brows got deeper. "But . . . divorcing me wouldn't have kept me safe, even if the threat you sensed had truly been a result of your work with the ATF."

Johnny shook his head reluctantly. "It's nothing as rational as that. I just . . . I don't know. I've been going off half-cocked a lot, ever since I got here. I don't always trust myself."

"That's too bad," Tessa said, holding his gaze steadily. "Because I trust you. With everything I am, and everything I have. And we might have work to do, a lot to learn about each other still, but I know one thing down to the bottom of my soul. I'm not better off without you. I've tried it, and I can survive. But I want more than that now. I want to live. I want to love, and be loved."

Johnny's hands were sliding up her back and curling her to him before he knew what he was doing.

Their mouths found each other, cool and sweet and clinging. The kiss did more to warm Johnny up than a wool blanket and a fifth of whiskey.

He cupped her face in his hands and told her what he'd realized in the moment when he thought he'd lost her.

"I do love you, you know. I didn't know I had any heart left to give, after my sister died. But whatever I have, whatever I am . . . it's yours."

Tessa, who hadn't cried once during the entire ordeal with her father, suddenly burst into tears. Johnny knew exactly how she felt. Everything he felt and wanted to say welled up in him, surging into his mouth like the waves crashing against the Coast Guard boat off the shoreline.

But as he held Tessa to his chest and savored the feel of her against him, there was really only one thing to say.

"Tessa. Honey."

She looked up, smiling through her tears, more beautiful to him than she was the day he first met her. "Johnny?"

With his thumbs, he brushed the tears from her cheekbones. Staring into the endless pools of her hazel eyes, he felt his life come full circle.

"Theresa Mulligan Alexander. Will you marry me? Again?"

Everything Tessa had ever wanted was right here, in her arms. The thought dried her tears in a hurry, although the emotion that started them remained just as close to the surface of her damp, shivering skin.

Standing on that sandy bank, she felt stripped down to the essentials, confronted with the reality of life's fragility.

How close they'd come to losing everything, to losing each other! Tessa felt the same stunned relief she would have felt after dodging a bullet.

Lacing her fingers together behind Johnny's neck, she said, "I will marry you, Johnny Alexander. As many times as it takes, until we get it right. But I think the second time is going to be the charm."

He laughed and kissed her again. Tessa closed her eyes and forced herself to memorize everything—the texture of his lips, the heat of his tongue, the rasp of his stubble. The joy in her heart, the desire in his hands, the love they shared.

It was a nearly perfect moment of happiness. But Tessa knew, better than anyone, that the marriage proposal wasn't the end of the love story. It was only the beginning. And as Johnny smiled against her mouth and held her tightly, Tessa opened her eyes and looked straight into her future.

Chapter 22

Tessa caught sight of herself in the bakery window as she locked up for the night. It was the first time Johnny had let her close the shop on her own in the two weeks since her father tried to kidnap her, and Tessa was determined to enjoy having her routine back in place.

Since her father tried to kidnap her. Those words still didn't make sense, when she tried to consider them too closely. In the past fourteen days, the outward marks of her ordeal had disappeared—the ring of bruises around her wrist had faded and the bump on her wrist had gone down.

But it was going to take longer for the invisible scars to fade, Tessa feared. As happy as she was, being engaged to her husband, she knew she'd be dealing with the emotional fallout of her family's implosion for some time to come.

With a shaky breath, Tessa turned her face to the golden light of evening. This was the first time she'd been alone for longer than a few minutes since she left the hospital, and it actually felt good.

She'd only been kept one night for observation after her dip in the freezing cold waters of the ocean, but Johnny hadn't left her bedside even though she spent most of her time in the hospital dozing off her medication. He'd been there every time the nurses came in to wake her and check her vitals, in case of concussion. He'd been the one to drive her home from the hospital, to Patty's house, where he'd promptly moved his things into her bedroom.

Tessa wasn't keen to let him out of her sight either, at first. She was shaky after her close brush with danger, she could admit that. And it was heaven to have him so close, in every way, after years of yearning. But after a week of coddling and hovering, Tessa had started gently trying to get Johnny to relax his hypervigilance a bit.

She'd suggested they finish out their couples counseling at Windy Corner, and to her surprise, Johnny had agreed without putting up a fight. "Dr. Voss got us this far," he'd said, smiling slightly and curling an arm around her shoulders to press a kiss into her hair. "Let's see what else she has to say."

One of the things Dr. Voss did was to give them homework. For instance, Johnny's homework was to let Tessa walk home from work by herself.

So here she was, meandering along the sidewalk on her way toward her love, and enjoying the cool, purple twilight . . . until she nearly crashed into someone right in front of Patty's stone walkway.

"Whoops!" Quinn Harper laughed, looking up

from her phone with a wide grin. "Man, I should not be multitasking. I can barely chew gum and walk at the same time, much less text. Are you okay?"

"Never better," Tessa assured her young friend. She and Quinn had bonded over the past couple of weeks. In a move that seemed to surprise everyone except Patty, the taciturn, unfriendly Marcus Beckett had all but moved in to help take care of the recuperating old lady. He was a better nurse than Tessa would have imagined. He did chores around the house, from changing lightbulbs to scrubbing toilets. He and Quinn played cards with Miss Patty by the hour. Between the two of them and having Johnny to help Tessa at the bakery, Miss Patty had never been better cared for.

"Things are definitely looking up around here," Quinn agreed cheerily. "Miss Patty seems to be doing really well."

"Thanks to you and Marcus."

"We're not the only ones! Everyone has pitched in."

They turned and started up the walkway together. Quinn was right. Patty's house was full of laughter and good wishes, with a constantly rotating cast of island friends bearing casseroles, salads, and gossip. Quinn had proven herself indispensable, her sunshiny smile cheering Patty up when her headaches came back, and her attention to detail helping to keep the many offerings of food organized and labeled with sticky notes to enable Patty to return the correct dish to its owner.

"That's one of the things I love about your home-town, Quinn. The way everyone comes together in a crisis to care for any member of the community that needs it. It reminds me of where I grew up . . . but with more acceptance and freedom to be yourself."

Tessa tried the front doorknob absentmindedly before remembering they were keeping it locked now. She fished in her purse for the keys she'd hardly ever used before the events of two weeks ago.

Quinn followed her into the house. "Sanctuary Island is pretty wonderful. I can't imagine ever wanting to live anywhere else. Hey, does this mean you and Johnny are staying?"

"That's . . . something we're still discussing."

It was a bit of a fib. Mostly, Tessa had avoided bringing up the issue of where they'd build their new life together after the small, private ceremony next week. As of right now, Johnny was still on paid administrative leave from the ATF, but that was going to be over soon. Things between them had been going so well, and they'd been working so hard on their relationship, Tessa hadn't been able to bring herself to rock the boat. But they were getting to the point where they needed to make a plan.

Mustering a smile to cover the nervous butterflies that danced in her stomach when she thought about how she might navigate that particular conversation, Tessa poked her head into the library.

Sure enough, Johnny was in there, pacing back and forth in front of the big bay window. It had swiftly become his favorite room in the house, with its walls lined with books and its comfy armchairs grouped around the fireplace.

Tessa's smile grew at the sight of her handsome . . .

husband? Ex-husband? Fiancé? Whatever label she put on him, he looked damn good in it. She stepped into the room, but before she could cross the thick, plush carpet to give him a hello kiss, she noticed he was on his cell.

Catching sight of her, Johnny smiled and held up a finger. Mouthing "One minute" to her, he turned toward the window.

Okay, then. Leaving her mysterious man to his private call, Tessa followed the sound of voices down the hall, toward the kitchen.

Patty's warm, homey kitchen was truly the heart of her household, where everyone tended to congregate. Tessa wasn't surprised to see that tonight was no different, but she was a little surprised to see Marcus Beckett standing in front of the stove with a red apron tied around his lean hips.

From her chair parked next to the butcher-block island in the center of the kitchen, Patty said, "I'm a little tired of tuna noodle, so Marcus said he'd make omelets."

Quinn's feet hardly seemed to touch the hardwood floor as she sailed over to Marcus. "You can cook?"

"No," he said shortly, then immediately contradicted himself by deftly flipping the delicate yellow omelet in the pan with a flick of his wrist.

"Oooh," Quinn cooed, slipping one hand around his waist. Marcus gave her a frown but didn't shift away from her.

Tessa smothered a grin. These two and their odd dance around each other was sometimes amusing, and sometimes frustrating—but most of the time, watching them made her glad she and Johnny had worked so hard on their communication with one another. It often sounded as though Marcus and Quinn were having two separate conversations, talking past each other.

With nothing to do but wait for Johnny to get off the phone, Tessa settled in the chair next to Patty's. She opened her mouth to interrogate her mentor about how she was feeling and whether she'd taken her meds that day when Marcus's harsh voice startled her into staring over at him.

"What do you mean, you're not taking the job?"

As Tessa's brows reached for her hairline, Quinn slowly removed her hand from Marcus and drew away a few steps, hurt tugging at the corners of her lips.

"I've already got a job. At the Buttercup Inn. With you."

Tessa swore she could hear Marcus's molars grinding from across the room. "But that's your dream job, you said. Working at the therapy riding place."

"Sure, a dream job. As in, a fantasy! I don't have the qualifications for a job like that. I'd need more school, certifications . . ."

Patty and Tessa exchanged a look. It sounded a lot like jack-of-all-trades Quinn was afraid to try a job that might lead to a real career. Choosing her words with obvious care, Patty said, "Oh, sugar, did they offer you a job over at Windy Corner? How lovely! Jo Ellen Hollister is no dummy, you know—I'm sure she knows exactly what your qualifications are. What did she say about it?"

Quinn shifted her weight. "She said Windy Corner

would pay for me to go back to school and get certified while I worked there full-time. But that's bonkers! Where did they get the money for that all of a sudden, when a few months ago they couldn't afford to pay me even part-time?"

A slight, aborted movement from Marcus caught Tessa's eye. She studied him over Quinn's shoulder. The way he was watching the younger woman, you'd think he never wanted to let her out of his sight, much less let her take a job with someone else.

But maybe he wanted what was best for Quinn, even at his own expense.

It was hard not to want the best for Quinn, who seemed to spend most of her time taking care of everyone around her.

"A new grant must have come through," Tessa suggested. "That's great!"

Quinn's mouth set in a mulish line. "It's great for them, but the point is, it doesn't matter where they got the money because I'm not taking the job. As soon as it opens, I'll be tending bar at the Buttercup Inn."

"That's a stupid choice," Marcus said bluntly. "Take your dream job and quit coasting through life."

Furious tears sprang to Quinn's eyes, magnifying them into deep blue pools, but she went toe-to-toe with Marcus anyway. "I'm not coasting! You need me! Especially now that Johnny is busy helping Tessa at the bakery. And we don't even know if he's sticking around yet! Sorry, Tessa."

Tessa caught her breath at the sting, but it was nothing more than the truth. They still had some big questions to resolve.

The blankness on Marcus's face as he stared down at Quinn was more chilling than any thunderous frown. "I don't need you."

Quinn gasped, and Patty hopped down from her chair. Threading her arm through Tessa's elbow, she said loudly, "You know what I could use? A cocktail. And don't give me any of that stuff about how the doctor says I can't have bourbon. What she doesn't know won't hurt her. Come on, Tessa, let's make a pitcher of manhattans. These two can handle supper."

They whisked out of the kitchen and down the hall to the library, where Johnny was putting his cell back into his pocket. "Hey there, pretty ladies. Is dinner ready?"

"Not yet. I need a drink first." Instead of making a beeline for the crystal decanters and silver cocktail shakers on her bar cart in the corner, however, Patty flopped down on the nearest love seat and stared up at Tessa with avid curiosity.

"Fifty bucks says they didn't even notice we left the room."

Tessa huffed out a laugh. "I've never seen two people so wrapped up together. It doesn't matter if they're making eyes at each other or fighting like two cats in a bag—there might as well be no one else on the planet."

"I've known a few other couples like that in my day," Patty mused, casting a sly glance between Tessa and Johnny.

The seed of happiness that lived in Tessa's chest sprang up into full bloom at the love shining clearly in Johnny's eyes as he laughed across the room at her.

"What are they fighting about now?" he asked, sauntering over to the bar cart and picking up the bottle of Miss Patty's favorite bourbon. "What fillings to put in the omelets? How many eggs it takes? Whether you have to break any eggs to make the omelets?"

"No, it seemed like more of a real fight this time," Tessa said, as Johnny poured out a small portion of amber liquid. Miss Patty frowned at it, then at Johnny, who shook his head and mutely refused to pour a bigger portion.

Taking the glass with a huff, Patty said, "It was one of the big three."

Tessa shook her head in response to Johnny's offer of a drink. "The big three?"

"Most married folks fight about their kids, their bills, or their jobs. Or all three."

Tessa tensed. The comment hit her right where she was bruised and raw from worrying about her job and Johnny's job and what it meant for where they'd live. She darted a glance at Johnny, but he didn't look concerned. He was shaking his head, like he couldn't understand why Marcus and Quinn were arguing about something so silly.

"All that stuff will work itself out," he said. "If Marcus and Quinn are serious about each other, if they love each other, all the rest of it will fall into place."

"Well." Miss Patty gave Tessa a look brimming with amusement. "That's a very optimistic viewpoint from a man who, until recently, didn't really believe in all that lovey-dovey stuff."

"I'm a changed man," Johnny declared, and Tessa knew it was true.

Oh, he'd always been a good man. The best of men, her own personal hero. But there was a lightness to Johnny now, a happiness, that he'd never had before. It warmed her down to her bones to think that she was a part of that. She never wanted to do anything to dim that light.

That made it hard to do what had to be done, but it was time.

"Johnny. I adore you for how much you believe love conquers all—believe me, nothing makes me happier than to hear you say that. But . . . we need to talk."

Chapter 23

Instantly realizing how dire that sounded, Tessa tried to laugh. "I mean, there are things we need to talk about! Not, like . . . we need to *talk*."

"What kinds of things?" Johnny asked, pausing in the act of pouring himself a finger of bourbon.

"The kinds of things that I'm afraid won't just work themselves out, no matter how much we love each other." Tessa bit her lip, hoping she didn't sound like she was angry. She wasn't—but this conversation did mean a lot to her. She felt a little tongue-tied and emotional, Johnny was looking at her with wary concern darkening his beautiful eyes . . . and Miss Patty was hauling herself up off the love seat.

"Well," Patty said loudly. "I think I'll go take me a stroll around my garden. A garden at dusk is a joy to be savored, my mama always said. Call me in for dinner, won't you? If dinner ever happens."

The last bit was mumbled on her way out the door, and Tessa had to laugh, although it felt strained. "Poor Patty. All these fighting couples, forcing her out of her own house."

Johnny set his glass down and crossed the carpet to take her hands in his. "Are we fighting? I don't want to fight with you, honey."

"I don't want to fight, either," she said firmly, gazing up into the face she loved best in the world. "But we do need to talk. About what happens next."

"What happens next is that we get married, for real this time, in front of the people who love you. The way you deserve."

They were technically still married, Tessa knew, since the divorce papers had been destroyed before they were ever made official, but she didn't argue the point. This would be their real wedding ceremony, the one they would remember for the rest of their lives, and they were both treating it that way.

But she couldn't let all of it go by without comment. "Us, Johnny. They love us, the people here. You as much as me."

Johnny smiled indulgently and brought her hands up to press a scratchy kiss against her knuckles. She could tell he didn't really believe her, but it was true. Patty had been a fan from the beginning, but she'd delivered her unabashed approval of Johnny in the past few weeks. Marcus was well on the way to becoming a true friend, now that the two of them had worked out their issues in whatever macho male way made sense to them. They were putting down roots here, on

Sanctuary Island. Both of them were. But how could she make Johnny see that? How could she hope he would value that over returning to his job at the ATF?

If their work together with Dr. Voss had taught Tessa anything, it was that a lot of their problems had come from keeping silent. Speaking up might be harder, it might start a fire that would be hard to put out, but it cleared the air and made new growth possible. So she took a deep breath and said, "I don't want to go back to D.C. I want to live here, with you, after we're married. I know that makes things hard for you, with your job—"

"I quit."

Tessa froze, her world rocked to the core. "You what?"

"I called Brad a week ago, and I resigned from the bureau." Johnny shrugged, but his eyes were sharp and watchful, waiting for her reaction. "I was going to tell you as a wedding present, but if you're worrying about it, I'd rather tell you now and ease your mind. Besides, I have something else in the works, that I'm hoping I can make happen as your wedding gift."

Shaking her head, Tessa tried to take it in. "You left the ATF. Johnny, I don't know what to say. You love that job."

"I love you. And this is where your life is. So this is where I want to be."

The words floored her. Not just the words themselves, but the certainty with which he uttered them. Overcome, Tessa dropped her head to his chest and simply breathed in the soap-and-leather scent of the man she loved.

The man who was rearranging his entire life for her.

Even though it was everything she'd wanted, guilt rose up to stifle her. "You didn't have to do that, Johnny. We could have figured something out together."

"You uprooted your entire life to follow me wherever my career led us for years," Johnny pointed out. "Some people might say it's your turn. But that's not even the main reason."

Tessa tilted her head up to look at him. "Oh?"

He paused, long enough to make Tessa wonder what he was about to reveal.

"I don't regret the work I did with the ATF. It was good work, and I know I did some good in the world. But I think it's time for me to figure out who I am when I'm not obsessed with trying to save everyone in the world all the time. That's an impossible goal, and it was driving me slowly crazy. I want to narrow my focus for a while—maybe try to save myself first. See if I can keep your heart safe. Work at the bar, take care of Patty and Quinn and Marcus—not that he'd admit he needs it. And who knows? Maybe we'll add a person or two to our little family as we go along."

Tessa's heart popped like a firecracker, whirling light and sparks and joy. "I like that idea. I like it a lot."

Sliding a hand into her hair, Johnny smiled, slow and wolfish. "Maybe we should skip dinner and get started on that project right away."

Tessa started to feel warm and a little dizzy with how much she wanted him. "Yes. Let's do that. Marcus and Quinn won't miss us, and Miss Patty will understand."

"Miss Patty understands everything," Johnny agreed, taking her by the hand and leading her up the stairs to the room they shared. "I don't know where we'd be without her."

"Let's hope she'll give Quinn and Marcus advice that's half as good as what she gave us." Tessa squeezed her once-and-future husband's hand. "And let's hope, for their sake, they listen, before they break each other's hearts."

Marcus was going to have to break Quinn's heart.

The last words he'd spoken hung between them in the silence like a handful of knives, waiting to slice them up.

I don't need you.

Marcus regarded Quinn as if she were on the other side of a deep, unnavigable ocean. Tears—tears he'd caused—stood in her eyes, trembling in her lashes, and all he wanted was to reach out and cup her head to draw her in close enough to kiss them away.

But he couldn't do that. Because he'd already screwed her life up enough. He'd broken his own rules and gotten in too deep, and now Quinn was throwing away the best chance she'd had at a real career so that she could pull pints and play house with Marcus.

Unacceptable.

"Maybe you don't think you need me," Quinn started, tilting that dimpled chin up defiantly. "But I'm a bigger asset than you think."

Marcus wished, for a fleeting instant, that he had

the skills to do this the gentle way. But he had to make it stick. So he gave her a calculated leer and said, "I know all about your assets, sweetheart."

That dried her tears in a hurry, but it didn't send her rushing out the door. Instead, it seemed to make her angry.

Okay. Angry was better than sad, and definitely better than infatuated.

"Don't be gross," she snarled. It was like watching a puppy face down a mountain lion.

Marcus forced himself to shrug. "Hey, I said I didn't need you, not that I don't want you. Feel free to come over anytime. This town doesn't have enough action for me to turn any down, especially action as good as you."

"Action. That's all I am to you."

He looked her straight in the eye. "I never said different."

Nodding slowly, Quinn scanned his face as if she were memorizing his features— probably so she could make an accurate voodoo doll later. "No, you've never said I mattered to you the way you matter to me. Not in so many words."

"Not in any way at all," Marcus clarified, his guard going up.

This wasn't going quite how Marcus had imagined it. And oh, yeah, he'd definitely seen this moment coming down the pike. Pretty much from the first moment he kissed Quinn, he knew they'd end up here eventually. He'd imagined more sobbing, more dramatic declarations. But Quinn had never done exactly what he expected, and she didn't start now.

"I may be young," she said softly, "but I'm not an idiot. And I'm not completely inexperienced. I know that what we have is something special."

Marcus couldn't afford to waver. Not now. "What we had," he corrected her firmly. "It's been fun, sweetheart, but you need to move on with your life. And so do I."

Her eyes narrowed, the fringe of her lashes stark black against the milky paleness of her freckled cheeks. "Why are you doing this?"

Because I need to get out now, while I still can.

The words tickled the back of his throat, nearly triggering his gag reflex, but he choked them back. Hoped his face conveyed nothing more than how little time he had for this crap. "It's for the best. You'll see."

A shrill shriek from above shocked them both into motion. It was the smoke alarm, and Marcus cursed as he turned back to the stovetop where his omelet was scorching sullenly to the bottom of the pan.

When he'd turned off the heat and moved the skillet to a cold burner, he glanced back to see Quinn on her way out the door. Despite himself, despite everything he knew to be true about himself and the way the world worked, the sight made his guts clench up. But he said nothing.

Instead, Quinn got the last word. Standing in the kitchen doorway, she gave him one last, very unimpressed look.

"You talk about how young and inexperienced I am," she said, meeting his eyes without flinching. "But time and life will take care of those terrible flaws. You—Marcus, you're a coward. And no amount of time is going to change that."

It was a good parting shot, and he let her have it. From down the hall, he heard female voices speaking softly, then the incredibly final sound of the front door closing. Moving on autopilot, Marcus picked up a spatula and walked over to scrape the disgusting, rubbery bits of egg into the sink. He couldn't help thinking of the last omelet he made, and the woman he made it for.

When an elderly lady's voice came from behind him, it almost could have been the voice from his memories, come back to haunt him the way she always threatened.

"What was that all about?" Miss Patty asked.

If Marcus could have smiled, he would have. Patty might remind him of his late boss, but there were differences. Mainly in that Patty sounded sympathetic right now instead of acerbic. God help him, but he missed the old bird.

Shoving down his emotions, Marcus set the clean skillet back on the stovetop and started cracking new eggs into a bowl. "It was time. She was about to make a choice she would have regretted for a long time."

"But it was her choice to make, don't you think?"

Marcus shrugged. "And it was my choice to end things between us and fire her. So now she can make her choice with better information."

"But not with *all* the information, hmm?"

His shoulders tensed so hard, they hurt. Slanting Patty a glance, he found her regarding him with a benevolent sort of exasperation that was so familiar, it gave him an instant of déjà vu. "What is that supposed to mean?"

"Oh, sugar." Miss Patty wandered closer to lay one frail hand on Marcus's forearm where he'd rolled up his sleeves before starting to cook. He knew she could feel the tension thrumming through his frame, but he couldn't make himself relax. The exasperated gaze turned pitying. "I knew it. You didn't tell her you donated the money for that position that *just happened to open up* at Windy Corner. Enough for them to pay for her certification, too?"

It was obviously no use denying it. Marcus nodded silently, then pinned the old lady with his more ferocious glare. "She doesn't need to know. Ever."

Patty sighed. "Oh, I won't tell her. But I hope you'll pardon an old lady for having an opinion, which is . . . you cocked this one up but good, now didn't you?"

Chapter 24

On the day of Tessa's first wedding, she'd been scared and alone, desperately grasping at the first kind hand extended to her. She hadn't had any friends to help her get ready. Her father would not be walking her down the aisle. She'd missed her mother.

Some things hadn't changed, she reflected as she gazed at her reflection in the old-fashioned beveled mirror in Miss Patty's guest room. Her father might be currently under treatment at a psychiatric facility instead of on his plot of land at the commune, but he still wouldn't be walking her down the aisle.

And Tessa still missed her mother, with a painful intensity of grief that had been stirred up by her recent experiences.

But this time around, she did have friends; she wasn't alone. In fact, this was the first moment she'd had to herself all morning. Between Quinn and Patty flitting around, helping her into her dress and insisting on doing her makeup, Tessa had never felt so pampered.

And this time around, she wasn't afraid, either. Johnny wasn't marrying her out of kindness this time. Today was all about love.

A tap at the door brought her out of her reflections. Shaking her head, she stood up from the vanity bench to let her friends back in.

"What now?" she called as she made her way to the door. "We still have an hour before we need to leave!"

"Tessa."

It was Johnny's deep voice, low and happy. Delight thrilled through her, and she leaned against the doorjamb longing for the time a few short hours from now when there would be nothing separating them any longer. "What are you doing out there? Don't you know it's bad luck?"

"Only if we see each other," Johnny said reasonably. "I'm staying out here, don't worry. We're taking no chances this time around. But . . ."

He paused, and Tessa frowned slightly to hear the hesitance and tension suddenly creep into his tone.

"What's wrong?" Was he having second thoughts?

"Nothing," Johnny assured her, easing the tight constriction around her lungs. "But I have a present for you. I wasn't sure it would get here in time, but it's here. And I wish I could be there with you when you . . . open it."

Giddy with relief, Tessa laughed. "Johnny! You're spoiling me. I don't need any more presents!"

"You need this one." His voice was very certain, rough with an emotion Tessa couldn't identify. "Here,

I'm going to leave it here in the hall and go down-stairs. Count to ten and open the door, I promise I'll be gone."

Tessa fought the urge to pout. "The best present would be getting to see your face," she said. "Maybe I'm not superstitious after all."

That made Johnny laugh. "Oh, but you are, though. I know you, and the minute you see me before the wedding, you'll start worrying about our seven years of bad luck."

"That's for broken mirrors," Tessa corrected him instantly, then scrunched up her nose. "I guess the fact that I know that sort of proves your point, huh?"

"I know you," Johnny said again, this time so tenderly, it made the tips of her ears burn and her eyes sting with tears. "And I'll see you very soon, honey."

"I'm counting the minutes." She leaned harder against the door, imagining him on the other side doing the same. She loved him so much, her heart felt sore and swollen with it.

"Just count to ten," he reminded her with another soft laugh. "And remember, I love you. No matter what. You'll never be alone again."

That was a little ominous, Tessa thought, raising her eyebrows as she listened for the sound of his footsteps retreating down the hallway. After ten seconds, Tessa reached for the doorknob and turned it.

The door swung wide, and there on the threshold stood Tessa's mother.

Naomi Mulligan was older, her face lined with the cares and trials of a lifetime of hard work and regrets. Her thick hair had gone fully gray, and her figure had rounded to a softness that had never been possible during the years of Tessa's bare-bones childhood. But it was unmistakably her.

Everything inside Tessa cried out in recognition. A sob tore its way from her chest. "Mom," she cried, and nearly fell across the threshold into her mother's open arms.

Naomi's embrace was as strong and sure as Tessa remembered. Tears came in a torrent, a flood that had been dammed up for years, suddenly released in a river of relief. She felt her mother's tears against her own cheek, and the two women clung together for several long minutes.

"My sweet girl," Naomi whispered, voice choked and thick with emotion. She pulled back far enough to frame Tessa's face between her hands. "You grew up so beautiful and healthy."

Tessa's heart broke a little. "Yes," she assured her mother. "I got treatment for the seizures, and they finally stopped completely a few years after I . . . after I left. I wrote letters, I wanted you to know I was okay."

Naomi dropped her hands from her daughter's face, pain tightening her features. "I never got those letters. I had left the community by then."

"I can't believe you left. I never thought you would."

A strange expression crossed Naomi's face. "Sweet girl. Do you really think I could have stayed? At that place, in that life—the life that had endangered my daughter and made her think she'd be safer running away than staying with us? And the worst part of it was that you were right. You were better off without us."

Tessa grabbed the tormented woman by the shoulders. "I had to leave, and I'm not sorry I did—I can't be sorry for any choice I made that led me here, to the life I'm building on Sanctuary Island with the man I love. But Mom, I wasn't better off without you. I missed you every day."

Naomi covered her eyes with her hands, shoulders hunching. "Oh. To hear you say that, after all the ways I failed you. I should have stood up to your father much sooner. I should have been stronger, I should have gotten us both away."

The words healed a ragged wound in Tessa's heart, allowing compassion and forgiveness to flow into the breach. "You were afraid. The community was the only way of life you knew. And Dad was . . ."

She broke off, suddenly unsure how much her mother knew about the events of the past few weeks.

"Your father is a bully," Naomi said bluntly. "He wants to control everything and everyone around him, even if it means crushing the life out of them. And don't worry, your young man filled me in on how far Abe was willing to go to get me back under his thumb. I'm so sorry, darling. So very everlastingly sorry that I couldn't protect you from him."

Tessa wrapped her mother up in a forgiving hug. "You didn't make his choices for him," she said, repeating the mantra she'd been working with lately. "And you did the best you could, under really difficult circumstances. I always knew that, Mom."

Blinking away tears, Naomi shook her head. "Where did you get that big, wide-open heart?"

"Well, not from Dad." Tessa smiled at her mother,

who tentatively smiled back. "Come on, come sit down with me. We have a lot of years to catch up on."

"Yes, I want to hear all about the man who tracked me down—the man you're marrying!"

"Technically, we're already married . . . it's a long story."

Naomi clutched her hand. "I'm not going anywhere. We have time."

The barn was crammed with people. Their "small, private" ceremony had bloomed into a town-wide celebration. Loyal bakery customers chatted to Windy Corner Therapeutic Riding Center employees on white folding chairs set up among the hay bales. Brad Garner, his buddy from the ATF, was there with his wife, and they'd gotten drawn into an animated conversation with Quinn once she finished handing out the programs and studiously ignoring Marcus Beckett. Marcus sat impassively at Miss Patty's side, in the very front row by the pile of saddles they'd moved to make room for the ceremony, and didn't move except to keep Patty from getting up to greet every new person who arrived.

Johnny stood underneath the hayloft, breathing in the scents of sweet hay, leather, and horses. They'd asked to say their vows at Windy Corner, because without that place, they wouldn't have made it this far. Dr. Voss had smiled so broadly when they asked, Johnny had thought her cheeks might split.

Now Johnny stared out over the smiling crowd of half-familiar, very friendly faces, and wondered when he was going to start feeling nervous.

God knew, he hadn't been smart enough to be nervous the first time he married Tessa. He'd been so sure he knew what he was doing, caught up in the practical implications and the satisfaction of helping someone who needed him. It wasn't until a few years later that he realized what he'd done—that he'd tied himself for life to a woman he couldn't touch. A woman who made him burn for her, without even realizing she was the spark that lit him up.

He'd assumed he'd be nervous in this moment, as their second wedding ceremony was about to begin. After all, now he knew what he was getting into. He knew how much Tessa meant to him. He didn't know exactly what their new life together would look like, but he knew it would be different from everything that came before.

Yeah, it seemed like he should be feeling some nerves. But he just wasn't, he mused as someone at the back near the open barn doors picked up a guitar and began to pluck at the strings. It was the man from the hardware store, Johnny recognized with a start. The one they called King, who wore a funny toy crown and sat playing checkers all day and picking up gossip. It turned out that checkers and gossip weren't King's only interests. The music he coaxed from that guitar sent warm chills down Johnny's spine. He felt as if the man's fingers were reaching into his chest to pluck at his heart.

A ripple went through the guests, and Johnny's heart quickened. Everyone stood up, so he couldn't see at first, but in the next instant, he caught a glimpse of Tessa. His wife.

She walked down the aisle between the chairs in a simple cream-colored sundress, and she was so beautiful, she dazzled him. Her smile was radiant, her eyes bright and clear when they locked on his. He couldn't look away, and it took him a full minute to realize that she was walking with someone.

Johnny's chest filled with satisfaction when he saw that Tessa was arm in arm with her mother. It looked like his gift had gone over well.

When the two women reached the front of the barn, Naomi hugged and kissed her daughter, then stepped close to Johnny. "Thank you," she whispered fervently as he bent down to embrace her. "For loving her as much as she deserves to be loved, and for bringing me here to be a part of this special day."

"I'd do anything for your daughter," he said quietly. "I'd give everything I am to make her happy."

"From what she tells me, you already have." Naomi patted his cheek and went to sit down while Johnny turned to Tessa.

She held out her hands to him, and he took them. In a husky undertone, he whispered, "It's a real struggle not to bend you back over my arm and kiss the breath from your body, right here and now."

He was rewarded with a shivery sigh and a slow lowering of Tessa's lashes. Her lips parted in the smile of a woman who knew all about pleasure. "Patience," she murmured. "Let's declare our love and commitment to each other in front of all the people who matter most to us in this world. And then you can have whatever you want."

"I already have everything I want," he told her. "I have a second chance. A new life. And you."

"We have each other," Tessa said, smiling with tears sparkling in her eyes. "Forever."

Epilogue

One month later . . .
The knock on the door roused Marcus from his intent contemplation of the last half-inch of whiskey left in the bottle.

"Go away," he growled, pulling the bottle closer. He wasn't sure where his glass was, but it didn't matter. He could drink straight from the bottle. He was alone.

As usual.

He settled deeper into the tattered, secondhand armchair that had come with the apartment over the bar when he bought it. The chair was uglier than sin, splotched with giant pink flowers on a mustard-yellow background, but it was comfortable and it reclined. He could sleep in it. Better than he slept in his bed, these days.

Marcus was just thinking about ditching the last of the whiskey in favor of shutting his eyes for a minute or two when the knock came again. Swearing violently, he swung to his feet and immediately rammed his bare heel into the heavy leg of the side table.

He kicked the offending table aside with a screech of wooden furniture on hardwood floor, and stormed over to wrench open the door.

"What?" he barked, and then he saw who it was.

Quinn Harper stood in his doorway with a backpack over her shoulder and a deeply unimpressed expression on her lovely face.

She looked good. He'd managed to successfully avoid her for weeks by throwing himself into his renovations. What with one thing and another, the way this island had sucked him in and distracted him with new friends and old ladies in jeopardy and whatnot, the opening of the Buttercup Inn was behind schedule.

In the last few weeks, he'd made real progress on his bar. His new life's ambition to become a hermit wasn't going as well, but it was a work in progress, too.

In a blur, Marcus realized what he probably looked like to Quinn. A sad, old man drinking alone in his darkened apartment, too out of it to bother with shoes or a shirt. Her gaze drifted down and Marcus became intensely aware of how low his unbuttoned jeans hung on his hips.

Meanwhile, she looked as fresh and wholesome as a glass of milk. Quinn hadn't spent the last few weeks drinking herself to sleep every night. She'd spent some of that time in the sun, if her new freckles were any indication. Marcus wanted to map them with his tongue, to see if her gold-tinted skin tasted any different than the creamy paleness he'd had his mouth on a month ago.

Quinn raised her brows and Marcus resisted the urge to button up, or to retreat inside for a shirt. Instead, he leaned his arm on the doorjamb above his head and regarded her with a defiant sneer to cover the way his body was suddenly working feverishly to metabolize the alcohol in his system.

"Couldn't stay away?"

Something flared in her blue-green eyes, like sunset glinting off the bottom of a pool. For the first time since they met, the open book of Quinn's expressive face was closed to Marcus.

"My parents came home this afternoon," she said briskly. "So now I need a place to stay and I happen to know the studio next door to you is available. I'd like to rent it, please."

Marcus snorted. "Right. I'm not one of your gullible little college boyfriends, sweetheart. Find someplace else."

He started to close the door in her face, but Quinn stuck her sneaker-clad foot in the crack and said, "You think I'd be here if there were anyplace else on this entire island available for rent? It's the high season. There's nothing. Give me the keys. I'm moving in next door, and you know my rent will be paid on time because I took the job at Windy Corner."

That was something, at least. Marcus tried to believe that result was worth the way he'd broken up with her. "Good. I'm glad."

She rolled her eyes at his reluctant semicongratulations. "I don't give a crap if you're glad. I didn't do it to make you happy."

This time, Marcus held back the snort of amusement. He knew damn well she didn't care about making him happy. If she did, she wouldn't be here right now trying to emotionally blackmail him into renting her an apartment. But he couldn't say any of that without admitting the truth.

He was weak, where Quinn Harper was concerned.

Apparently, he'd stood there silent long enough for her patience to run dry. She pressed her lips together, her jaw tight. "Please," she ground out. "I can't stay in my parents' house. My mother and I get along better when we don't share a roof, I need my own place, and this is it."

Weak. He was weak.

Without a word, Marcus reached into the bowl on the table by the door and grabbed the keys Johnny had dropped off a few weeks ago. He tossed them to her and she caught them one-handed.

The smile she gave him didn't reach her eyes, but that was for the best. A real smile might've forced him to reconsider this incredibly stupid, self-hating move.

"Thank you. I'll be the perfect tenant," she promised, already backing across the hall to her own—God, what had he done?—her own apartment. "You'll never even know I'm there."

"Good," he said, and slammed his door closed. With a deep sigh, Marcus leaned his forehead against the smooth, cold wood. Very cool. Very mature.

From outside his door, he heard the distinctive

sounds of the key jiggling around in the studio apartment's tricky lock. Quinn cursed softly under her breath, but before Marcus could talk himself into going out there and helping her, she got it.

The door across the hall opened and closed, leaving silence behind. But it wasn't the same empty silence that had messed with Marcus's head for the past four weeks.

No, this silence was full of Quinn, seething and jumping with all the things they still hadn't said to each other, all the things he still wanted to do to her. Abruptly, Marcus missed that hollow, crushing silence from before. It had hurt, like having a car flipped over to crush his chest, but it had been bearable.

This? The knowledge that Quinn Harper was in the apartment right across the hall? This was going to be a nightmare.

And if anyone knew about nightmares, it was Marcus Beckett.

ORLAND PARK PUBLIC LIBRAR

Catch up on the Sanctuary Island series
by Lily Everett!

Available now from St. Martin's Paperbacks

Don't miss the Hero Project trilogy
by Lily Everett!

Available now   Coming March 2017

from St. Martin's Paperbacks